Charles Townsend

Charles Townsend is a Member of The Magic Circle and particularly enjoys devising new magic tricks. He has now retired from a long career running companies. In 2012 he took over a pub with his eldest son and has since built a brewery and distillery in the pub's outbuildings. He lives with his wife Hayley in an historic house in old Harwich and has five children.

The magic tricks described in this book are all performable. The way the tricks are described are exactly what the spectator would observe. The only things missed out are the secret moves or slights that make the tricks work. This leaves it to the reader to puzzle out how the tricks were done.

The Magic Lantern

Charles Townsend

Book 3 of Illusions of Power

The Magic Lantern

Copyright © (Charles Townsend 2022)

All rights reserved

First published 2022 by Charles Townsend, West Street, Harwich, England

The story so far in "The Magician's Secret" - Book 1 of Illusions of Power

Practical Joker Delvin had been learning Magic from his friend the travelling magician Borlock.

Borlock was murdered by a black magician who wanted to get Borlock's magician's stone, but he failed to find it. The black magician had been sent from the Guild of Magicians who wanted to control all magician's stones and gain power through them.

Delvin inherited Borlock's magic tricks and decided to set up as a magician himself in the city of Hengel. However, he didn't know about the magician's stones, and when strange things started to happen, Delvin began to wonder if he was performing real magic and not just tricks.

Princess Jarla, the ruthless daughter of the Duke of Hengel, heard about him and decided to use him to help her stop a war with Argent, the neighbouring country.

Delvin eventually discovered the special powers of the magician's stone which was among the things he had inherited from Borlock. With the stone he found that he could project thoughts into people's minds and so control them. Also, if another person with a magician's stone projected a thought, if he was touching his stone at the time, the thought came through as a clear message.

Delvin and Jarla were pursued by the black magician who had killed Borlock. The black magician had discovered that Delvin had Borkock's magician's stone and was determined to take it from him.

Grimbolt, the Duke of Hengel's fixer was also pursuing them. He thought that Delvin had kidnapped Princess Jarla and Princess Fionella of Argent.

Eventually Delvin and Princess Jarla managed to rescue the Duke of Argent who had been held captive by the magicians and also stop the war between Hengel and Argent.

The story so far in "The Three Card Trick" - Book 2 of Illusions of Power

Disturbing news had come from the Duchy of Argent, and Delvin, Grimbolt and Princess Jarla travel there to investigate. As they arrive a riot is taking place fermented by the Guild of Magicians who are using their magician's stones to make people rebel against the duke. A magician's stone allows the person holding it to compel other people to do what that person wants.

The rioters kill Prince Carlo heir to the Duke of Argent, and Delvin and the others only escape with the help of a street urchin called Nippy.

On returning to Hengel, they find the same thing is happening there, and Prince Gustov heir to the Duke of Hengel is also murdered by rioters. The magicians now control both Hengel and Argent, ruling Hengel through Princess Stella and Argent through Princess Fionella.

Together with Nippy they rescue Princess Stella and flee towards Pandol. Princess Stella and Jarla are riding ahead of the others and come across a village being attacked by slavers. Princess Stella hides, but Jarla attacks the slavers and is captured and taken over the Grandent Mountains to a slave market at a gathering on the other side.

Delvin and Nippy follow over the mountains and manage to rescue Jarla and the slaves.

On returning to Hengel they hear of an old magician at a disused diamond mine, but when they investigate, they are captured by the black magician who doesn't realize who they are. To stop him killing them, Delvin tells the black magician that Nippy is Jarla's son and Jarla is Nippy's tutor.

They are imprisoned at the mine with the old magician who is called Golbrick. He is able to tell them more about the magician's stones, where they came from and what they do.

They escape and head for Argent. They manage to hoodwink the Magician Drandor, who is controlling Argent, into returning to Norden the Guild of Magician's country. With him gone they rescue the duke and get Argent back under his control.

Returning to Hengel, they overcome the magician Meldrum who is in control there.

For his services, Delvin is made a knight by the dukes of both Argent and Hengel.

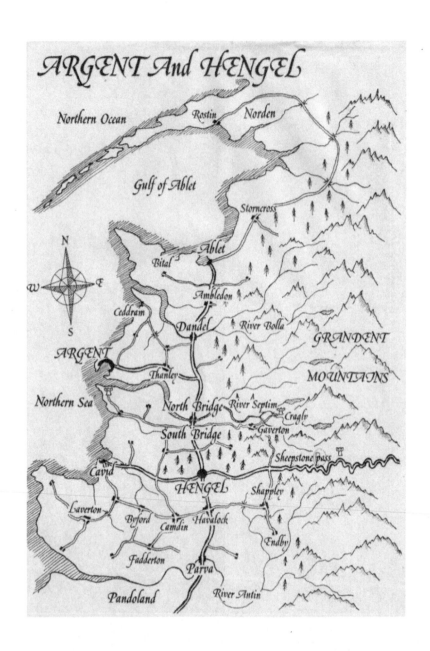

HENGEL

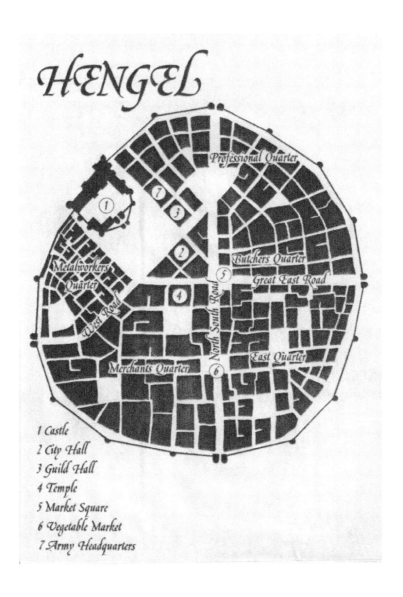

1 Castle
2 City Hall
3 Guild Hall
4 Temple
5 Market Square
6 Vegetable Market
7 Army Headquarters

HENGEL CASTLE

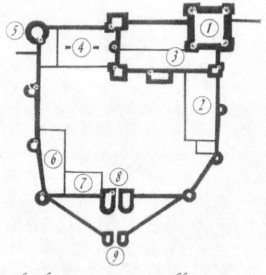

1 Hengel's Keep   6 Stables
2 Great Hall   7 Servants' Wing
3 Rooms of State   8 Great Gate
4 Kitchen and Offices   9 Barbican
5 Lyles Tower

HENGEL CASTLE

Ground Floor 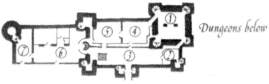 Dungeons below

1 Armoury   5 Royal Dining Room
2 Court   6 Kitchen
3 Grand Hall and Stair   7 Servants' Hall
4 Blue Drawing Room

First Floor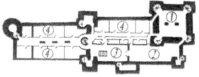

1 Guard Room   3 Lobby
2 Throne Room   4 Offices of State

Second Floor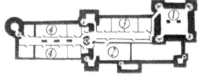

1 Duke's Drawing Room   3 Royal Bedchambers
2 Library   4 Bedchambers

Third Floor

1 Duke's Bedchamber

13

CAVID

1 Castle
2 Boat yard
3 Fisherman's Square
4 Fish Market
5 Market Square
6 Town Hall
7 Merchant's Quarter

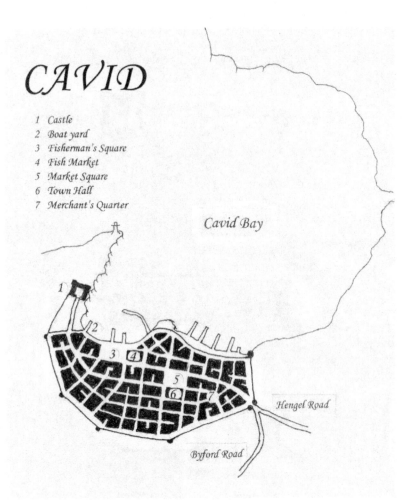

CAVID CASTLE

Ground Floor

1. Entrance Hall
2. Great Hall
3. Library
4. Drawing Room
5. Dining Room
6. Kitchen
7. Servant's Hall

First Floor

1. Bedchambers
2. Great Hall
3. Store Room

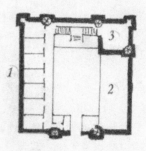

Second Floor

1. Servant's Rooms

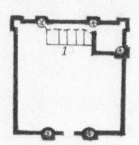

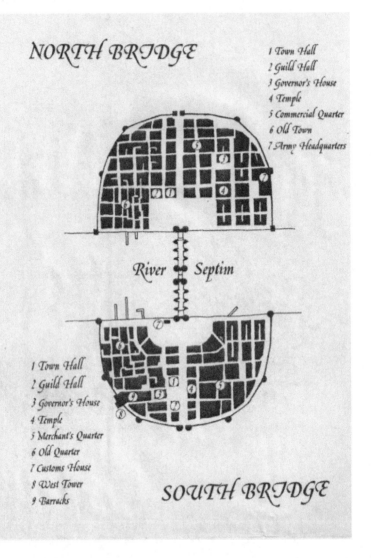

NORTH BRIDGE

1 Town Hall
2 Guild Hall
3 Governor's House
4 Temple
5 Commercial Quarter
6 Old Town
7 Army Headquarters

River Septim

1 Town Hall
2 Guild Hall
3 Governor's House
4 Temple
5 Merchant's Quarter
6 Old Quarter
7 Customs House
8 West Tower
9 Barracks

SOUTH BRIDGE

ARGENT

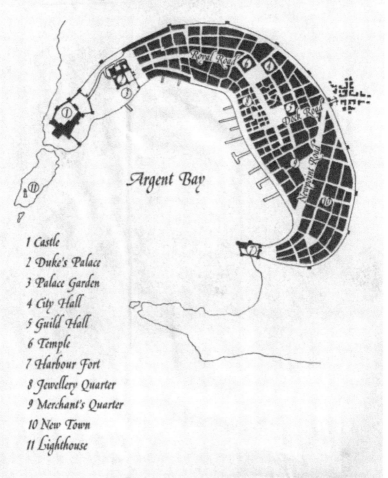

Argent Bay

Royal Road

Dock Road

Newport Road

1 Castle
2 Duke's Palace
3 Palace Garden
4 City Hall
5 Guild Hall
6 Temple
7 Harbour Fort
8 Jewellery Quarter
9 Merchant's Quarter
10 New Town
11 Lighthouse

ROSTIN

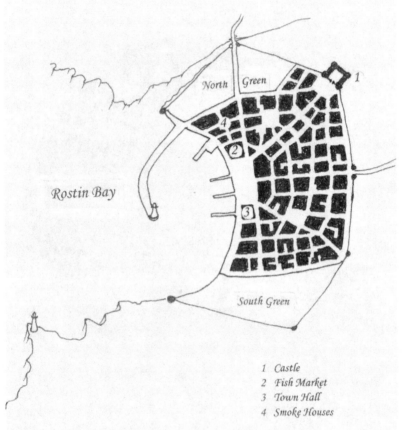

North Green

Rostin Bay

South Green

1 Castle
2 Fish Market
3 Town Hall
4 Smoke Houses

ROSTIN CASTLE

Ground Floor

1 Great Hall
2 State Dining Room
3 Small Dining Room
4 Kitchen
5 Steward's Office

First Floor

1 Great Hall
2 Study
3 Drawing Room
4 Library
5 Servant's Hall

Second Floor

1 Principle Bedchambers
2 Bedchambers
3 Servant's Bedchambers

Third Floor

1 Bedchambers

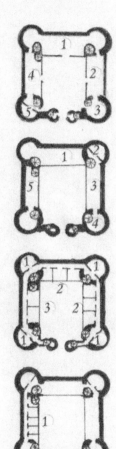

Chapter 1

Delvin felt happy as he walked with his apprentice Nippy back to Mistress Wilshaw's house where they lodged with his friend Greg. His magic and magic lantern show had gone well. He had not only got his fee of three carls, but had got a tip of one carl as well. Nippy was learning fast, and together their show was earning itself a good reputation.

Delvin had come to Hengel the previous year. He had been brought up in the village of Byford and had always loved it when Borlock the travelling magician had visited the village. Borlock had sensed his interest in magic and had taught him several magic tricks. When Borlock was murdered he had left everything to Delvin, including all his magic props. Delvin had decided to try his hand at being a magician, so he had set out to Hengel with his friend Greg and set up performing shows and doing fortune telling at Mistress Wilshaw's house. He was starting to do well despite being only twenty and not having the look of ancient wisdom that people normally associated with magicians. He was of average height with blond hair, an open face and a cheeky smile. More the look of a farm-lad than a magician.

Nippy, Delvin's apprentice, had been a street urchin in the city of Argent. He was only about ten and was small and thin for his age, but he made up of his lack of years with his streetwise skills and cheeky ways.

Twang!... "Arhhh!"

Delvin spun round and moments later saw Grimbolt emerging from a doorway behind him with a crossbow in his hand.

"I think I only winged him. Come on! We need to catch him!"

Delvin looked the other way but could see nothing.

"Come on! Quick! Give your props to Nippy."

There was the sound of horses' hoofs as Delvin handed his props to Nippy. Then running to catch up, he followed Grimbolt as he disappeared around the corner.

"Lost him. Sheffs! He must have had horses hidden round the corner. Come on, we need to try to follow him. He is probably heading out of the North Gate. We need to get some horses. Come on!"

Grimbolt dashed off through the lanes of the East Quarter and was soon pulling open the gate to a yard and stable behind a small neat house. This was Grimbolt's safe house that they had used last summer when hiding from the magicians. Grimbolt's real name was Major Grybald, but everybody called him Grimbolt behind his back. He was the Duke of Hengel's fixer in chief. His appearance was deceptive. He was short and wiry and slightly bowlegged. He had a round fleshy head that was bald on top. His lopsided smile hid an iron determination, and Delvin knew he was enormously capable. Last year, together with Delvin and Princess Jarla the duke's daughter, he had managed to stop two attempts by the magicians of the Guild of Magicians to take over the Duchy of Hengel.

They soon had two horses saddled and out of the stables. They quickly mounted them and clattered out of the yard. Moments later they were heading down the North South Road towards the North Gate of the city of Hengel.

"What was that?" shouted Delvin as they manoeuvred their horses past the horses, carts and people thronging the road.

"It was the black magician. He had a crossbow aimed at you. I had to shoot him before he fired. Otherwise, I'd have waited and got a clean shot at him."

"The black magician? I didn't think he was after me any longer. I thought the magicians believed I'd given my magician's stone to the Duke of Argent."

Delvin still had his magician's stone and had not actually given it to the Duke of Argent. The magician's stones were very powerful. If you were touching a magician's stone, you could project thoughts into other people's minds and so make them do whatever you wanted. However, if that person also had a stone and was touching it. That thought projection would come out as a clear message in their mind rather than compelling them to do anything. The secret of the magician's stones was fiercely guarded by the Guild of Magicians. Apart from Delvin, the only other stones were in the possession of magicians who were members of the Guild, and they desperately wanted Delvin's stone.

The black magician was a member of the Guild of Magicians. His task was to kill anyone who learned the secret of the magician's stones and take back Delvin's stone.

"I am fairly certain the magicians believe that the Duke of Argent has your stone," said Grimbolt. "But the black magician has a personal grudge against you. And of course, you know the stone's secret. That makes you a target. I had a feeling he would come after you, so I had a person keeping watch. He came to tell me he had seen a figure in black around Mistress Wilshaw's house, so I thought I'd stake it out."

Delvin remembered that when the black magician had tried to take the stone from him the previous year, he had escaped by setting a swarm of bees on him. That would certainly be enough to give him a grudge against him, he thought. Delvin had set the bees on him after discovering that he could control animals and insects with the magician's stone as well as being able to control people.

They were nearing the North Gate when suddenly Delvin sat up straight.

"Hold on a minute."

Grimbolt pulled up his horse and looked at Delvin inquiringly. Delvin was looking into the distance with a look of concentration on his face. He had picked up a faint message in his mind. *'Princess Jarla you are paralyzed. You must do as we say. Follow us.'*

"It's Princess Jarla," said Delvin, and told Grimbolt the message.

"Sheffs! The magicians are kidnapping her!"

"Do you think the black magician was trying to kidnap Nippy as well as killing me?"

"Maybe. They still seem to think Nippy is Princess Jarla's son… I think that the black magician had more than one horse with him, so you might be right. Come on, I reckon they'll be heading for the North Gate. We'll get ahead of them. When the kidnappers come past with Princess Jarla, we'll be able to see where they are going, and that way it won't look like we're following them. This looks like a coordinated attack. If it is, they should lead us to the black magician as well."

They had now reached the North Gate. The guards on the gate recognized Grimbolt, and let them through ahead of the carts and other people leaving the city.

Once outside the city walls, they set off on a slow canter on the road to South Bridge.

It was not long before Devin sensed the message. *'Out of our way. Let us through.'*

"They are coming," said Delvin. "I think they are going through the gate now."

Ten minutes later a group of four riders streamed past. The rider in their midst had her hands tied behind her back, her dark hair streaming behind her and a furious expression on her face. Delvin immediately recognized Princess Jarla.

"Right, we need to keep them in sight," said Grimbolt.

They were soon at the edge of the forest. The riders ahead had slowed slightly, and Delvin and Grimbolt were able to keep them just in view.

"It's fairly late," said Grimbolt. "They won't have time to get to South Bridge before the town gates shut for the night. That means they will have a camp somewhere, probably in the forest."

Sure enough, a short while later the riders pulled off the road into the trees.

Grimbolt kept his eyes on the point where the riders had left the road. Shortly before reaching it, he pulled up and signaled for Delvin to stop too.

"On foot from here," he whispered.

They tied their horses to a tree and moved cautiously through the trees. It was starting to get dark, but there was still sufficient light to see their way.

Only a little way ahead they could hear voices. They crept ever more carefully through the trees and saw the kidnapper's camp ahead of them. A fire had been lit in the centre of the camp, and by its light they could see a clearing with four tents. One of the riders they had been following was still mounted. As Delvin looked closer, he could see that the mounted rider was Princess Jarla. Two of the others were bending over another figure on the ground.

They could now faintly hear their voices.

"He needs a doctor."

"Bind it up as well as you can. We'll find one in North Bridge."

"What do we do with her?"

"Put her in that tent." The speaker nodded to a tent on the edge of the camp.

Two of the riders went over to Princess Jarla and pulled her down off her horse. Then they bundled her across the clearing and into the tent.

"One of you stay in the tent with her and keep guard."

Grimbolt and Delvin crawled closer.

"We need to rescue her tonight," whispered Grimbolt. "They'll be gone at first light."

"I can't use my stone to paralyze them," replied Delvin. "There're two magicians with magician's stones there. The one that captured Jarla and the black magician. I can't overcome two magician's stones with my one."

"There's too many of them to fight," muttered Grimbolt thoughtfully. "And we can't cut through the side of the tent as that guard will see us and raise the alarm."

"I have an idea," whispered Delvin.

Chapter 2

Delvin and Grimbolt waited and watched for the camp to settle down. The kidnappers had cooked a meal in a pot over the fire, and Delvin could smell it from where he lay. Some of the food was taken into the tent where Jarla was being held. After a while someone went into the tent to retrieve the empty dishes. It was now completely dark, and the kidnappers were sitting around the fire and talking in low voices.

Grimbolt nodded to Delvin, and they crept carefully round the camp so they were behind the tent where Jarla was being kept, trying to make as little sound as possible.

In the magic show that afternoon, Delvin had performed his trick where he made his rabbit Freda appear. He normally made her appear from a box painted to look like a genie's palace. But today he had been performing for a family who owned a fashion business. So instead of the genie's palace he had made her appear out of a hat. It had gone down well, so he thought he would do that in his shows more often.

He had taken to carrying Freda around in a sling. When he had rushed off so quickly with Grimbolt after the attack that afternoon, he still had Freda in her sling around his neck. He now took her out, turned to Grimbolt and grinned.

Delvin placed Freda on the ground then began projecting the thought to her that there was some lovely tasty grass by the tent. He had found that when he projected thoughts and images to animals, other magicians with magician's stone didn't pick it up like they did with messages.

Freda hopped happily towards the tent. When she reached the tent, Delvin projected the thought that the grass was inside the tent. Freda immediately started burrowing under the side.

This is the difficult bit thought Delvin, holding his breath as Freda disappeared down her burrow under the tent's wall. He started projecting the thought that ropes were really tasty things, and tried to send an image of the ropes round Jarla's wrists. If this works, he thought, Freda will bite through the ropes and free Jarla. He then sent a second thought that if there was a sudden movement, Freda should run back under the tent and return to him. He hoped that when Jarla's hands were free, the sudden movement of her hands would be enough to get Freda to come back to him.

Delvin was confident that Jarla would be able to deal with the guard, as despite being a princess, she was a formidable and ruthless fighter. Earlier that year he had seen her kill several people. Jarla had grown the fingernails on her forefingers so they projected an inch from her hands and then had sharpened them so they were like knives. He shivered as he imagined what she might do to the guard with them.

Now he had to wait. He kept projecting the thought of tasty rope to Freda.

Freda suddenly came lolloping out from her burrow. Delvin sent the thought there was tasty grass near him, and Freda ran towards him.

Moments later a knife slit the wall of the tent, and Jarla came through, her hands and fingernails bloody. She looked quickly around and saw Freda. Then followed her towards where Delvin and Grimbolt hid.

"You took your time Grimbolt," she whispered.

"Major Grybald, if you please Princess," whispered Grimbolt. He always insisted on Princess Jarla calling him by his proper name, and not the nickname Grimbolt.

Jarla looked at Delvin.

"When I saw that rabbit, I knew you must be here," she whispered. "At least your rabbit was useful."

Delvin smiled sweetly back at her and returned Freda to her sling.

"Right, back to the horses," whispered Grimbolt.

They crept as silently as they could back to where the horses were tethered.

"I suppose I have to share a horse with you," said Jarla as she mounted Delvin's horse.

"And with my useful rabbit," replied Delvin as he hauled himself up behind her.

"We need to get to the Castle to tell your father what's happened," said Grimbolt, as they made their way back down the road towards Hengel. They had to ride slowly at first to make sure they stayed on the road, since it was dark and the trees obscured the dim light from the moon.

When they emerged from the forest, they were able to speed up. They then rode as quickly as they could, since they did not know how long it would be before the kidnappers realized Jarla had escaped.

The city gates were shut when they reached Hengel. But a yell from Grimbolt got them open, and they made their way through the streets of Hengel to the Castle.

Chapter 3

They rode through the Castle barbican and the Great Gate, the guards recognizing them and saluting as they rode past. On reaching the main Castle buildings, Jarla threw her horse's reins to a groom and marched in. She went straight through the Grand Hall to the spiral stairs in the corner of the keep, Delvin and Grimbolt having to run to keep up.

"My father will have finished his dinner and be in his drawing room," said Jarla over her shoulder.

They climbed past the first floor. When they reached the second floor, there was an iron studded door with a guard outside.

"Open it," commanded Jarla.

The guard opened the door to admit them to a sumptuously furnished chamber. There was a sofa and several matching chairs arranged around a massive fireplace. Sideboards inlaid with gold fittings bore small sculptures, and gold framed pictures adorned the walls. The room was lit by several candelabras and by the flickering flames of the fire. Seated in one of the chairs was an extraordinary figure. He was wearing an elaborate purple robe, but his most arresting feature was his hair. It had been set in giant spikes that radiated from his head like the rays of the sun drawn by a child. On the tip of each spike was a small bell that tinkled as he moved his head. The spikes on his head were complemented by his beard that was also in the shape of a spike, and it too bore a small bell.

"My dear," said Duke Poldor the Duke of Hengel, looking up and seeing his daughter Jarla as she entered. The bells on his hair tinkling as he did so.

Jarla was a striking figure. Aged twenty-one she was tall with long dark hair and pale skin which made her face seem gaunt and rather severe. She was slim and muscular moving with an almost catlike athleticism. Her most striking feature though were her long sharpened fingernails.

"Ah, Major Grybald and Sir Delvin," said the duke seeing Delvin and Grimbolt as they also entered the room.

The Castle was the only place where Delvin was known as Sir Delvin. The duke had knighted him the previous year for his services in defeating the magicians who had taken control of Hengel. Delvin didn't use his title when performing his magic shows and reading people's fortunes, since it would only lead to questions that would be difficult to answer without revealing he had a magician's stone.

"Your Grace," said Grimbolt and Delvin bowing to the duke.

"I was wondering where you had got to my dear," said the duke looking at Jarla. "You were not at dinner, and you do look a bit...disheveled... Have you hurt yourself? Your hands are covered in blood." The duke looked concerned.

"The blood is not mine. I was kidnapped father."

The duke's eyebrows rose. "Not your blood? Kidnapped?"

"Yes father."

Jarla and Grimbolt explained to the duke what had happened.

The duke looked hard at Grimbolt. "You think it was a coordinated attack, and they might have intended to kidnap that boy Nippy...Nippold as well?"

"I do Your Grace."

"There have been these idiotic rumours about Princess Jarla having a son," said the duke softly. "Do you think the magicians believe Nippold is Princess Jarla's son?"

"I do Your Grace."

"How do these ridiculous rumours get around?" growled the duke. "If I knew... I would deal with them..." Delvin inwardly blushed. It was him who had started the rumours earlier that year to save Jarla and Nippy from the black magician.

"What do you think the magicians are up to?" asked the duke.

"I don't know Your Grace," replied Grimbolt. "But it seems to have been coordinated and specially timed. I think the magicians had been waiting in the forest for the right time to strike. I have a nasty feeling it's a prelude to something else. But I don't know what."

"You may be right," mused the duke. "We shall have to be on our guard."

"I think it is time we took the initiative," broke in Jarla. "We have always been reacting to what the magicians do.

We should hunt down the magicians and finish them once and for all."

"That is easier said than done my dear. We have already got rid of that Magister Meldrum who was here in Hengel, and my brother duke, the Duke of Argent, got rid of that Magister Drandor in Argent. We don't know of any others, apart from the ones in Norden... Norden is an independent country. How do you propose to hunt them there?"

"Delvin and I could go there in disguise."

"My dear, you and Sir Delvin have already spent too much time going round the country in disguise. Do you realize what it has done to your reputation? How do you think you will find a husband? There are also the rumours and stories that you have killed several people, on top of the rumours that boy is your son... And looking at your hands, it now appears you have killed somebody else. You really can't carry on like this my dear. You can't go on killing people. All potential suitors are terrified of you."

"I don't want a husband father. I don't want someone who thinks he can order me around and hangs around me all day."

"My dear you need a husband. With Gustov dead you are the heir to the duchy. You need to produce an heir to carry on after you."

"Stella can produce an heir. It looks like she is going to marry Prince Elden down in Pandol."

"Yes, it does look like she will marry Prince Elden. But any child will be brought up in Pandoland. Any future

Duke of Hengel needs to be brought up in Hengel. Also, these rumours of Nippold being your son could cause problems for any son of hers who became duke here. No, my dear, you need a husband. That is why you must try to stop killing any more people."

"Do you expect me to just lie back and let people kidnap me?"

"No, my dear I do not. But going in disguise into a hostile country with the aim of killing magicians will not get you a husband. And it will not dispel your current reputation. You need to start spending time with suitable people and start getting to know them. So, despite today's incident, you must still go to Cavid tomorrow to spend time with Lord Cavid."

"I do not want to marry Lord Cavid," said Jarla determinedly.

"It has taken me a long time to negotiate this visit," said the duke. "I suspect Lord Cavid does not want to marry you either. But he is in debt, so I have been able to bring pressure to bear." The duke gave a grim smile.

"So, you are forcing him to marry me?"

"No, I have forced him to allow you to visit him so you can get to know each other better. When you go there you must be at your most charming. Then if he does not propose… I suspect he can be persuaded…"

Jarla gave a furious look at her father.

"So, you have paid him to just allow me to visit?"

"And to stay… and get know you."

"If I wasn't a girl, you wouldn't treat me like this."

"Oh no! I am treating Lord Cavid in just the same way as I'm treating you."

Just then Freda the rabbit popped her head out of the sling around Delvin's neck and looked around the room.

"Well, well," said the duke his eyes wide in surprise.

"So this is the rabbit I have been hearing so much about."

"I am sorry Your Grace," mumbled Delvin. "We came straight here. There was no time to take him to my lodgings."

"You were right to come straight here."

The duke turned to Jarla and fixed her with a steady stare. "My dear," he said, "you will go to Cavid tomorrow."

Jarla turned and stalked out of the room.

The audience with the duke seemed to be over, so Grimbolt and Delvin took their leave of the duke and made their way out of the Castle.

Neither Delvin nor Grimbolt had had any dinner, so they called into an inn on the edge of the East Quarter and ordered a bowl of stew and an ale each.

As they ate their dinner, Grimbolt turned to Delvin.

"We need to keep a keen look out, I feel something is about to happen."

Delvin nodded his agreement. "I wish we knew what it was."

It was late when Delvin got back to his lodgings at Mistress Wilshaw's house. She came out of the kitchen as he came in.

"Master Delvin, where have you been? You have missed your dinner. I was getting quite worried about you. Do you want me to make you something? We can't have you fading away. Now come into the kitchen and sit yourself down and tell me what kept you." Mistress Wilshaw gave a little wriggle of anticipation.

"No thank you. I met some friends and grabbed a bite to eat with them. I've had a tiring day. I think I had better go up and get to bed. But thank you very much."

He had told Mistress Wilshaw and his friend Greg about being given the title of Sir Delvin the previous year. But since then, he had used his magician's stone to get them to think he had just been playing a practical joke. When he did his magic shows and fortune telling he wanted to be just Delvin the magician.

Delvin went up to the room he shared with Nippy and Greg. They were both asleep and Greg was snoring softly.

Delvin got himself ready and climbed into his bed. But it was sometime before he got to sleep, as he kept turning over the events of the day in his mind and wondering if the magicians were plotting something.

Chapter 4

Delvin woke just after dawn the next morning. He stretched and rolled out of bed. As he put his breeches on, he was thinking about the magic show that he was performing that afternoon. His feet went into the legs, but then stopped suddenly and wouldn't go any further. He looked down. Knots had been tied in both the legs. Laughter was coming from his room-mate Greg's bed.

"That's for putting salt in my hot leaf yesterday," laughed Greg.

"Well, you shouldn't have been day-dreaming," laughed back Delvin.

"Look who was daydreaming when they tried to put their breeches on," returned Greg.

Delvin laughed again and untied the knots. Then he finished dressing and went down to the kitchen for his breakfast of hot leaf and rolls. Greg and Nippy followed shortly after.

After breakfast Delvin spent some time teaching Nippy his apprentice some more magic. Nippy was starting to build up quite a good repertoire of tricks, and had a natural ability when it came to slight-of-hand. Maybe that came from his skill at picking pockets from when he had been a street urchin in Argent, thought Delvin.

A little later a lady and a gentleman came to have their fortunes read. He had got quite proficient at doing fortune telling. Starting by making general statements that everyone would think applied to them, then surreptitiously drawing information out of them, and feeding it back in a way that made it look like he had a special insight.

In the afternoon he performed a magic and magic lantern show. The audience at this show were mainly children, so he made Freda appear from his box that looked like a genie's palace rather than from a hat. Then he wove fantastical stories around the slides he showed with his magic lantern. The show went well. He loved the smiles and laughter of the children, and their parents were happy too. Again, he received a good tip at the end.

The following day he had no bookings in the morning, so he dismantled his magic lantern and experimented with the lens. He tried putting the lens in different positions and combining it with a mirror. He wanted to understand exactly how it all worked.

He had a show booked for that afternoon at a grain merchant's house close to the Professional Quarter. It was for the merchant's wife's friends, so he decided to try making Freda appear out of a merchant's hat again.

"We'll be back at tea time," shouted Delvin as he and Nippy went out through the front door.

"Don't you get chatting to your friends again," replied Mistress Wilshaw coming out of her kitchen with her hands covered in flour. "I'm cooking a nice chicken pie for dinner, I know it's your favorite, so don't be late."

"We won't," he called back.

Delvin and Nippy made their way through the lanes of the East Quarter and out onto the North South Road.

"What was all that the other day?" asked Nippy. "Are you getting mixed up with them magicians again?"

"Something like that," said Delvin. He had been trying to avoid Nippy's questions all the previous day. Then he suddenly thought, if they had been trying to kidnap Nippy, he really should know about it.

"Nippy, you know when I told the black magician that you were Princess Jarla's son to stop him killing you?"

"Yeh, I was Prince Nippold. I liked that."

"Well, I think they may actually believe it. That attack might have been an attempt to kill me and kidnap you."

"Wow! I'm a prince!"

"No, you are not a prince. It seems they just think you are."

"Prince Nippold the first."

"We need to be careful."

Delvin then explained what had happened after he had left Nippy to take their props back to Mistress Wilshaw's.

"Wow, it's 'citing being with you."

"And dangerous, so be careful."

They had now reached the grain merchant's house. It was a large square house with a door flanked each side by bay windows. Next to it was a warehouse. It had big double doors which were open, and inside Delvin could see piles of sacks filled with grain.

Delvin knocked on the door and it was opened by a serving girl.

"Delvin the magician at your service. Mistress Salient is expecting us," announced Delvin.

The girl's eyes grew round in her face.

"This way magister."

The girl led Delvin and Nippy to a large room where Mistress Salient's friends were all assembled.

One of the walls of the room was painted white. Perfect thought Delvin as he set up his magic lantern to project onto that wall.

When everything was set up and with his audience facing the wall, Delvin went to the front and announced his show.

"I am Magister Delvin, magician extraordinary, and this is my assistant Nippold."

"Prince Nippold the first," announced Nippy. Delvin gave him a quelling look.

"Today I shall make scenes and stories appear before your eyes," continued Delvin. "You will be transported to far off lands, see the world's wonders and experience tales of daring do and adventure. Then, after a short interval I shall perform feats of magic and prestidigitation the like of which you have never seen before. You will tell your friends, your children, your grandchildren about what you have seen, and they will not believe it, because you too will not believe what you are going to see."

Delvin drew the curtains across the window, lit his magic lantern and began his show.

He was nearing the end of the lantern show when there was a loud rapping on the door.

There was the sound of the door being opened and then a voice.

"In the name of the duke I must speak with Sir…Magister Delvin immediately."

Seconds later Grimbolt burst into the room.

"You must come now! I have horses outside."

Chapter 5

All eyes in the room were on Grimbolt.

"Now! We have no time to lose!" demanded Grimbolt.

Delvin turned to Mistress Salient whose eyes were wide in astonishment.

"I apologize mistress, but it seems I must go. My assistant Nippold will pack up my things."

"Can I come too?" asked Nippy eagerly.

Grimbolt looked at him a moment.

"You can follow. I'll leave a horse for you. Take the Cavid Road."

"Can I do some of the magic before I come?" asked Nippy eagerly.

Mistress Salient gave Delvin a hopeful look.

"Alright," said Delvin. "Just do the main part of the act."

Nippy grinned and Mistress Salient looked pleased.

"Mistress Salient," said Delvin. "Please would you send a message to my lodgings to say I may not be in for dinner."

"Come on!" said Grimbolt.

Delvin followed Grimbolt out of the door leaving a room of open-mouthed ladies. They will certainly have something to talk about, thought Delvin.

Moments later Grimbolt and Delvin were mounted and heading for the West Road and the West Gate.

After they had gone through the gate, they picked up speed.

"What's happened?" called Delvin.

"They've invaded," replied Grimbolt.

"Who has invaded?"

"It seems to be a mercenary army. They have a magician with them. I think the magicians are behind it. I'm sure that's what those kidnap attempts were leading up to."

Delvin suddenly picked up a faint message in his mind. *'There is a huge army in front of you and another on your flank. You are frightened. You will stop fighting. You will run away.'*

Delvin immediately projected a counter message. *'You are brave. You will fight. You will win.'* He shouted across to Grimbolt to tell him about the messages. Then he began to wonder. Was the message about the huge army in front and on the flank just an illusion? Were they really there? Maybe the mercenaries' magician was creating an illusionary army.

He shouted across to Grimbolt, "I think the magician's projection about the huge army may be an illusion. They might not really exist. It might be like my lantern show, but projected into people's minds rather than projected onto a wall."

"Counteract that too," shouted back Grimbolt. "Sheffs! let's hope we aren't too late."

Delvin projected a message counteracting the illusion of a huge army and of an army outflanking them.

Another message came into his mind. *'A magician! I was told there was someone in Argent with a magician's*

Stone, but they said there wasn't anyone here in Hengel who had one.'

Delvin responded, *'Think again. I am here and we will drive you into the sea. If you want to save yourself, leave Hengel now.'*

There were no more messages. Delvin told Grimbolt about the exchange. He grimaced.

"We need to find General Gortly," he said.

As they rode, they passed several units of Hengel's soldiers marching towards Cavid. There was also a stream of refugees coming the other way, their carts piled high with their possessions. Frightened faces looked at them as they passed.

It was not long before they reached the fighting. They could see soldiers in the fields, and on the side of the road soldiers were having their wounds tended. Shouts and yells were coming from ahead.

"Where is General Gortly?" shouted Grimbolt to an officer who was starting to lead his unit forward.

"Over there," he shouted back, pointing to a group of men standing by a farm house.

Delvin followed Grimbolt has he spurred his horse towards the men.

A short stocky man with a weather-beaten face and short grey hair sticking straight up from his head, looked up as they approached. He was wearing a leather jerkin and looked more like a workman than a soldier.

"Sir Delvin, Major Grybald," said the man. "You took your time. Have you stopped them using their sheffs awful magician's stone?"

"I have General," said Delvin. "They now know we have a stone as well."

"Can you do anything else? Can you make them retreat?"

"I don't think I could make them retreat. Their magician would simply counteract any suggestion or compulsion I tried to put on them. I could possibly get both sides to stop fighting and then to pull back. I don't know how well it would work though, or if it is possible."

"Do it," commanded the general.

Delvin thought hard then projected a message. *'We both have magician's stones. Any more fighting will be a stalemate. If you stop fighting and withdraw. We will stop fighting too.'*

Delvin waited anxiously for a reply. General Gortly and Grimbolt looked at him expectantly.

'You will just use the delay to bring more troops forward.'

'We will bring more troops forward,' replied Delvin. *'That will happen whether we stop fighting or not.'*

Delvin decided to bluff. He knew that the magicians thought he had given his magician's stone to Argent. *'We are bringing Argent's magician's stone down to join mine. It should be here in less than a day, maybe even by tonight. Then the stalemate will be broken. With our two stones against your one, we will crush you. If you don't take this opportunity there will be no quarter. You will all be destroyed.'*

Delvin glanced nervously at General Gortly as he waited for the reply. Would his bluff work?

'You do not have two magician's stones.'

'Yes, we do. There is the one I gave to Argent and there is Meldrum's stone.' Meldrum's stone was the magician's stone that had belonged to the magician Magister Meldrum who Delvin had defeated the previous year. The duke's dog Aspro had grabbed it and run off and buried it. They had spent a long time looking for it but had never actually found it.

'Meldrum's stone was lost.'

'It has been found. Otherwise, how have I got a stone when Argent have also got one.'

Delvin realized he was holding his breath.

'We will stop fighting and withdraw if you stop fighting and do not pursue us.'

Delvin told General Gortly the proposal, and the general nodded his agreement.

'Agreed,' projected Delvin.

Delvin let out a huge breath of relief. He heard General Gortly barking orders to his officers, and Delvin projected his own message to the soldiers. *'Prepare for a truce. Prepare to stop fighting. Do not pursue the enemy.'* He picked up a similar message from the other magician.

"Right," ordered General Gortly. "Tell me exactly, word for word, what messages you and that magician exchanged."

48

Delvin told him. As he spoke, the yells and clash of battle began to reduce.

General Gortly looked towards his officers with a look of grim satisfaction and relief on his face.

"For the moment we will hold our position here. Draw up a defensive line. If this falls through, I don't want them advancing any further." He turned to Delvin and Grimbolt.

"Sir Delvin, Major Grybald, follow me. We need to decide our next move."

General Gortly marched into the farmhouse that they were standing outside. They went through to the farmhouse kitchen where there was a map of the area laid out on the table. Two officers stood by the table.

"Captain Blenson, Captain Cortel, send scouts to check exactly where the enemy forces are and how many there are. Also, if they start moving, I want to know."

"Yes sir," said the two officers in unison and marched out of the room.

"Right, Sir Delvin, you said you bluffed them, making out there was a second stone in Argent besides yours. How long will that bluff hold?"

"It's hard to say," replied Delvin. "It will certainly hold for one day, maybe longer."

"So, we need to get them shifted out of Hengel as fast as possible, and we can't attack them, since it will then be apparent that we haven't got a second stone," growled the general.

Noises and orders came from outside, and moments later the door burst open and the Duke of Hengel strode into the room, the great spikes of his hair waving as he moved.

"General Gortly, what is the situation? Why has the fighting stopped?"

"Your Grace," began General Gortly. "The enemy landed at dawn, captured Cavid and made a dash for Hengel. I think they hoped to take Hengel before we could put enough troops in place to stop them. They have a magician with them who was making our men stop fighting and retreat. Sir Delvin says they also created an illusion that there were far more men than they actually had, and that they were outflanking us. He has now countered their magician, and bluffed them to stop fighting and withdraw."

"So, they created an illusion," mused the duke. "Just like that…" He looked at Delvin. "Like that lantern thing in one of your shows?"

"Yes, Your Grace. Similar to my magic lantern. But projecting the illusion onto people's minds."

"You said they agreed to withdraw." His gaze became fierce. "How far did they agree to withdraw?"

"It was not specified, Your Grace," muttered Delvin.

"Not specified." repeated the duke menacingly. "Not specified… I want them out of Hengel, not camped two paces down the road."

"I could bring troops up behind them," suggested General Gortly. "Sir Delvin's agreement did not say we could not change out troops disposition, only that they should withdraw, and we would not pursue them." He grinned an evil smile.

The duke nodded, the spikes of his hair waving.

"I like it General. If they are surrounded, it will be a strong encouragement for them to withdraw back to Cavid... Even if we do only have one magician's stone, they would not want to be surrounded..." He smiled a cruel smile then fixed General Gortly with a fierce stare. "And how about my daughter Princess Jarla? What are you doing about her?"

"Princess Jarla?" asked General Gortly in surprise.

"Yes, Princess Jarla. She left for Cavid yesterday morning."

"I didn't know she was in Cavid, Your Grace."

"With luck the enemy don't know either," whispered the duke. "But knowing her, she'll get herself involved in something sooner rather than later... Then they'll know... We need to get her out... fast... We don't want to give them anything else to bargain with... And we need them out of Cavid."

The duke looked around the room. His gaze eventually fell on Delvin.

"Sir Delvin?"

Delvin gulped, "Yes Your Grace."

"Could you get Princess Jarla out of Cavid?"

"I could possibly smuggle myself into Cavid, Your Grace. And I might be able to smuggle her out again...

provided she agreed to come with me." What was he getting himself into, he wondered?

"You could tell her I ordered her to go with you."

"Yes, Your Grace," said Delvin dubiously, knowing Jarla's reaction to being told to do anything.

"What do you need?" asked the duke.

Delvin thought quickly about how he might get into Cavid.

"I imagine that farm carts with vegetables and other things will still be going in and out of the town," he said. "I can go in as a farmer with a farm cart."

"You won't be able to go down this road," said General Gortly.

"No, I'll take the other road. The one that goes through Byford. I come from Byford. I know the people there. I'll buy a cart and the vegetables from them, then drive it into Cavid."

Just then there was a noise outside. They looked up as a slightly flustered officer came in.

"Your Grace, General, I am sorry to interrupt, but a small gentleman is insisting he speaks with Sir Delvin. I tried to put him off, but he seems rather skillful at getting round the guards."

The duke raised his eyebrows.

"It will be my assistant Your Grace," said Delvin.

"Will he be useful in this venture?"

"I believe he may be Your Grace."

"Show him in."

52

The officer left the room and moments later Nippy came in grinning.

"Ah yes, Nippold I believe," said the duke eying him distastefully. "Sir Delvin is going to smuggle himself into Cavid, he said you might be useful."

"Smuggle into Cavid?" said Nippy grinning. "I can do that, easy."

Chapter 6

It was already late afternoon and the sun was beginning to set. Delvin and Nippy took their leave of the duke and General Gortly and rode as fast as they could towards Byford. Nippy had attached all the magic props from their show to his horse when he had left Hengel, including the magic lantern which now clanked as it moved against the other props. Delvin fervently hoped they would all survive the journey.

"How were the ladies after I had to leave?" asked Delvin, shouting across to Nippy.

"They loved it. Gave them some excitement. Even gave me the full fee... Can I keep it?"

"All right," said Delvin smiling.

By the time they reached the village of Camdin it was dark. But the moon was nearly full which gave them just enough light to keep going, though they did have to slow their pace.

The evening was late by the time they reached the village of Byford. They rode into the yard of the Ploughman's Inn and dismounted. A stable lad ran out and stopped in surprise when he saw them.

"Delvin," he exclaimed. "Is that you?"

"Hi, Anton, are they treating you well?"

"Yeh... It's great to see you. Does Berman know you're here?"

"No, we have just ridden in. Can you see to the horses for us and give my rabbit Freda here some oats?" He took

Freda out of her pouch and handed her to Anton who gave a wide grin.

"Trust you to have a rabbit with you. Have you come here to play a trick on someone?"

"No, not today, unless that stuck up village chief elder comes in." Delvin's mind flashed back to when the chief elder had tried to have him hung.

They left Anton to look after the horses and went through into the inn. Berman the landlord looked up as they entered the common room.

"Delvin! What brings you here? It's wonderful to see you." He smiled broadly. "Do your mother and father know you're here?"

"No, I've just ridden in. I haven't had time to call on them yet."

"I'll send a boy over to tell them. And who is this?" he said seeing Nippy.

"I'm Prince Nippold," said Nippy brightly.

"No, he's not," said Delvin. "He's my apprentice Nippy."

Berman laughed, shook his head and turned to Delvin. "Let me pour you an ale. Have you had anything to eat?"

"I'd like an ale too," said Nippy grinning at Berman.

Berman just smiled, shook his head again and poured Nippy a lemonade.

The other people in the common room had seen them come in, and they now came over asking Delvin how he was doing, so it was a little while before he was able to sit down with his ale and the plate of pie and vegetables that

Berman had ordered for him. Nippy was already happily tucking into his portion of pie.

Just then Delvin's mother and father came in. They rushed over, and as Delvin got up from the table his mother flung her arms around him.

"You didn't tell us you were coming."

"I didn't know till this afternoon."

"Who is this?"

"Nippy my apprentice."

The next few minutes were taken up with Delvin giving his parents a rather edited account of what he had been doing since he left Byford, interspersed with many questions.

"Will you be staying with us tonight? I could get a bed ready," asked his mother.

"I don't want to put you to any trouble. If Berman has a room free, we will stay here. We need to be up very early in the morning." Delvin called across to Berman. "Do you have a room free?"

"Aye, I do."

Delvin turned to his mother. "I would love to stay with you. But I really don't want to put you to any trouble."

His mother nodded smiling, and when Delvin said he hoped he would be back in the village again very soon, his mother gave him another hug. Not long after, she and his father took their leave, as they had been half way through eating their dinner when they had got the news that Delvin was at the inn.

Delvin looked around the common room. In the corner he could see the chief elder drinking a mug of ale. Smiling wickedly to himself, Delvin touched his magician's stone and projected the thought that the chief elder's arm would twitch just as he was taking a drink. The chief elder spluttered as his ale poured over his face and down his front. It was with some difficulty that Delvin managed to keep a straight face.

Delvin finished his ale and walked over to Berman at the bar.

"I'd like that room you have, and I have two horses in the stable. Let me know how much that is. I also need a farm cart loaded with vegetables. I'll pay for it. Do you know anyone who might sell me one?"

"Whatever do you need that for? Not another of your practical jokes, is it?"

"No, not this time." He took a deep breath. But he knew he could trust Berman. "I need to smuggle myself into Cavid."

"Smuggle yourself into Cavid? I hear there's trouble there. Why ever do you want to do that?"

"It's a mission for the duke. I can't say any more."

"For the duke eh. In that case… we may be able to do something. When do you need them for?"

"As soon as possible. Ideally by first light in the morning, but I know that might be difficult… I need to get into Cavid as soon as I can."

Berman thought for a few moments sucking on his teeth, then he leaned across the bar and called to a man drinking with his friends at a table against the far wall.

"Jolyan, are you taking a cart of vegetables to Havelock tomorrow?"

"Aye," called back the man.

"Would you sell them to Delvin here?"

"Sell them?"

"Yes, including the cart."

Jolyan got up and came over to the bar.

"What do you want with my cart and vegetables?"

Delvin thought quickly. He knew Jolyan and knew he could be trusted.

"I need to smuggle myself into Cavid."

"Into Cavid eh? It's not one of your practical jokes again, is it? Well, I can tell you something. I wouldn't go there. A person came through earlier and said some foreign army has invaded."

"I need to go there. It's a mission for the duke."

"Ahh… The duke is it… In that case I'll sell them to you. Do you need a horse as well?"

"No thank you, I have a horse."

Jolyan thought for a moment… "Seven royals."

"Agreed," said Delvin, and he reached into his purse and counted out the money.

"I need to set off as early as possible in the morning. Can you bring it round here at dawn?"

"Aye. The cart is already loaded. We were going to Havelock first thing. What are you going to do with it when you get to Cavid?"

"I hadn't thought," replied Delvin.

"Go to Enson's. They're vegetable wholesales. Enson's a really good person and totally loyal to the duke. Enson will buy the vegetables off you and give you a fair price."

"Thank you," said Delvin.

"You'll need to know how to get to Enson's."

Jolyan gave Delvin a set of directions.

"Tell Enson I sent you... What are you planning to wear on this mission of yours? You'd look strange with a cart of vegetables wearing those clothes." Delvin was still wearing his magician's clothes from his show.

"I thought I might see if my father had anything to spare."

"Aye, he might well have. But you're a bit taller than him. I'll bring a couple of smocks for you and that boy."

Delvin thanked him again. They shook hands, and Jolyan returned to his seat.

"When you've done what it is you are doing, will you be coming back this way?" asked Berman.

"Probably," replied Delvin.

"Will you be able to tell us what you've been up to?"

"Probably not," replied Delvin grinning.

"I guessed not. Right let's get that room fixed."

Delvin paid Berman for the room and stabling, and agreed with him that he would leave one of the horses with him until he returned.

Delvin took his leave of Berman and signaled to Nippy who was just finishing his second portion of pie to follow him. Then he made his way up to the room.

The room Berman had given him was the same room that his friend the magician Borlock had occupied when he had been murdered by the black magician. It had happened only about a year ago, but to Delvin it seemed more like a lifetime.

It was a while before Delvin got to sleep as his mind was racing, trying to think how he might rescue Princess Jarla.

Chapter 7

Delvin and Nippy were up before dawn. After a hurried wash and grabbing a roll each from a sleepy kitchen maid, they went out into the yard, their breath making clouds in the chill air.

Jolyan was already there with his cart. The cart was filled with stacks of large wooden crates containing a wide variety of vegetables.

Delvin went into the stables and got out one of his horses. Then he and Jolyan harnessed it to the cart. Delvin then packed the props from his show and his magic lantern in the back of the cart. He covered them with some sacking so that they were hidden from view.

Anton the stable boy came out with Freda, Delvin's rabbit. Delvin thanked him for looking after her, gave him a copper and tucked Freda into her sling. He and Nippy then slipped off their jackets and replaced them with the smocks that Jolyan had brought, packing the jackets with the magic props under the sacking.

"Aye, you look more the part now," said Jolyan standing back and surveying them as they climbed up on to the cart. "You just need a straw in your mouth to look the perfect yokel." He gave a mischievous grin and handed Delvin a straw of wheat. Delvin grinned back and put it in his mouth, then immediately spat it out with a gasp. The straw had been coated in mustard.

Jolyan was roaring with laughter. "That's for that trick you played on me last year."

Delvin, spluttering and his eyes streaming tears, laughed back. "You caught me out properly that time."

Delvin climbed down to get a quick drink of water to rinse out his mouth before mounting the cart again. Then to more laughs, he thanked Jolyon for the cart and vegetables, and with a grin, flicked the whip and began to move the cart out of the yard and onto the road towards Cavid.

Although it was already spring, it had been a cold night, and the air had not yet warmed up. Delvin rubbed his hands together to keep the circulation going while Nippy tucked his hands into his sleeves.

As the sun rose higher it began to warm a little. There were few other travelers on the road as it was still quite early in the morning.

This was familiar countryside to Delvin, having worked on farms in this area until only a year ago. It was an area of gently rolling hills. Meadows were interspersed with fields where the crops were starting to grow strongly. Occasional woods dotted the landscape, and farms and cottages nestled in orchards or stood amid barns down muddy tracks.

After just over two hours they reached the village of Denbig. It was a small village with an inn beside a village green. The village was at the junction of the roads that led to either Laverton or Cavid. They took the Cavid road and drove through the village without stopping. Delvin wanted to get to Cavid as early as possible.

The land was now becoming hillier with the road following the valleys between the hills. Most of the fields were now pasture with only a few planted with crops. As they neared the sea, they could begin to smell the tang of salt in the air.

It was nearing noon when they came over a rise and saw Cavid Bay and the town of Cavid below them.

Cavid was quite a large town. It was surrounded by a high wall with a large turreted gatehouse and several towers. It was Hengel's main port, and they could see several ships tied up at its many wharves with warehouses in the roads behind. On the other side of a low headland there was a small bay with a harbour. Beyond the harbour fishing boats were hauled up on the beach. Past the fishing boats the land rose up as a cliff. Perched on the top of the cliff, at the far end of the town and connected to the town wall, was a square grey stone building. It looked like it had once been a fortress, but the multitude of chimneys now showed it had been converted to domestic use. Delvin knew this building was known as the castle and was the home of Lord Cavid. This was where Jarla would be staying.

Out in the main bay, Delvin could see a fleet of some twenty ships. These must be the invader's ships he thought. They looked sleek and fast and were all painted black. Their sails were furled and small boats rowed between them and the shore.

Delvin took Freda out of her sling and handed her to Nippy who smiled back at him. They had used Freda in the past to distract guard's attention and make them seem normal and unthreatening, so then the guards wouldn't think of checking what was in the cart.

Delvin and Nippy drove the cart down towards the gate. The road they were on joined with the road between Cavid and Hengel just before the two roads reached the gate.

On the Hengel road squads of soldiers were marching towards the city while units of cavalry rode the other way. Did this mean the invaders were withdrawing to the town, wondered Delvin? He had not picked up any projections from the invaders' magician after the truce had been agreed.

On reaching the gate they were stopped by the guard.

"What's in the cart?"

"Vegetables. We are delivering them to Enson's."

"I haven't been notified of any deliveries."

"Well, if you want the town to starve, I can take them away."

The guard called for his sergeant who came over to them.

"You've got vegetables for Enson?"

"Aye," replied Delvin.

"And who's this?" said the sergeant seeing Freda.

"That's Freda my son's rabbit," replied Delvin. "He takes her everywhere." Nippy stroked Freda and smiled up at the sergeant. The sergeant smiled back.

"Will you be staying in the town or leaving later?"

"Aye we'll need to get back to the farm when we're done."

"When will that be?"

"Maybe tonight. Maybe tomorrow. I've a repair needs doing to the cart before I drive it back. Might not be ready till tomorrow."

"Right go through. You'll need a pass to get back out again. No civilians are allowed to leave the town." He took a pad from his pocket and wrote on it. "Here's your pass. Show it to the guard when you leave."

"Thank you," said Delvin taking the pass and putting it in his pocket.

"Walk on," he said and drove the cart into Cavid.

"Easy, works every time," grinned Nippy once they were out of earshot of the guards.

Delvin took back Freda and put her back in her sling.

"It does. Freda's a great distraction. I don't know anyone who can resist looking at an animal, then they stop thinking too much about other things." He grinned back.

Enson's yard was easy to find. They went down the main road and turned left at the market square. A short distance down the road there was a large green sign written in red and gold letters over the entrance to a yard, declaring 'Enson's Fruit and Vegetables'.

Delvin drove the cart into the yard. The yard was quite big with a warehouse at the back and what looked like offices to one side.

As they drew up a middle-aged lady came out of the offices. She had long brown hair tied up on the top of her head. She was wearing a tight green jacket that showed off her small waist and good figure. She strode confidently over and looked up at Delvin as he climbed down from the cart.

"Good day to you, magisters. What have you here?"

"A load of vegetables. We have come to see Magister Enson?"

"There is no Magister Enson. I am Mistress Enson."

Delvin was momentarily lost for words but he quickly recovered.

"My apologies. Magister Jolyan in Byford just told us to ask for Enson and to mention him to you."

Mistess Enson smiled.

"Aye, I know Jolyan. He's a good man. But he does like playing little tricks on people. I take it he didn't say I was a woman."

Delvin realized Jolyan had played another trick on him. He was certainly getting his own back for the tricks Delvin had played on him in the past.

Mistress Enson looked enquiringly at Delvin.

"Now why would you be driving Jolyan's cart?"

"May we talk in your office?" asked Delvin.

Mistress Enson looked at him of a moment then nodded.

"This way."

Delvin told Nippy to stay with the cart and followed Misress Enson into her office.

The office was a large room. One wall was filled with shelves containing folders of papers. There was a desk against the far wall also covered in papers and a big pine table in the centre of the room with chairs around it.

Mistress Enson indicated the chairs around the table and took a seat at the head of the table herself.

"Right, now tell me what all this is about."

Delvin took a deep breath. He remembered that Jolyan had said Enson was loyal to the duke.

"We are on a special mission for the duke. We needed to smuggle ourselves into Cavid. I guessed that with the invasion, not many local farmers would be coming this way, so any that did would be welcome and would be able to get in. I come from Byford myself. I bought the cart and vegetables off Jolyan with the duke's money so I could get into the town."

"On a mission for the duke, eh?" Mistress Enson looked Delvin in the eye, weighing him up. She seemed to come to a decision. She stood up and looked out of the window.

"This invasion is dreadful," she said thoughtfully. "It was all so sudden. It happened just before dawn yesterday. The garrison didn't see it coming. None of us did. It is absolutely awful." She turned back towards Delvin. "Do you know what the duke is doing about it?"

"The invaders tried to make a dash and take the city of Hengel by surprise," replied Delvin. "The army managed to stop them before they got there. The duke is with the army now."

"Thank goodness for that… Right, I've known Jolyan a long time. I know he's a good man and loyal to the duke, so if he sold you his cart for this, I reckon you are alright too. I would really like to do something about these invaders. How can I help?"

"We need to somehow get into the castle."

"Oh, that's not going to be easy. I've heard the invaders' general is staying there. And some magician person. There are invaders' men guarding the gate."

"Ah, that's a problem. I was going to offer to do a magic show and get in like that. But if a magician is there. That's probably not going to work."

"Are you a magician?"

"Yes."

"Do you tell fortunes?"

"Yes."

"I know Lady Cavid is very superstitious. I think she might just like to have her fortune told…"

"How do I get an invitation to do it? If there are invader's guards on the gate, I'm sure I'd need an invitation to get past them."

"I think I might be able to arrange that. I know the butler there… quite well. Your vegetables are the first fresh vegetables we have had in two days. We make regular deliveries of vegetables to the castle kitchen. I'll take a delivery of them there myself and have a word with the butler. I reckon I can get you an invitation." She smiled. "I've been wanting to do something against these sheffs awful invaders ever since they landed."

"Thank you," said Delvin. "That would be fantastic."

"In the meantime," said Mistress Enson, "we need to get you sorted. I'll buy those vegetables off you. how about three royals for the lot?"

"Fine," said Delvin.

Mistress Enson pulled open a drawer in the desk and counted out the money.

"You can leave your cart in the yard here and use our stables for your horse. Do you have anywhere to stay?"

"I had thought of staying with my landlady's sister who lives in the town, but I don't know her, and I was worried about getting her into trouble."

"I have a house just next to the yard here. My tenant left two weeks ago, and I haven't relet it yet. You can use that."

"That would be great," said Delvin.

"Right, I'll get one of the men to unload your cart, then we'll get your things and get you moved in there."

They went back out into the yard. As they came out, Nippy appeared from the warehouse munching an apple.

"What are you doing young man?" said Mistress Enson.

"Exploring," replied Nippy between bites. He gave Mistress Enson a wide grin.

"No more exploring," said Delvin and Mistress Enson almost together. Nippy gave another grin as he produced another apple from his pocket.

Mistress Enson gave him a severe look.

"He's my apprentice," said Delvin apologetically.

"I'm Prince Nippold," said Nippy with a grin.

"No, he's not," said Delvin shaking his head. "His name is Nippy."

Mistress Enson shook her head too. Then she called to one of her men to start unloading the vegetables off the cart.

Delvin began to unload his things from under the sacking, and Mistress Enson went to help him. She raised her eyebrows and looked slightly surprised when she saw Delvin's magic props and magic lantern.

"The props are for my show," explained Delvin.

They soon had all their things out of the cart and into the house next door.

Mistress Enson then left them, as she had tasks she needed to do as well as arranging the delivery to the castle, but before she left, she gave Delvin a wink and a smile. He grinned back.

Delvin explored the house. It had a room at the front with three easy chairs around a fireplace, and a kitchen at the back. Narrow stairs led to two bedrooms, one at the front and one at the back. The bedroom at the front had a double bed, the one at the back two single beds. Both rooms had a small table, a chair and a washstand.

After looking round the house, Delvin left Nippy in the house while he went looking for a shop to buy some food. He was soon back with two pies, a loaf of bread, some cold ham and a flagon of ale.

Delvin and Nippy sat down at the small table in the kitchen and ate their lunch.

After lunch Delvin went out again to buy some essentials, since he hadn't had time to pack anything when he had rushed off from his magic show.

On getting back to the house he washed and shaved. After that there was nothing else to do until Mistress Enson came back from the castle.

It was mid-afternoon when Mistress Enson knocked on the door and came in. She was smiling broadly.

"Good news. They want a magic show as well as fortune telling. It seems the magician staying with them is an old man and keeps to his room most of the time. He even has his meals there. Those invaders are not allowing anyone to leave the castle, and they are all getting rather bored, so Lady Cavid is looking for something to entertain everyone."

"That's great," said Delvin. "What time do they want us?"

"Two hours after dusk, after they've finished dinner."

"That leaves us a few hours," said Delvin smiling at Mistress Enson.

"It does indeed," said Mistress Enson smiling back, raising an eyebrow and glancing towards the stairs.

Chapter 8

An hour after dusk Delvin and Nippy presented themselves at the castle gate. Nippy was carrying the magic lantern, and Delvin had a pack holding his other magic props. Close up the castle looked very forbidding. Grey stone walls with small windows rose up without any decoration or ornamentation. The one feature that relieved the stark look were the highly ornamented chimneys. They rose up in spirals like candles on a child's birthday cake. The early spring evening was cold, and smoke drifted up from several of the chimneys.

Two men from the invading force were on guard. One was wearing mismatched armour and had a wicked looking sword at his side, the other looked to have a foreign uniform. When Delvin told them who they were, the guard in the uniform ordered the other guard to tell the butler that they were at the gate. The guard ran across the courtyard to a door on the other side. Shortly after he re-emerged with a stately looking gentleman.

The uniformed guard waved them through. The courtyard was surrounded by buildings on all sides. In the corner on the right was what had obviously been the keep of the original castle. Its square shape rose above the buildings to either side, and it still had its battlements and corner turrets. Opposite the gate was the doorway the guard had run to. It was very impressive. Three wide steps led up to a double door with a stone canopy above it.

"The butler," grunted the gate guard, nodding towards a stately looking gentleman who had just emerged from the door and was now waiting for them at the top of the steps.

"Magister Delvin, good evening," said the butler as they approached. "Lady Cavid, Lord Cavid and their guests are having their dinner at the moment. If you would care to come through to the drawing room, we will have the show in there." With that he turned and entered the building.

Delvin and Nippy followed the butler through the door. Inside was a large hallway. The floor was black and white checked tiles, and a wide staircase rose up in front of the door with branches to the left and right half way up. Marble statues stood in niches around the walls.

The butler opened a door on the left and led them into a sumptuously furnished room. There were groups of comfortable chairs and sofas, and a large fireplace opposite the door they had come through in which burned a log fire. Small tables and sideboards lined the walls with paintings in gold frames above them. Candelabra on the sideboards added to the light from the fire.

Delvin looked around to see where he could hold his magic lantern show. With all the pictures there was no area of plain white wall, and the fire would make it difficult to get the room dark enough.

"Have you a white sheet and a screen we could use?" asked Delvin.

"I will see what I can find," said the butler, and he withdrew the way they had come.

73

"I'm going to explore," said Nippy.

"Be quick and don't get caught, that butler will be back soon," replied Delvin.

Nippy grinned and tried a small door in the same wall as the door through which they had entered. The door was unlocked and Nippy disappeared through it.

Delvin meanwhile began to arrange the room for his show. He arranged the chairs facing where he would perform and placed a table for his lantern at the back, with another table for his magic props at the front.

Just as Delvin finished arranging the furniture, Nippy came back through the door.

"That's a service passage through there. Leads to the keep. Room with books in the keep."

"That's called a library," said Delvin.

"Yeh. Went through there up… stairs." He made a spiraling motion with his hand. "Room above is storeroom. Room above that is empty. Then you get out on the roof. It's really neat. There's a little round room in the corner off the top. It's got a pointed roof like a pointed hat."

"That's called a turret," said Delvin.

"It was locked… but picked lock… was empty."

Just then the butler came back in with two other servants. One was carrying a screen the other a large white sheet.

Delvin thanked them and placed the screen in front of the fire to shield the room from most of the fire's light. Then he hung the sheet between two of the pictures.

When he had everything just as he wanted, he filled the magic lantern's oil burner with oil from a large jar. Then he lit it, and got the lantern into focus on the sheet.

Nippy was just about to go off exploring again when Delvin stopped him. He could hear noises coming from behind a large door in the wall to the left of where they had entered.

Moments later the door opened, and the party who had now finished their dinner, came through from the dining room next door. They were led by a lady of late middle-years. She had grey hair elaborately curled and decorated with combs and jeweled pins. She wore a yellow dress that hugged her ample body. A jeweled necklace sparkled beneath her several chins. This must be Lady Cavid thought Delvin. He knew she was widowed, and she fitted the description he had been told about her.

Behind Lady Cavid came Jarla. She wore a scarlet dress that clung to her slim muscular body, and had a single red ruby on a chain around her neck. Her dark hair was loose and hung over her shoulders. She had a furious look on her face. When she saw Delvin, there was a glint of recognition in her eye, but she showed no other sign that she knew him.

Close behind Jarla, and seemingly trying to catch up and walk next to her, was a short gentleman wearing one of the most elaborate uniforms Delvin had ever seen. It had epaulettes and gold braid, tassels and a red sash. He had a full head of chestnut coloured hair that didn't seem quite right for his face, and his mouth was set in a lascivious sneer. This must be the invader's general, thought Delvin.

The last person in the group was a young man in his twenties. He seemed to be trying to keep as much distance from Jarla as he could. He was of slight build with dark hair and was dressed in black with no decoration. He had a slightly haunted expression on his face. This must be Lord Cavid who Jarla had been sent to get to know better, thought Delvin grinning to himself.

The party took their seats and Delvin strode out to the front and began.

"My lords and ladies, today I shall show you scenes and sights that only great travelers have seen. Wonders and displays. Stories and tales that will stay in your memories for years to come. Then after a short interval I shall perform feats of magic and prestidigitation the like of which you have never seen before. You will be amazed, bewildered astonished and entertained. You will tell your wives, your husbands, your children and your grandchildren and they will not believe what you tell them… for I am Delvin the magician."

He gave an elaborate bow, then blew out the candles at the front of the room, moved to his magic lantern, blew out the rest of the candles and began.

Delvin gave his usual overblown description of the slides. He did hear a snort from the general at one point, but otherwise it seemed to go down well. He relit the candles and they had a short break.

In the second part of the show, he performed his trick with cups and balls where balls disappear from under one cup to reappear under another. His trick with an egg and a small bag, in which the egg is put under his arm to reappear in the bag and then disappear again. A trick with a rope that he cut in two with his knife only for it to magically become whole again. A trick with a piece of paper that he tore up and scrunched into a ball, but when he spread out the ball of paper it had restored itself. He ended the show by producing Freda his rabbit from a hat.

Delvin bowed and received polite applause from his audience.

Chapter 9

Lady Cavid stood up, walked to the front of the room and turned to face her guests.

"Thank you, Magister Delvin. Now, as an extra treat, Magister Delvin has said he will read our fortunes. That is if you want them read," she added looking at the general. The general smiled. "I enjoy having my fortune told."

"I will go first," said Lady Cavid. "We shall do it in the library." She beckoned to Delvin. "Come, this way." She looked at the others. "You stay here. When I am finished, I shall come back here and the next person can go and see him."

Delvin quickly told Nippy to pack up their props, and then followed Lady Cavid out of the drawing room, through the entrance hall and into the library.

A servant, who had been at the back of the drawing room during the magic show, had run ahead and had lit two of the branches of candles on the library tables. A fire warming the room was already burning in the fireplace. When Lady Cavid and Delvin came in, the servant bowed and retreated out of a side door. Lady Cavid shut the library door behind them.

With the light from the fire and just two branches of candles, the library was a place of dark corners and shadows. This suited Delvin. It gave the room a mysterious feeling. The library walls were lined with shelves filled with rows of leatherbound volumes. There was a desk with papers and an ink stand. On a small table was placed a decanter and wine glasses. And in the centre of the room were three leatherbound armchairs and another small table.

Lady Cavid took one of the armchairs, and Delvin took one opposite, pulling up the small table in front of him. He didn't have his crystal ball with him, so he had decided he would use mainly cards and palm reading instead. He had prepared his cards that afternoon.

Delvin brought his pack of cards out of his pocket.

"I shall use the cards to give me a feeling of the future. Of what may shortly happen. Of dangers and pitfall to avoid and of opportunities to grasp. I shall then read your palm to tell me more about you and of what will come to pass."

Lady Cavid gave a little wriggle of anticipation.

Delvin took the pack of cards in his left hand.

"I am going to riffle through these cards. You must tell me when to stop." Delvin cut the pack and riffled through them with his thumb.

"Stop."

Delvin stopped and placed the top half of the pack on the table, then took hold of the card on top of the bottom half.

"This is the card you stopped at."

He turned over the card. It was the queen of clubs.

"Ah…the queen of clubs… There is an important lady. A dark…strong lady. The queen of clubs is a strong card… but it is not always a good one. This important lady is somehow… not right… Does this make any sense to you?"

"Oh yes," breathed Lady Cavid. "There is a lady… a strong lady… but she is not right for my boy."

Delvin took the cards, cut and shuffled them then placed them on the table.

"Let us try another card. This time I want you to cut the cards and place the cards you cut off, onto the table."

Lady Cavid cut off half the pack and laid it next to the remainder on the table.

Delvin placed one pack crossways across the other and looked up. Lady Cavid looked up too.

"Cutting the cards yourself helps the strength of the message, and this adds to the message of the queen of spades." Delvin removed the top pack of cards leaving the other half of the pack on the table. "Turn over the card you cut to."

Lady Cavid turned over the card. It was the seven of spades.

"Another spade. That strengthens the connection to the queen. It means there are seven things to do with the queen. The lady has seven secrets or seven incidents. They are spades… It means there is… something wrong."

"Oh yes," gasped Lady Cavid even more breathlessly.

Delvin knew that there were rumours going round that Jarla had killed seven men. He hoped he hadn't gone too far.

"Let me see your hand. We can go back to the cards later if you wish."

80

Lady Cavid laid her hand in his. Delvin peered at her hand then began to make statements and ask purposely ambiguous questions. These drew information from her that he then fed back as if he had seen it in her hand. It was a technique that he had learned from the magician Borlock and which he used in all his fortune telling.

It became apparent that Lady Cavid had heard the rumours about Jarla and was terrified for her son, but his gambling debts had forced her to agree to this visit.

Eventually Delvin came to the end and looked up. Lady Cavid looked up too, her eyes round in wonder.

"That my lady, is your fortune."

"Oh," breathed Lady Cavid getting unsteadily to her feet.

Delvin rose too and saw her to the door. When she had gone, Delvin reset his cards and waited for who would come next.

The next person to enter the library was Lord Cavid. He looked slightly frightened and glanced nervously round the room as he came in.

Delvin rose from his chair and seated Lord Cavid opposite him. He smiled at Lord Cavid who smiled wanly back.

Delvin then started as he had with Lady Cavid, cutting the cards, riffling through them and asking Lord Cavid to say "stop".

This time though, the card cut to was the queen of hearts.

"The queen of hearts. The queen of hearts can denote love, and even marriage. But it can also mean blood. We will need to see the next card to see if it tells us more."

In the same way as he had done with Lady Cavid, Delvin asked Lord Cavid to cut the cards. He laid one half of the cards across the other. This time the seven of hearts was revealed.

"The seven of hearts... That cannot be love seven times... Could it be blood?... Blood seven times?... Surely not..."

Lord Cavid had gone white.

"Let me read your palm."

Delvin again went into his routine of statements and questions. It was soon apparent that Lord Cavid was terrified of Jarla. He had heard all sorts of stories about her, and his friends had joked any man marrying her would be dead or emasculated within a week. He had only agreed to her coming to Cavid after the duke had paid off his most pressing gambling debts. He was planning to leave the country if the duke tried to force him to marry her.

Delvin painted a rosy future for him after his present troubles had passed, with a kind wife and several children. By the time he had finished, Lord Cavid was looking much more relieved.

Lord Cavid rose and left the room. Who would be next thought Delvin as he again reset his cards?

He did not have long to wait. Jarla entered the room, looked around then shut the door.

Delvin had risen and strode over to her.

"Just a minute," he said. Then standing very close to her, he projected very softly and tightly, that any suggestions and compulsions the magician had put on her were removed.

Jarla gave a slight start.

"What was that you just did?"

"Removed any suggestions the invaders' magician might have put on you."

"Will he have detected you using your magician's stone?"

"I don't think so. That's why I was standing so close, so I could do it very softly."

"Right. I presume my father sent you. What are your instructions?"

"To get you out of the town and away from these invaders, whoever they are, as soon as possible."

"Well, that will at least get me away from that idiot Lord Cavid."

"Aren't you two lovebirds getting on?" said Delvin with a grin.

Jarla gave him a disparaging look.

"Do you know who these invaders are?" asked Delvin. "They seem to be mercenaries. The magicians must have hired them... I tried to get away from this place when the invaders first came, but I couldn't seem to get past the door, or even through the windows which I also tried. Have you any ideas for getting me out of here?"

"The reason you couldn't go through the doors or windows, must have been a suggestion that magician put on you. I've removed that, but we still have to get you past the guards on the gate… No, I haven't got any ideas about that at the moment."

"Well while you think, remember back in Hengel, I said it was time we stopped reacting to the magicians and took the initiative ourselves. I said rather than the magicians hunting us, we should hunt them. Well now we know exactly where one of the magicians is. He is right here in this castle. I want to hunt him down before I leave."

"Hunt him?"

"Yes, hunt him down and kill him. He has been responsible for the deaths of all the Hengel soldiers killed by these mercenaries. If we don't kill him, he will cause more deaths."

"How do you propose to do that?"

"I am not sure… He's not going to be easy to get at. He spends nearly all his time in his room and locks the door."

Suddenly Delvin's face lit up.

"I have an idea," he said.

Delvin told Jarla his idea, and she grinned wickedly.

"There's another thing," said Jarla. "I've been trying to find out from that horrible general what the mercenaries' plans are, but I couldn't get anything out of him. Is there any way you could use your stone to get him to talk?"

"Not without alerting that magician…"

Delvin suddenly grinned again.

"I have another idea. I am not sure if it will work, but it would get you out of the castle as well."

Delvin told Jarla his second idea.

"It might work. We'll try it."

"Right, you had better get back to the drawing room. Then after the general has come down, we can get started."

Jarla left the room with a slight spring in her step and a gleam in her eye, leaving Delvin waiting for the general to come and get his fortune told.

He didn't have long to wait. The door opened again and the general strode in. He shut the door, took one look around the room, strode purposefully to the chair opposite Delvin and sat down.

"Right," said the general. "Let's get started."

Delvin again took out his pack of cards, and as with the others got the general to say "stop". The card stopped at this time was again the queen of hearts.

"The queen of hearts," said Delvin. "That donates love and passion. There is a lady that is highly attracted to you. Do you have a lady here?"

"No," said the general. "You are wrong."

"The cards do not lie. It must be a secret desire. There is someone here attracted to you."

"Probably some old bat," muttered the general.

"We'll ask the cards her age."

Delvin riffled through the cards twice more, each time asking the general to say "stop". He placed the cards the general stopped at face down on the table. He turned them over. They were the two of hearts and the ace of diamonds.

"She is twenty-one," announced Delvin.

The general started to look interested.

"Let me see your palm," said Delvin. He needed to move away from the cards, he had only one force card left and he might need that later.

Delvin looked at the general's palm and began his series of statements and questions, this time angling them towards the general having a secret admirer who secretly wanted to have an affair with him.

"Who is this lady?" demanded the general.

Delvin thought quickly. He was going to have to use the cards again, but he needed to be able to do it without using his last force card.

"Let us see if the cards can indicate her name," said Devin.

He spread the cards face up on the table and secretly noted the position of the jack of hearts. Then he brought the cards together again.

"Let us see what the cards can tell us."

Delvin riffled through the cards again, and when the general said "stop". The card stopped at was the jack of hearts.

"The jack of hearts. Hearts for love and desire. J for jack. The lady's name begins with J."

"Are you sure," growled the general.

"The cards do not lie."

"How do I know you do have the power and you aren't just some trickster?"

"What would you have me do."

"Make a prediction I can test."

Delvin thought fast and had an idea.

"Certainly," he said.

Delvin went over to the desk and took a sheet of plain paper and the inkstand and brought them over. Then he got one of the wine glasses and placed a playing card in it so it divided it into two compartments.

"You say you want me to make a prediction that you can test and verify. I shall make two. I am going to write a prediction on this piece of paper, of a name you are going to think of, and then place it in the glass."

Delvin tore a small piece off the sheet of paper, wrote on it, folded it and placed it in the side of the glass facing the general.

"I now want you to think of the name of a person, any person at all... Have you thought of it?" The general nodded. "There is no way I could have known in advance the name you would think of." The general nodded again. "Good. What was the name you thought of?"

"Eliza," said the general.

"Right, I shall make my second prediction," said Delvin.

He tore off another piece from the sheet of paper, wrote on it and placed it in the wine glass. This time in the side of the glass facing himself.

"My second prediction is the card you will stop me at."

Delvin again cut and riffled through the pack, and the general again said "stop". This time it was the ace of spades.

Delvin looked up and the general looked up too. "There was no way I could know in advance the name you would think of and the card."

"No," said the general.

"Let us look at my predictions."

Delvin took the piece of paper from the side of the glass facing the general and opened it. 'Eliza' was written on it. He took the piece from the compartment facing himself and opened that too. 'Ace of spades' was written on that piece. Delvin looked the general in the eye.

"Two predictions."

The general looked dumbstruck. Muttering something Delvin couldn't quite hear, he got up. Then glancing briefly back at Delvin made his way out of the library.

Delvin gave a sigh of relief. He had not been sure he would be able to convince the general that Jarla was attracted to him and wanted him. But it looked like he'd managed to do it.

Now for the next stage of the plan.

Chapter 10

Delvin went out of the library and found Nippy in the entrance hall waiting for him with their props and the magic lantern. He quickly explained his plan to Nippy.

"Easy," said Nippy grinning. "I've been exploring. Found clothesline in store room at end there."

"Great," said Delvin. "Right let's get started."

Nippy went out, and bending down picked up several small stones from the ground. Then he ran across the courtyard to the store room returning to the hall again with a coil of clothesline.

Meanwhile Delvin was rummaging through their props and took out the bottle of oil that they used for the lamp in the magic lantern.

Having got what they needed, Delvin and Nippy went back into the library, over to the spiral stairs in the corner and climbed up to the floor above. Once there they went down the servant's passage leading to the bedrooms.

The castle was quiet. Delvin hoped the servants would have all gone to bed needing to get up early in the morning.

They peered out of the door at the end of the servant's passage. The door led to the wider bedroom passage. Through the servant's passage door, they could see down the bedroom passage and see the doors of the principal bedrooms that led off it. They left the door open a crack so they could observe the bedrooms without being seen. Now they had to wait.

Only a short while later one of the bedroom doors opened and the general came out. He walked to the bedroom two doors down, straightened his collar and knocked on the door. The door was opened and he went in.

Delvin held his breath as he waited. Only moments later, Jarla, now dressed in riding clothes, came out of the door the general had gone to, and beckoned to them.

Delvin and Nippy, moving as silently as they could, crept down the passage.

Nippy went to the room at the far end. They knew from Jarla that the room at the far end was the magician's room, and that he habitually kept the door locked. Nippy pushed several of the small stones he had collected, through the keyhole into the lock. Delvin smiled grimly, when the magician tried to unlock the door, the stones would jam the lock and he wouldn't be able to get out.

Delvin entered Jarla's room. The general was lying on the floor unconscious. Jarla had rolled him onto his back and she was standing over him unbuttoning his jacket.

"Help me get his clothes off. Good you've got some rope. Where did you find that? I thought we were going to have to use his belt to tie him up with."

"It's clothesline. Nippy found it," said Delvin removing the general's trousers.

They soon had the general's jacket and trousers off, and Delvin tied his hands and feet. Jarla handed Delvin a towel, and he stuffed it in the general's mouth to gag him, holding it in place with more of the clothesline.

"Don't forget his wig," said Jarla.

Delvin grinning removed the general's wig. Underneath he was completely bald. There was a large bump on the back of his head where Jarla had hit him.

Nippy had joined them in Jarla's room. He now held the door open while Delvin and Jarla carried the general between them out of the room and down the passage. Nippy closed the bedroom door behind them.

Going as quickly as they could, they went back through the door into the servant's passage. Nippy again closing the door behind them.

When they reached the spiral stairs in the corner of the keep, they started to climb. By the time they reached the roof and battlements they were both out of breath. The general was beginning to come round and started to struggle.

"Put him down," ordered Jarla.

Delvin dropped his end, and Jarla stood over the general. She held her sharpened fingernails an inch from his right eye.

"Any more struggling and I will prick your eyeball. Nod if you understand."

The general's eyes moved from left to right, but there was only the implacable face of Jarla above him. He nodded and stopped struggling.

"Get the door open," ordered Jarla.

Nippy grinned and went over to the corner turret and picked the lock like he had done when he had originally explored.

"Easy," he said.

They bundled the general into the turret, closed the door and Nippy locked it again. He then pushed more small stones into the lock to make sure the lock would jam, and nobody would be able to open it and get the general out.

Delvin let out a great breath.

"That's the first part."

Jarla gave a brief smile and headed for the spiral stairs.

"I'll go and get changed," she said.

"Right Nippy, it's over to you now," said Delvin.

"Easy," said Nippy with a grin.

The magician's room was at the end of the bedroom passage. It was at the opposite corner of the castle from where Delvin and Nippy stood on the keep. Smoke was coming from several of the bedroom chimneys, including the furthest chimney on the opposite corner. That will be the chimney for the fire in the magician's bedroom thought Delvin. He pointed the chimney out to Nippy.

"I knew that," said Nippy disparagingly. With that, Nippy was over the battlements and moving across the roofs with astonishing speed.

It seemed only moments before Delvin saw Nippy reach the chimney of the magician's room. The chimney, like the other castle chimneys, was ornate and built in a great spiral of bricks. Nippy was up it almost as if it had been a staircase. A moment later Delvin saw Nippy take the top off the bottle of oil that he used as fuel for the magic lantern's light, and then drop the whole bottle down the chimney.

As Nippy climbed back down the chimney, Delvin heard a faint whomph from inside the building, and a cloud of smoke, soot and sparks flew out of the top of the chimney into the night sky.

Nippy was on his way back, and soon he was clambering up over the battlements onto the keep where Delvin was watching. He was slightly out of breath but grinning from ear to ear.

"Did you hear that go off?"

"I did," said Delvin smiling back.

"Enjoyed that. Was easy."

"Right," said Delvin. "Now we need to go, and make it look like nothing has happened."

They were quickly down the spiral stairs and through the library into the entrance hall. There they picked up their props and magic lantern and strolled towards the gate.

The guards on the gate were the same ones who had been there when they had arrived and did little more than nod to them as they went out.

Once through the gate they made their way down the hill towards the town. When they reached the first buildings they stopped and stood in the buildings' shadow. From there they had a clear view of the castle. They put down their loads and waited.

They did not have to wait long. They heard the cry of "Fire!" and through the castle's gate they could see people starting to run around. The sound of crashing came from where the magician's room was. They are breaking the door down, thought Delvin. The fire was starting to get hold, and through the small windows of the magician's bedroom, which were still shut, they could see a flicker of flames.

He hasn't escaped through the window, thought Delvin. He'll probably have been overcome by the smoke by now.

In the courtyard Delvin could see a chain of buckets being passed hand to hand from a pump in the corner.

A thought suddenly struck Delvin. Jarla had been influenced by the magician to stop her leaving the castle. If the other people in the castle had been influenced too, they wouldn't be able to escape if the fire spread. He quickly sent a projection to remove any influences the mercenaries' magician might have put on the other people in the castle.

Servants, many in their nightclothes, now began to spill out of the castle through the gate. Delvin felt a surge of relief that he had removed any influences from them.

Another figure came into view. The ornate uniform and chestnut hair were unmistakable. The figure came through the gate, stopped and turned back to look at the fire, feet apart, hands clasped behind. Then the figure turned away from the fire and came towards them.

As the figure came next to where they were, Delvin called out, "Over here."

"There you are," said Jarla, taking the lumps of rolled up cotton material out of her mouth that had made her face more the shape of the general's face. "Right, let's get this ridiculous uniform off."

She rapidly took off the uniform and wig. Under it she was still wearing her riding clothes.

Delvin folded up the uniform and added it to his bundle of props. Then keeping to the shadows as much as they could, they made their way to Mistress Enson's house.

. They let themselves in and went up the stairs. When Jarla saw the slightly dishevelled double bed she gave Delvin a withering look.

"Do you have a woman in every town?"

"I haven't stayed overnight in Parva yet," he replied grinning.

Jarla snorted and shut the door.

Delvin and Nippy went to the other room and got ready for bed. They had to be away early in the morning.

"Enjoyed that. Was easy," said Nippy happily as he climbed into his bed.

Chapter 11

They were up before dawn. After eating a hurried breakfast from the remains of the food that they had bought the previous day, they went next door into Enson's yard. Mistress Enson was there before them, and was already hitching their horse up to their cart.

"I reckoned you would want to make an early start."

She looked up from where she was getting the cart ready and saw Jarla.

"Good morning…I suspect it is probably best if I don't ask who you are," she smiled, and Jarla smiled back. "Are you planning to smuggle her out of the town?" she asked Delvin.

"Yes," he replied smiling too.

"Right, in that case we need to rearrange these vegetable boxes."

The wooden boxes that had contained the vegetables that they had brought into Cavid were neatly stacked in the back of the cart. Mistress Enson nimbly jumped onto the cart, and with Delvin and Nippy's help, soon had them arranged so there was a gap between them big enough for a person to lie in.

"Right if you lie down here my lady, we can put these other crates over the top, and no one will see you."

"In the past," said Jarla, looking at Delvin and then at the small gap between the crates in the cart. "You have disguised me as a corpse, a whore and almost as a stuffed toy. Now I see it's going to be a turnip. I dread to think what it will be next time."

"Don't worry, I'll think of something," retorted Delvin grinning.

Jarla scowled at him and then climbed up onto the back of the cart and lay down in the gap.

Delvin heaved several crates over where she lay covering up the gap.

"I think maybe a little dirt to get you to blend in better," grinned Delvin. "Or maybe a few cabbage leaves."

"Don't you dare," came Jarla's voice from beneath the crates.

They finished packing everything onto the cart. When everything looked right, with both Jarla and Delvin's magic props well out of sight, Delvin thanked Mistress Enson for all her help. She smiled at him and gave him a long kiss. Delvin and Nippy then climbed onto the cart, and they were away. As they drove out of Enson's yard and into the road, Delvin took Freda his rabbit out of her sling and handed her to Nippy to hold.

They reached the town gates as the sun was coming up. The guards on duty came over to Delvin and saw Freda.

"I remember you. You're the ones with the rabbit who came in yesterday."

Delvin smiled at the guard and handed him the pass they had been given when they came in.

The guards looked at the pass, returned the smile and waved them through.

They took the road back towards Byford. It was the road they had arrived from, and Delvin thought it would look suspicious if they took a different road going back. Besides, he could see several squads of the mercenaries' soldiers on and around the road leading from Cavid directly to Hengel.

The road climbed slowly up the hill away from the town. When they had gone over the top of the hill, and Cavid was well out of sight, Delvin pulled the cart off the road and onto the verge. He and Nippy climbed onto the back of the cart and removed the crates from above the space where Jarla was lying.

Jarla got up stiffly and dusted the dust and dirt off her riding clothes.

"Well at least you got me out of there."

"The turnip express," said Delvin grinning.

"Well, the turnip express is much too slow. I need to get back to General Gortly and my father as soon as possible to let them know the situation. We need another horse."

"We can try to buy one at one of these farms," suggested Delvin. "But before we do anything, I need to check if their magician is still alive."

Delvin concentrated and projected a message towards the town. *'All invaders, you must now leave Cavid. Leave Hengel. Go back to your ships and leave.'*

Delvin waited, holding his breath to see if there would be a reply or a message counteracting his message, but there was nothing.

"I think their magician is dead," he announced. "I'll keep on projecting messages telling them to leave Cavid, and I'll add that they will probably die if they stay. Without their magician, and with their general disappearing, hopefully they will go."

"Good," said Jarla with a smile. "Right, let's find a farm and see if we can buy a horse."

"Oo look! You've got a worm on your head," interrupted Nippy pointing at Jarla's head.

She brushed a small worm off her head and looked at Delvin accusingly.

"Was that you? Did you drop that down on me when I was in the back of the cart?"

"No," replied Delvin. "I hadn't thought of doing that."

Jarla glared at him. "So, you would have done it if you'd thought of it."

"I didn't say that," said Delvin innocently.

"Right," said Jarla turning back towards the cart. "We need to get going."

They climbed back on to the cart and set off again.

A short distance ahead there was a farm set back from the road down a short track. A group of buildings were set around a yard with a neat farmhouse to one side. A field with cows in it was next to the track leading to the farm. Delvin pulled the cart up onto the verge, climbed down and walked down the track to the farm. Jarla followed behind him while Nippy stayed with the cart. A lady came out of the farmhouse.

"Good day to you, magisters, mistress, what may I do for you?"

"Good day mistress," began Delvin. "Do you have a horse we can buy from you?"

"A horse?" said the lady in surprise. "We only have the horses we use on the farm, and we need those for the farm."

"We would be prepared to pay a good price," said Delvin. He touched his magician's stone and started to project to the lady that perhaps they could make do with one less horse.

"I'll get my husband," she said and moved off towards the yard. "Zeph! Zeph!" she called.

While they waited for the lady to find her husband, Jarla leant against the fence of the field containing the cows.

Delvin grinned to himself and projected to one of the cows that Jarla's ear was a tasty bit of grass. The cow ambled over, and with its tongue, gave Jarla's ear a huge lick.

Jarla leapt forward with a surprised cry.

"Delvin, was that you?" she growled.

"That cow?" said Delvin trying to look innocent. "Maybe it was your new cabbage perfume."

Jarla began to move menacingly towards Delvin, but was stopped by the farmer's wife and her husband Zeph coming out of one of the buildings. Jarla was then only able to glare at Delvin.

"This gentleman wants to buy a horse," said Zeph's wife.

"Ain't got no horse for sale," said Zeph.

Delvin again touched his magician's stone and projected the message that perhaps he could manage with one less horse.

"I'll pay a good price," said Delvin.

"How about old Daisy," said Zeph's wife.

"Aye, we could probably manage without old Daisy. I'll go and get her and see what the gentleman thinks."

He went into one of the barns and came back out with a heavy plough horse. He led her over to Delvin.

"She ain't young no more, but she's good and placid."

"How much would you like for her," asked Delvin examining the horse. She was old but appeared to be sound. He guessed that an old horse like that would probably cost seven gold royals from a horse dealer.

"I'd not really thought. Hadn't thought about selling her."

"I'll give you twenty royals for her," said Delvin.

"Ahh," said Zeph, his face lighting up.

The deal was soon done, and Delvin was able to buy an old saddle and bridle as well.

"Shall we saddle Daisy up for you?" said Delvin to Jarla with a grin, imagining Jarla trotting down the road on a heavy plough horse.

"I'll be taking the other horse," said Jarla giving him another disparaging look.

They unhitched their horse from the cart, and while Nippy put the saddle on it, they put Daisy in its place to pull the cart.

Delvin gave a wave to Zeph and his wife, and they set off.

"I won't get you to buy any horses for me," said Jarla as they got back onto the road. "You paid far too much for that old nag."

"Perhaps, but you wanted a horse and you got one," said Delvin. He had been given a purse of money by the duke's aide when they set out, and he was happy the farmer had got a good deal.

Without looking back, Jarla set off down the road at a fast canter and was soon out of sight. Daisy plodded along behind, quite happily pulling the cart.

Delvin continued projecting messages towards Cavid, ordering the mercenaries to leave and saying they would die if they stayed.

It was nearing noon when Delvin drove into Byford.

Chapter 12

Delvin pulled into the yard of the Ploughman's Inn and Jumped down from the cart. Berman the landlord came out from the inn to greet him.

"Delvin, you're back. I see you still have the cart, but your horse seems to have grown a bit."

Delvin smiled. "This is Daisy. Do you think Jolyan would like his cart back. I've finished with it now."

"I'll send a lad over to ask him. Are you staying here or moving through?"

"I am afraid I need to move on. Please could you look after the cart and Daisy while I quickly go and see my parents? Nippy, do you want to come with me?"

Berman smilingly agreed, and Delvin with Nippy beside him, walked quickly the short way to his parent's house where he had grown up. Delvin's mother was in, and when he walked through the door, she leapt up, exclaiming in delight and flung her arms around him.

Delvin's mother then noticed Nippy and she welcomed him too with a motherly smile.

Suddenly there were shouts from outside, and Delvin's father burst in saying, "Look what's coming down the road." He then noticed Delvin, and with a huge smile shook him by the hand.

They all went out to see what the hubbub was all about. Coming down the road at some speed was a considerable cavalcade of horses. At the front was a squad of cavalry carrying the blue and white banner of Hengel. Behind them were several figures. But the figure that most arrested the attention was a man sitting straight in his saddle dressed all in black. Each of the huge spikes of his hair were tipped with ribbons which streamed back in the wind as he rode.

"Is that Duke Poldor?" gasped Delvin's mother.

"Yes," replied Devin. "I had better get back to the Ploughman's. I have a feeling he might want to see me."

"Why would he want to see you?" asked his mother in a surprised voice.

"I've been doing a job for him," replied Delvin. "I haven't got time to tell you about it." With that, he bade his mother and father a quick goodbye. His mother, still with a surprised look on her face, gave him one final hug before he and Nippy dashed back to the inn.

The duke's party had pulled up at the inn. As Delvin ran across, he saw that Jarla and General Gortly were also in the party with the duke.

A small crowd had started to gather. It was the first time that anyone could remember that Duke Poldor had come to Byford.

"There you are," said the duke testily as he saw Delvin run up.

"I only arrived a moment ago," said Delvin breathing hard.

"We'll get a bite to eat here, then on to Cavid," announced the duke. "Sir Delvin, join us."

When the duke called Delvin, Sir Delvin, the jaws of the onlookers dropped in astonishment. They had only known him as Delvin the farmhand who had always been playing tricks on people.

The duke strode into the inn with Jarla, General Gortly and Delvin following closely behind. Berman showed them into the common room and sat them down at a table. Then he rushed off, coming back a moment later with a bottle of wine and glasses. He glanced at Delvin, who mouthed the words 'ale please' and smiled. Berman smiled back. He knew Delvin preferred ale, and quickly poured a tankard of ale for him.

Meril, Berman's wife, brought out bread rolls and cold meats, bowing to the duke as she did so.

"Princess Jarla has told me about you possibly killing their magician," said the duke turning to Delvin as he ate his lunch. "Do you know for certain that you killed him?"

"I think we have Your Grace," replied Delvin. "I have been sending messages all morning telling the mercenaries to leave and they'll get killed if they don't. There have been no counter messages or anything from their magician, so I am fairly certain that he's dead or that at least he's incapacitated."

"So, if you have projected a message telling them to leave," growled General Gortly, "there is a good chance that they will have done so. Will your message also have been picked up by their army outside the town?"

"Probably," replied Delvin. "But I did project it towards the town as I was trying to check if their magician was still alive. Its effect won't be quite as strong outside Cavid."

"Princess Jarla said you had incapacitated their general too," mused the duke, "so they won't be able to get any counter orders from him."

"It will be worth giving their men outside the town an extra push to make them leave," said General Gortly. "With your permission, Your Grace, I'll order our army to move forwards as quickly as possible. That should get them to move."

"Certainly General," said the duke.

The general excused himself and they could hear him bellowing orders to his officers to advance on Cavid. He returned with a look of satisfaction on his face.

"If they leave Cavid, and we can take the town back without having to storm it, that will save a lot of casualties. Cavid has strong walls."

The duke nodded, the spikes of his hair waving as he did so. They continued their meal. As soon as they had finished, the duke rose from the table.

"On to Cavid as quickly as we can," he said striding purposefully out of the inn.

"I need to get my horse saddled," said Delvin running towards the stables. "I'll be with you shortly."

"No time for that. Use the remounts," growled General Gortly and shouted at a trooper to bring two of the remounts forward.

Delvin hardly had time to grab his necessities from the cart before they were off.

The ride to Cavid was done at a brisk canter. As they came over the brow of the hill and saw the town below them, they could see boats full of mercenaries being rowed out to the ships in the bay. A whisp of smoke rose up from the castle. There was no sign of any mercenaries outside the town or manning the walls.

"We should wait here till my men clear the town," said General Gortly.

It was not long before they saw columns of men and squads of cavalry, under the blue and white banner of Hengel, advancing on the town down the Hengel Road. They watched as the soldiers entered the town. There was no noise of battle. Just an occasional yell as one of the tailenders was caught by the advancing Hengel soldiers.

"Your message to the mercenaries seems to have worked," growled General Gortly. "Right. Time to go in."

Chapter 13

The duke and his escort trotted down to the town gate. Two of Hengel's soldiers were now manning the gate. They saluted as the duke and general rode past.

"We need to talk to that general of theirs," said General Gortly, "and find out what's happened to our garrison."

They rode through the town towards the castle. People peered out of their windows, and as they saw who it was, cheered and waved their arms. Others heard them, and soon people were pouring out of their houses and cheering the duke as he rode past.

The duke sat straight up in his saddle, a slightly sardonic look on his face, acknowledging the cheers with slight inclinations of his head.

They reached the castle and rode under the arch of the gate into the courtyard.

The fire in the magician's room seemed to have been contained and not spread to the rest of the castle. Part of the room's roof had fallen in, and blackened timbers protruded from the roof tiles on either side of a large hole.

As the duke dismounted, the butler, closely followed by Lady Cavid, rushed out from the door.

"Your Grace," began Lady Cavid looking very flustered. "I fear you have found us in a considerable state. There was a fire last night as you can see." Lady Cavid then noticed Jarla. "Princess Jarla, I am so thankful you are safe. We were so worried. We didn't know where you were. We hunted everywhere for you. We feared that mercenary general had taken you away. He's disappeared too. It's been terrible."

"I believe I can find the general for you," said the duke. He turned to Jarla. "My dear, lead the way."

To Lady Cavid's astonishment, Jarla led the duke, General Gortly, Delvin, and a detachment of soldiers into the entrance hall and from there to the library and up the spiral stairs. Lady Cavid followed, and Nippy tagged along behind, avoiding the butler's attempts to shoo him away.

They reached the battlements and Jarla strode over to the corner turret.

"He's in there," she said.

"There's nothing in there," said Lady Cavid looking around slightly wildly.

General Gortly stepped over and tried the door.

"It's locked," said Jarla, "and the lock will be jammed."

"Break it down," ordered General Gortly to two of the soldiers.

The men stepped forward, and after several kicks and hitting it with their shoulders, the wood holding the lock gave way, and they pulled the door open.

The mercenary general was in a bad way. He had got very cold without his jacket and trousers and not being able to move.

"Get him warmed and cleaned up then bring him to us," ordered the duke. He turned to Lady Cavid. "We will use the library."

"Yes, Your Grace," she said looking bewildered.

They went back down the spiral stairs into the library where the duke sat himself down on one of the easy chairs, General Gortly and Jarla took the other two. Delvin looked round the room and pulled out the chair that was by the writing desk and offered it to Lady Cavid. She waved it away and approached the duke.

"Your Grace, is there anything you need or anything I can do for you?"

"After we have interrogated this general, we will have dinner… After your fire, do you have any rooms fit to sleep in?"

"I believe we can find three, Your Grace. We could also probably find a room in the servant's wing."

"Princess Jarla, General Gortly and myself will take those three. Sir Delvin, see what you can find for yourself."

The butler had anticipated that they would want some refreshments and came in with a tray of glasses and a decanter of wine. He set it down on a side table and poured wine for them all.

It was not long before two soldiers came in supporting the mercenary general between them. He was now looking a little better, and there was some colour in his cheeks. They had given him a dressing gown to wear, and he had a blanket over his shoulders. He was still unsteady on his feet and needed the support of the two soldiers to stop him from falling.

Delvin brought over the chair from the desk, and the soldiers sat the general in it.

"Sir Delvin make him tell us everything," ordered the duke.

Lady Cavid, now looking at Delvin more closely, suddenly realized he was the same person as the magician who had performed for them the previous night. Her hand went to her mouth in shock.

Delvin projected the thought that the general must tell the duke, who had hired the mercenaries, how many of them there were, what their plans were and answer any other questions.

The general began to speak. His eyes flashed backwards and forwards, and a grimace came over his face as he tried to fight the compulsion that Delvin's projection had placed on him. He could not overcome it, and he started to tell them everything.

"We were hired by the Guild of Magicians."

"I thought so," growled General Gortly.

"I have twenty-two ships and thirteen hundred men. There are another twenty-four ships outside Argent. There are about fourteen hundred men on those ships."

"Outside Argent?" said the duke in surprise.

"We all assembled outside Rostin up in Norden. The magicians put one magician with my fleet and two with the fleet going to Argent. They said that Hengel and Argent together had only one magician, and he was in Argent. That was why two magicians went with the Argent fleet, so that they could counteract Argent's magician. The plan was that my fleet would attack Hengel. We would take Cavid by surprise, then make a rapid march on the city of Hengel. The magician with us would make sure any troops that did manage to deploy in time wouldn't be any problem by projecting an image of a much larger army outflanking them."

"An illusion like your magic lantern," growled General Gortly looking at Delvin.

"We would then take Hengel before they could put up a proper defence," continued the mercenary general, his face contorting as he tried to fight Delvin's projection.

"The plan was to then march on Argent. The Guild of Magicians had placed another magician in North Bridge. He was there in case the magician from Argent tried to stop us crossing the bridge between South Bridge and North Bridge. He would counteract Argent's magician if he tried to stop us crossing the river. As soon as we were across, the other fleet with their two magicians would land in Argent. Then we would make a pincer move trapping Argent's army between us. We would have three or even four magicians against one. We would have taken both Hengel and Argent with hardly losing a man."

There was a slightly stunned silence from both General Gortly and the duke.

"So that's what this was all about," said General Gortly.

"We must warn Argent," said the duke.

"There's another magician in North Bridge," said Jarla, her eyes sparking as she flexed her fingers. "We shall have to deal with him."

"That is not in our country," said the duke.

"We can always pay a visit," responded Jarla.

"You are on a visit here to get to know Lord Cavid," said the duke severely. "That is what you will continue to do. It is not your job to go chasing off after magicians."

Jarla smiled sweetly back, but her slightly faraway look suggested she was planning something completely different.

"What did you do with our garrison?" demanded General Gortly.

"They are in the barracks. The magician put some sort of compulsion on them to keep them there."

General Gortly growled and looked towards Delvin who nodded back. He would need to remove the compulsion later.

They continued questioning the mercenary general for some time but found out little more that was useful. Eventually the duke turned to one of the soldiers.

"Take him back to Hengel, and lock him in the dungeons." He then turned to Lady Cavid who was standing in the background. "It's time for dinner." He turned back towards Delvin. "Sir Delvin, after dinner check that the mercenaries' magician actually is dead... But first we will have dinner. Lady Cavid, please show us the way."

Lady Cavid gave a little bow and led them through the entrance hall and drawing room into the dining room.

The butler had again anticipated things and the table was already set. They took their seats around the table. The duke glanced around with a look of query on his face. "Where is Lord Cavid? I had hoped he might have had an announcement to make about him and Princess Jarla."

"I don't know," said Lady Cavid. "He was here earlier... Denam," she addressed the butler, "find Lord Cavid and send him down."

"Yes, my lady," said Denam and withdrew.

When Denam returned a little while later he had a worried expression on his face.

"I can't find him, my lady. We have looked everywhere."

"Oh Dear! Not another person disappearing," said Lady Cavid in some agitation. "Have you checked the stables?"

"I have my lady. His horse is missing."

"I do apologize, Your Grace," said Lady Cavid. "I expect he didn't realize you were here."

"I rather expect that he did," said the duke sardonically. He turned to Jarla. "My dear, you seem to have scared off yet another suitor."

Jarla smiled back sweetly.

Lady Cavid looked embarrassed. "I'll send someone after him to see if they can find him. Denman, send someone to see if they can find Lord Cavid."

"Yes, my lady."

114

The meal continued with Lady Cavid frequently looking at the door, as if she hoped her son might come in.

When dinner was finished the party moved through to the drawing room. Delvin had hardly been included in the conversations over dinner, so he decided that now was a good time to do the tasks he had been set.

"I'll check the mercenaries' magician and then go over to the barracks and take any suggestions or compulsions off the garrison," he announced.

"Take one of my men. He'll show you where the barracks are," said General Gortly.

Delvin bowed and left the room. Denam was just outside.

"Do you know where my apprentice Nippy is?" asked Delvin,

"I believe he is in the kitchen sir," replied Denam.

Nippy grinned as Delvin walked into the kitchen. Nippy was performing some of the tricks that Delvin that had taught him, giving an impromptu magic show across the kitchen table. Delvin's pack of magic props lay open on the floor beside him, and there was a hat on the table that already had some coins in it. Delvin smiled at him and left him to it.

Delvin decided he would check the magician first. He turned to Denam.

"I need to look at the room where the fire was," he said.

Denam hardly raised his eyebrows, but simply nodded and led Delvin up the stairs and along the bedroom passage.

The floor of the bedroom at the end of the passage was still intact, although the room was open to the sky. As Delvin entered, he wrinkled his nose at the strong smell of burnt wood and smoke. He walked over to the remains of the bed and quickly checked to see if there was any sign of the mercenary magician's magician's stone. There was nothing there.

"Where is the magician's body?" asked Delvin.

"We took him to the room next door. He was lying on the floor. It looked like he had been overcome by the smoke," replied Denam.

"Please take me to him."

They went through to the next-door room. There was still a strong smell of smoke, and the wall next to the magician's room was charred and at one point had been burnt right through. On the bed lay the body of the magician. It looked partly burnt.

Delvin took a deep breath to steady his nerves, then went over to the body and bent down to examine it. There was a chain around the body's neck and on the chain was his magician's stone.

Delvin carefully removed the chain and stone from around the body's neck. The stone was blackened from the fire, and part of it seemed to have burnt away. Delvin wondered if it still worked.

Delvin stood up and went back out of the room. He realised he had been holding his breath and took in a gulp of air.

"Thank you," he said to Denam who had been waiting outside the room. "Please could you show me to where the soldiers are."

"Certainly sir."

Denam turned round and began to lead Delvin down the passage.

As Delvin followed him, he quickly rubbed the soot and dirt off the stone. Then, making sure he was not touching his own stone, he projected the thought to Denam that he would give a quick skip and a jump.

Nothing happened. The heat of the fire and the part that had burnt away must have stopped the stone working, thought Delvin. He put the stone in his pocket and followed Denam to where the soldiers were guarding the castle gate.

One of the soldiers on the gate was quickly detailed to be his guide, and with the soldier showing the way, Delvin made his way to the barracks. It took him only moments to release the soldiers there of the compulsion that the mercenaries' magician had put on them.

As Delvin walked back to the castle, he again tried using the mercenaries' magician's stone, this time on the soldier who was accompanying him. But again, nothing happened.

Delvin knew he must report straight back to the duke, so on reaching the castle he made his way to the drawing room.

The Duke, Jarla and General Gortly were sitting around the fire. They looked up as Delvin walked in.

"Your Grace, General," began Delvin, "I have removed the magicians influence from the soldiers in the barracks."

General Gortly gave a grunt of approval.

"I have also checked that the mercenaries' magician is actually dead, and he is. I managed to recover his magician's stone, but it was damaged in the fire and now doesn't seem to be working."

"Really?" said the duke. "Show me." He held out his hand.

Delvin handed him the damaged stone. The duke looked at it and handed it on to Jarla.

"I take it you have tried using it?" asked Jarla.

"Yes," replied Delvin.

"Is there any way we can get it to work again?" asked General Gortly.

"I don't know of any," replied Delvin. "Part of it seems to have burnt away."

"We could really have done with having another stone," growled the general. The duke nodded his head, the great spikes of his hair waving.

Jarla handed the damaged stone back to Delvin. He didn't feel like continuing the conversation, so he bowed and asked the duke if he would excuse him, then retreated out of the room.

Delvin had not yet been allocated a room in the castle. He was feeling depressed that the mercenaries' magician's stone was damaged and didn't work. He didn't feel like staying in the castle, so he decided instead he would head towards Enson's yard, hoping he might catch Mistress Enson before she retired for the night.

The gates of the yard were shut when he got there. He stood a little way back and looked up at the building. There was a light coming from a window above the offices. Delvin grinned to himself and picked up a small stone and threw it at the window. After the third stone the window opened and Mistress Enson's head peered out.

"Oh, it's you. What do you want?"

"The company at the castle is rather boring."

"Did you hope to find more interesting company here?"

"Something like that," said Delvin grinning.

"Oh, you do, do you?"

Mistress Enson shook her head and gave an exasperated sigh.

"Wait there."

A few moments later a door to the side of the yard's gates opened.

Delvin smiled and went in.

Chapter 14

Delvin was up early in the morning. He didn't know what time the duke wanted to leave, so he needed to get back to the castle in good time, but before that, he wanted to pay a quick visit to Mistress Wilshaw's sister before he left Cavid.

He gave Mistress Enson a quick kiss as he left her house. Then with a spring in his step went to find where Mistress Wilshaw's sister lived.

Mistress Wilshaw's sister lived in a street behind the fish market. It turned out to be a small, neat house with window boxes and a brightly painted blue door.

Delvin knocked on the door. I was opened by a lady who was a complete contrast to Mistress Wilshaw. While Mistress Wilshaw had ample proportions, her sister was very thin.

"Good day," said Delvin. "My name is Delvin, and I lodge with your sister Mistress Wilshaw in Hengel. I was in town, and I thought I should pay my respects before I leave later today."

"Ooo! You're the magician, aren't you? My sister told me all about you. Ooo! a real magician! That's really exciting. Come on in and have a cup of hot leaf and tell me all the news. And you must tell me my fortune. My sister said you did fortune telling."

Delvin quickly realized that while Mistress Wilshaw and her sister might look different, they both loved gossip and talking.

As Delvin drank his hot leaf, Mistress Wilshaw's sister questioned him about Mistress Wilshaw, about Hengel and about what was going on there, and also told him all the gossip of Cavid.

"Now," she said, "you must tell my fortune." She gave a little wriggle of excitement.

Delvin took out his cards and performed a quick fortune telling. He was starting to get worried about being late back at the castle. He didn't want to miss the duke leaving Cavid. Just as he was wondering how to get away, Freda his rabbit popped her head out of her pouch and looked around. Mistress Wilshaw's sister stopped talking in surprise. Delvin quickly took the opportunity of the break in conversation to thank her for the hot leaf and said he would pass on her complements to her sister. Then he got up, bowed and took his leave. As he walked quickly down the road towards the castle, he let out a sigh of relief. When he arrived back at the castle, the duke's party was already in the courtyard starting to get ready to leave. Nippy had saddled both their horses and packed the props they had brought with them.

Delvin approached the duke and explained he needed to return to Hengel via Byford, since in the rush to get to Cavid, he had left a horse and cart there together with some other of his magic props.

The duke gave a dismissive wave of his hand.

Delvin quickly mounted and joined the duke's party as they trotted out of the castle and through the town. The crowds cheered them as they passed, thankful to have been delivered from the invading mercenaries.

After passing through the town gate, the duke and his cavalcade headed down the main road to Hengel, while Delvin and Nippy took the road to Byford.

They reached Byford at lunchtime and went straight to the Ploughman's Inn. Berman the landlord greeted Delvin warmly and poured him a tankard of ale. Nippy looked hopefully at the ale, but Delvin just ordered him a lemonade.

"Now then," said Berman, "what's this about being called Sir Delvin? You haven't been playing tricks on the duke, have you?"

"No." replied Delvin. "The duke knighted me for services I did for him."

"Can I ask what those services were?"

"I'm sorry, but I can't tell you." Delvin thought he had better not mention that he had also been knighted by the Duke of Argent as that would lead to even more questions and speculation.

Berman gave him a long look.

"It's caused a lot of comments, the duke calling you Sir Delvin."

Delvin gave him a rueful look and took a sip of his ale.

The inn's common room was quite full, and it seemed Delvin was quite the topic of conversation as people's eyes kept glancing towards him.

Delvin saw the chief elder sitting in the corner and grinned to himself. Just as the chief elder took a drink of his ale, Delvin projected the thought that he would sneeze. The chief elder practically exploded.

Berman the landlord looked at Delvin narrowly. Delvin tried to look back innocently. Nippy was giggling.

Berman gave a slight shake of his head.

"I spoke to Jolyan after you left yesterday," said Berman. "He said he'll buy back that cart, and if you don't want the horse, he'll buy that too."

"Great," said Delvin. "He can have them for eight royals."

"That seems very fair," said Berman. "I'll send one of the boys over to tell him. In the meantime, do you want some lunch?"

"Yes please," replied Delvin. Nippy hearing the mention of lunch grinned eagerly.

Delvin and Nippy were just finishing their lunch when Jolyan came in. He greeted Delvin with a smile.

"How was Mistress Enson," he asked grinning.

"She was very well," replied Delvin grinning back. "Fancy not telling me Enson was a lady." They both laughed.

"I hear you don't need the horse and cart any longer."

"No, I've done what I needed to do."

"Berman said eight royals?"

"Yes, that's right," replied Delvin. They shook hands, and Jolyan handed over the money. Then going out to the stables, Delvin retrieved his magic lantern and other props that were still in the cart.

After thanking Berman, Delvin made his way to his parent's house, where again he was embraced by his mother and shook hands with his father.

"Are you able to tell us what you have been up to? And being called a sir, is that true?" asked his mother a look of concern in her eye. "Everyone's been talking about it."

"I'm sorry, I really wish I could tell you, but I can't," Delvin replied. It was important that his parents didn't know about his magician's stone, since knowledge of it would put them in danger.

They chatted for a little longer, then he and Nippy mounted their horses and set out for Hengel.

Chapter 15

It was almost dark when Delvin and Nippy got to Hengel. They left the horses at the Castle, then made their way back to Chandler's Lane and Mistress Wilshaw's house. It had been raining, and there was a slight smell of damp vegetables in the air as they crossed the market square.

They arrived at Mistress Wilshaw's house and went in.

Mistress Wilshaw rushed out of the kitchen.

"Oh, there you are Master Delvin. We were wondering where you had got to. That gentleman is here to see you again. Ooo, you are not going to get mixed up in anything again, are you?" She gave a slight twitch as she spoke.

"I had better see what he wants. May we use the parlour?"

"Ooo yes. I'll sent him through."

"Delvin went into the parlour, and a moment later Grimbolt came in."

"Hello Major Grybald," said Delvin tiredly.

"You can call me Grimbolt when we are in private," said Grimbolt giving his lopsided smile. "Princess Jarla has asked that you come over to the castle as soon as you get in."

"I've only just come from there to drop off your horses," replied Delvin in exasperation.

"You know Princess Jarla."

"Have I time to grab a bite to eat?"

"If you are quick."

Delvin was about to go through to the kitchen, when a thought struck him, and the tiredness suddenly went. He looked up. "There's something wrong."

"What's the problem?" said Grimbolt now fully alert.

"Mistress Wilshaw gave a twitch not a wriggle when she spoke."

"Do you think the back magician has been here?"

"Yes. I think he might have put some sort of compulsion on her and she was somehow fighting it. We need to check."

They went back to the kitchen. Mistress Wilshaw was putting on her coat. Delvin touched his magician's stone and projected a thought to her that she was released from any suggestions. She gave a twitch and looked at him in surprise.

"Ooo! Master Delvin, that was very strange. I seemed to be doing things I didn't want to."

"Has a man in a black cloak been here?"

"Yes, Master Delvin. He was here yesterday."

"What did he ask you to do?"

"He said, that when you came back, I was to go to The Black Horse Inn to tell him. He also wanted one of your socks."

"Did he say anything else?"

"He asked if I knew where you were. I said I didn't know. Ooo Master Delvin! He was a nasty man. I didn't like him at all. He was quite rude."

"Well, you don't need to go to The Black Horse Inn."

Delvin gave Grimbolt a questioning look.

126

"We will deal with him," said Grimbolt returning Delvin's look.

Mistress Wilshaw gave a little shake and seemed to pull herself together.

"Now Master Delvin," said Mistress Wilshaw. "You sit down and have some dinner. It's chicken pie. I know it's your favourite. I cooked it hoping you would be home tonight. Come on, sit down." She looked at Grimbolt. "There's plenty for you to have some too."

Nippy, on hearing there was chicken pie had immediately sat down and was looking hungrily towards the oven.

"We really should be going out," said Delvin.

"Have you had any dinner?"

"No," said Delvin.

"Well, I'll have no more excuses then. You sit down and have some dinner. You too," she said looking at Grimbolt. "Come on, sit down."

Delvin and Grimbolt both obediently sat down at the table, and Mistress Wilshaw handed them and Nippy large plates of chicken pie.

Just then Greg, Delvin's room-mate came in. The next few minutes were spent greeting each other and telling each other their news. Greg was excited, since he had been given the job of taking two horses down to Pandol and was setting off the next day. He hadn't been to Pandol before and was looking forward to going there. Delvin told him he had been to Cavid, but he wasn't able to tell him much more, since he didn't want Greg to know he had a magician's stone, as it would put him in danger.

While Greg was speaking, Delvin sent a projection releasing him from any suggestions and influences that the black magician might have put on him. He was relieved to see no twitch. It seemed that he hadn't been in the house when the black magician had visited.

In between all the talk, Delvin managed to eat most of his pie.

Nippy had finished his plateful of pie while they had been talking, and now hopefully held it out for a second helping. Mistress Wilshaw gave him a motherly smile and filled his plate again.

Grimbolt too had finished most of his pie and was now looking slightly impatient. Eventually he tapped Delvin on the shoulder.

"We had better be going."

"You mustn't go yet," said Mistress Wilshaw, "neither of you have finished your pie." She looked at Grimbolt accusingly.

"It was lovely Mistress Wilshaw," said Delvin getting up from the table, "but I really do have to go."

Grimbolt got up too, and they eventually managed to get out of the door. Mistress Wilshaw entreating Delvin to come back quickly.

It had started to rain again, and Delvin pulled his collar up to stop the rain running down his neck.

Grimbolt headed further into the East Quarter.

"Aren't we going to the Castle to see Jarla?" asked Delvin.

"She'll have to wait. Before that, we need to see if we can fix that black magician once and for all."

"Can't we do that later?"

"The longer we leave it, the more likely it is he'll visit Mistress Wilshaw again. Then he'll know we are on to him. Also, if we go to see Princess Jarla first, she'll want to come too. It's going to be dangerous. I don't want her in any more danger than I can help."

"She won't like it."

"True. But this way there is nothing she can do about it." Grimbolt smiled his lopsided smile.

"Where are we going now?"

"To my house to pick up my crossbow."

They soon arrived at Grimbolt's house. This was the safe house they had used the previous year. It didn't take long for Grimbolt to find his crossbow, and they were on their way again.

The Black Horse was an inn on the edge of the Butcher's Quarter, just off the Great East Road. It was an ancient building, its upper floors overhanging the pavement below, and with an arch leading to the stable yard behind.

"What do we do now?" asked Delvin as they stood on the street corner looking at the inn.

"We need to find out what room he is in then go up there," replied Grimbolt. "You'll need to do it. I can't walk in asking questions with a loaded crossbow in my hands."

Why do I always get myself into these things, thought Delvin as he crossed the road and entered the inn?

He went through the front door. The door opened into a passage that went through the inn to the stable yard behind. On his right was the common room. Through its open door he could see it was filled with drinkers, and he could hear singing over the sound of many voices. He made his way down the passage towards a flight of stairs at the end. A serving girl came out of what looked like a kitchen on the left. She was holding two plates of food.

"I'm looking for a gentleman who dresses in black. Do you know what room he is in?" asked Delvin, sending a very tight projection to the girl with an image of the black magician.

"Up the stairs, last door on the right at the end of the passage," said the girl walking past him and through into the common room.

"Thank you," said Delvin to her retreating back.

He went through the inn into the stable yard, and then back through the inn's arch out into the street. Grimbolt was waiting for him at the corner.

"Upstairs, last door on the right at the end of the passage," said Delvin.

"Right," said Grimbolt. "Let's go."

Delvin led them through the arch to the back door of the inn. Then he peered inside to make sure the coast was clear.

"No one there," he whispered.

They ran through the door and up the stairs.

"If we'd had more time, I'd have got one of the maids to put a sleeping draft into his food," muttered Grimbolt. "But as it is, it looks like we'll just have to make a frontal assault."

They reached the top of the stairs and looked down the passage. A dog lay asleep part way down.

As they crept down towards the end, the dog raised its head, sniffed the air and began to bark.

"Shh!" hissed Grimbolt, but the dog ignored him.

They stepped over the dog and moved quickly to the end of the passage. There was a large black painted door on the right.

"Right," said Grimbolt taking hold of the door handle.

He turned the door handle and pushed open the door, levelling his crossbow as he did so.

Thwang… "Arhh!" Grimbolt reeled back clutching his shoulder and dropping his crossbow. As the crossbow hit the floor the bolt was knocked off and the crossbow was discharged with another thwang.

Looking through the partly opened door Delvin could see the black magician. His left arm was in a sling and he held a crossbow in his right hand. He dropped the crossbow and drew his sword.

Grimbolt gave a bloodcurdling yell, and despite a crossbow bolt sticking out of his shoulder and blood pouring down his arm, he charged forward drawing his sword. Delvin drew his belt knife and followed him.

The black magician seeing them both coming through the door, let go of his sword and dashed for the window. A coil of rope had been tied to the centre window mullion. The black magician leapt through the window holding onto the rope with his right hand. By the time Grimbolt had reached the window, the black magician was on the ground. He looked up towards Delvin and Grimbolt with a sneer on his face. A message came into Delvin's mind. *'I didn't get you this time, but I will get you Magister Delvin. Don't think you can escape me. Then you will experience pain like nothing you could even imagine. Keep looking over your shoulder. I will be there. I am going to get you and destroy you.'* With that the black magician turned and disappeared into the night.

Delvin reeled back in shock.

"Did he project a message to you?" asked Grimbolt.

"Yes, he said he was going to get me, and I should keep looking over my shoulder as he'd be there."

"Well, we now know one of the things he is aiming to do."

"Yes… Thanks," said Delvin dubiously. He looked at Grimbolt and saw the blood dripping down his arm. "We need to get you to a doctor."

"We'll go to the Castle and get a doctor there," said Grimbolt with a grimace. "Grab his crossbow. We don't want him ambushing you with that. Get his sword too."

"Do you think he'll come back here to get his things?"

"He might do. Or more likely get someone else to get them for him."

Delvin picked up the black magician's crossbow and sword and started back towards the door where Grimbolt was picking up his own crossbow.

As they were about to leave, Delvin saw his sock that the black magician had taken when he had visited Mistress Wilshaw's house. He went over and picked it up.

"What did he want my sock for?" he asked.

"To get your scent," replied Grimbolt. "He will have given a suggestion to that dog to bark when he smelt that scent. That's why it barked when we came down the passage, and why he was ready for us when we broke through the door."

"So, he's starting to use animals like I do," said Delvin, wondering what other animals the black magician might use.

They left the room and went back down the stairs. At the bottom, Delvin checked there was no one in the passage before they went out into the stable yard, then through the inn's arch and out into the street. Delvin offered to support Grimbolt if he felt weak or couldn't make it, but Grimbolt waved him away.

It was still raining and few people were about. Those that were on the streets were huddled in their coats trying to stay dry, and were just concentrating on getting where they were going.

They reached the Castle without incident. The guard on the barbican recognised Grimbolt and saluted as he passed. When they reached the Great Gate, Grimbolt opened the guardroom door at the base of the left-hand tower.

"One of you get the surgeon. Tell him to go to the tower room off the lobby… You!" Grimbolt looked at one of the other guards. "Find Princess Jarla. Tell her to go to the lobby tower room as well."

The guards ran off on their errands as Grimbolt and Delvin crossed the courtyard and entered the main Castle building.

They went up the stairs into the lobby and then into the tower room. The room was sparsely furnished with just a wooden table and four wooden chairs. Grimbolt sat down in one of the chairs and dropped his crossbow down on the floor.

"Cut my jerkin off," ordered Grimbolt. "You won't get it over the shaft of that bolt."

Delvin dropped the black magician's crossbow and sword, and took out his belt knife. Then as carefully as he could, he cut through the jerkin. Although his knife was very sharp it was tough going. The jerkin was thick leather and had heavy padding underneath. He eventually managed to open the seams and had almost got the jerkin off, when the door opened and Jarla strode in.

Jarla took one look and strode over to Grimbolt. "Give me that knife," she demanded.

Delvin handed her the knife, and she deftly finished cutting Grimbolt's jerkin and shirt off.

"What have you been doing? I expected you and Delvin here ages ago."

"We heard the black magician was at The Black Horse Inn," said Grimbolt. "We went there to try to deal with him."

"You should have come back here like I told you to. What happened?"

Grimbolt briefly told Jarla what had happened.

"If you had come back here and I'd been with you, we would have got him rather than you getting shot like this."

"Even you wouldn't have been quick enough to stop him escaping through the window," said Grimbolt.

"You could have had Delvin under the window to get him when he tried to escape."

"Delvin?" replied Grimbolt incredulously. Both Grimbolt and Jarla knew Delvin's lack of fighting skills.

"Perhaps not," said Jarla. "Unless he stood under the window with his knife pointing up so the black magician landed on it." She gave half a smile.

Just then the surgeon came in. He took over from Jarla who had been using Grimbolt's shirt to stem the blood. He removed the shirt and examined the wound.

"You've been lucky," said the surgeon. "Your padded jerkin seems to have taken most of the force. I don't think the bolt has gone in too deep. But first we must get it out. Bring me some hot water and clean towels."

Delvin thankfully retreated from the room and went down to the kitchen to get the water and towels. By the time he had returned, the surgeon had got the bolt out. He deftly cleaned the wound, stitched it, and bound it up.

"Not much more than a flesh wound. You should be fine in a few days." The surgeon bowed and left.

"Right," said Jarla. "As I said before, until now we have simply been reacting to what the Guild of Magicians does. It is time we took the initiative and we started hunting the magicians down and eliminating them. Unless we do that, they are just going to keep on attacking both us and Argent. This invasion was their third attempt. They're not going to stop until we have eliminated all the magicians who've got magician's stones… We now know the rough whereabouts of two of them. So, which one are we going to hunt first? The black magician here in Hengel, or go to North Bridge to hunt the magician there?"

"The black magician will probably have gone to ground for the time being," said Grimbolt.

"We could stake out The Black Horse Inn," suggested Jarla. "Or use Delvin as bait to get him to come out."

"He's going to be very careful about going back to the inn," said Grimbolt. "I doubt we'd catch him there again. As for using Delvin. He is always going to be bait wherever he is. We don't need to stay here for that."

"That's true," said Jarla. "Right, it's decided then. We'll go to North Bridge and hunt down the magician there. We leave at dawn. Be ready."

"Shouldn't we have more of a plan?" asked Delvin.

"You can be thinking about that tonight. I'll see you at dawn."

With that Jarla marched out of the room leaving Delvin and Grimbolt looking at each other.

"Looks like I'll be seeing you in the morning," said Grimbolt. "I'll bring you a horse."

"Will you be all right?" asked Delvin concerned.

"As the surgeon said, just a flesh wound," replied Grimbolt.

"Well, if you're sure you're alright, bring a horse for Nippy too," said Delvin. "He may be useful."

"If you are going back to Mistress Wilshaw's house now, I'll get a couple of guards to go with you," said Grimbolt. "I don't think the black magician will try to ambush you on your way home. But it's better to be careful."

"Thank you. And at least he hasn't got his crossbow," responded Delvin.

Delvin took his leave, and with Grimbolt's two guards accompanying him, made his way back to Mistress Wilshaw's. It was still raining, and he was quite wet when he got in. Mistress Wilshaw appeared from the kitchen.

"Master Delvin, you'll catch your death of cold in wet clothes like that. Take them off at once. I'll dry them by the fire. Come on, I've seen it all before."

"Thank you, Mistress Wilshaw," said Delvin retreating up the stairs. "I'll take them off up here."

Mistress Wilshaw followed him up the stairs, and Delvin only just managed to make it to his room before Mistress Wilshaw caught up with him. Once in the room he took off his outer garments and opening the door a crack handed them through to Mistress Wilshaw.

"And the rest," said Mistress Wilshaw.

"Those aren't wet," replied Delvin.

"Well don't you catch a chill. I don't want to go chasing up and down the stairs looking after you."

"I'll be fine, thank you Mistress Wilshaw."

His room-mate Greg was sitting on his bed grinning.

"She almost got you there," he laughed.

Delvin smiled back but his mind was racing. With the black magician after him, he knew he needed to get Greg and Mistress Wishaw to safely in case the back magician visited again while he was away.

"When you go to Pandol tomorrow with those horses, you should take a break while you're down there. My magic shows have been doing well recently. Here's ten royals. Stay for a few days and have a good time on me." Delvin touched his magician's stone and reinforced what he was saying with a projection telling Greg to accept the money and agree to having a break.

"Thank you," said Greg in a surprised voice. "I think I will take a break while I am down there."

Delvin then sent a projection to Mistress Wilshaw, telling her that she should visit her sister in Cavid. That the invasion might have upset her sister, and she should go to make sure that her sister was all right. He also added that she should leave first thing in the morning.

Having ensured the safety of his friend and Mistress Wilshaw, Delvin felt much better.

"Where did you go to when you rushed off?" asked Nippy who had already got into bed.

"I'll tell you tomorrow," replied Delvin giving a knowing look towards Greg.

Nippy rolled his eyes.

"You and I will be off at dawn," said Delvin.

"Will we be going with that Grimbolt and…"

"Yes," replied Delvin, cutting him of before he could say Jarla's name.

Nippy grinned.

Delvin grinned back and got ready for bed. It would be another early start in the morning.

Chapter 16

Delvin and Nippy were up before dawn. As they got dressed, the noise woke Greg.

"What time is it?"

"Just before dawn. We have to be off early."

"Ahhh," said Greg stretching. "I need to be up early too." Greg rolled out of bed. "I'm meant to be leaving for Pandol at dawn."

When they came downstairs, Mistress Wilshaw was already there. She had heard them get out of bed, and hot leaf and rolls were ready for them on the kitchen table.

"Get your breakfasts. I want to be off and catch the early coach to Cavid."

Greg was the first to leave, giving Delvin a cheery goodbye as he set off for The White Bear where he worked.

Mistress Wilshaw already had her coat on and bag packed, when there was a knock on the door. It was Grimbolt.

"Good morning Major Grybald," said Delvin. "How's your shoulder?"

"Stiff and sore, but I'll live," replied Grimbolt.

Delvin said goodbye to Mistress Wilshaw and wished her a safe journey. Then he and Nippy followed Grimbolt out of the door.

Jarla was waiting in the lane with the horses. She was dressed as a young man in black leather riding gear and with a blond wig covering her long hair.

Delvin and Nippy fixed their bundles onto their horses, then they mounted and were on their way, trotting towards the North Gate just as the sky began to lighten.

Delvin turned to Jarla.

"What does your father think of you going off with a single man again. He seemed concerned about your reputation."

"He doesn't know. Anyway, I am in disguise, so nobody should have recognized me when I left the Castle, so with any luck he won't find out."

"It's too late to worry about her reputation," muttered Grimbolt. Jarla gave him an icy look.

Just then Delvin's rabbit Freda popped her head out of the sling she was being carried in and looked around.

"You're not bringing that rabbit again?" said Jarla in exasperation.

"What's wrong with my rabbit?" asked Delvin. "She's got you out of some difficult spots."

"She may have done, but whoever's heard of hunting a magician using a rabbit?"

"You use dogs to hunt things."

"Dogs hunt rabbits," muttered Jarla.

"Anyway, I have to bring her. There's nobody else to look after her. Everyone else is going away."

When they reached the North Gate, it had only just opened, and they had to wait while the farm carts carrying their produce into the city came through. Jarla drummed her fingers impatiently.

Once through the gate the road was clear, and they set off for South Bridge at a brisk canter.

South Bridge came in sight around mid-morning. South Bridge was quite a large walled town on the Hengel side of the River Septim. The river was the border between Hengel and Argent. As they approached, they could see North Bridge on the far side of the river. A great multi-spanned bridge crossed the river between the two towns. The bridge was impressive. There were two towers and a drawbridge at the Hengel end of the bridge, then three arches, before two more towers supported Hengel's side of a central double drawbridge wide enough to let large ships pass through. Argent's side was similar, with two towers supporting their side of the central drawbridge, three more arches, and a further drawbridge and two towers leading into North Bridge.

The guard on the South Bridge town gate let them through into the town after simply enquiring what their business was.

"What was the point of that?" muttered Jarla. "We could have said anything to that guard."

They rode through the town down the main street which led to the square in front of the bridge. The street went past the guild hall, town hall and temple and was lined with several inns and shops. When they reached the entrance to the great bridge, the guard, like the one on the town gate, let them through with few questions.

"We need to tighten up," muttered Jarla again as they trotted over the bridge.

The guard at the North Bridge end of the bridge was more thorough. He questioned them in some detail about who they were and what they were going to do in Argent. They said they were family members going to a funeral of a relative in Argent. Eventually he let them through.

"That's more like it," said Jarla as they trotted off the bridge and across the square on the other side.

"Right," said Grimbolt. "We need to find an inn away from the main roads to use as a base."

They turned into one of the side roads on the left of the square. This was the old quarter. They soon found a suitable inn, The Prancing Pony. It was an ancient building with overhanging eves and black beams surrounding panels of brickwork set in a herringbone pattern. They rode through an arch into the inn's stable yard. Grimbolt dismounted and entered the inn to arrange rooms. He reappeared shortly after and nodded to them. The stable lad had been waiting to see if they were staying. As they dismounted, he ran forward to take the horses.

"Brush them down and give them oats," said Grimbolt. "I'll be out later to check."

The stable boy nodded looking slightly frightened.

Delvin handed him Freda, and giving him a copper, asked him to give her a run and some oats. The stable lad nodded again.

They entered the inn and Grimbolt led the way to the rooms he had booked. They followed him up the stairs and down a narrow dark passage. Grimbolt showed Jarla her room which faced the stable yard. It had a lumpy looking double bed, washstand, chair and a carpet that had seen better days.

"Is that the best you can do?" complained Jarla.

"We need to be inconspicuous," replied Grimbolt.

The other room had three beds, a large washstand, three chairs a reasonable carpet and faced the road. Jarla looked at it enviously.

They set their things down in their rooms and gathered in the larger room to plan what they would do.

"Right Delvin," said Jarla. "How are you going to find this magician?"

"Me?" replied Delvin. "I don't know how to find a magician. Do you have any ideas?"

"Let's see if we can tackle this logically," suggested Grimbolt. "Let's go round looking for advertisements put up by magicians offering their services. If any of those people have recently arrived, that would be a good indication. Then we can check them out."

"Do you really think a magician newly arrived from the Guild of Magicians would worry about earning a few carls," said Jarla.

"Probably not. But it's worth trying. Do any of you know anyone who lives in North Bridge who might know anything?"

"I know this lady," said Delvin.

"What a surprise," muttered Jarla.

Delvin ignored her. "She's called Aggie and works in service. I know the bar where she drinks."

"It would be worth you talking to her," said Grimbolt. "Right, Sir Delvin you go and see your lady-friend. Jarla, you and I will look for advertisements for magicians. Nippy, see if you can ask around. There may be gossip on the streets about a magician. Sir Delvin, could you also listen out for any messages that the magician might be making. That might give a rough indication of where he is."

"It might be late evening before she comes into the bar," said Delvin. "Assuming she still uses that bar. I'll check the bar at regular intervals and do a bit of snooping around as well."

"We'll meet back here in three hours," said Grimbolt. "If none of us have found out anything, Sir Delvin can go out again to see if his lady-friend has come into that bar."

They set out on their various tasks.

Delvin decided to try talking to people in other bars to see if anyone knew of a magician who had recently arrived in North Bridge.

It was still well before noon and the first bars were only just beginning to open. He found an open bar in one of the side streets. He went in and ordered an ale. Two locals were leaning against the bar.

"Good day gentlemen, I'm new in town. How are things here?"

"They are all right at the moment, but there is worrying news from down in Hengel."

"Aye," said the other. "I've heard some foreign army invaded."

"Really?" said Delvin. "I've been in Argent. I don't think the news has got through there yet. What happened?"

"Not much information. Just heard some foreign force came. But it's unsettling. Not good for business... What do you do?"

"I'm an entertainer," said Delvin. "I give magic lantern shows and perform a bit of magic. I thought I would see if it would be worth moving here. Do you know if there are any magicians performing in North Bridge?"

"Not heard of any," said one.

"There was a children's entertainer who used to do children's parties. I don't know if he is still doing them."

"Oh, I remember him. I don't think he is doing them anymore. I think he died a few years ago."

"Aye, I think he did."

The conversation carried on for a bit longer, but it was soon apparent that the people he was talking to didn't know of any magician in North Bridge. Delvin made his excuses and moved on.

As he was walking down one of the side streets, he suddenly stopped. A black-cloaked figure was walking down the road ahead. Was it the black magician? Delvin kept to the shadows and followed him. After a little way the figure stopped a passing man. A faint message came into Delvin's mind, *'Have you seen any of these people?'* There followed images of him, Jarla and Nippy. The passer-by shook his head. The black figure moved on with a snarl, leaving the passer by looking shaken.

It was the black magician thought Delvin. He must have been watching Mistress Wilshaw's house in Chandler's Lane then followed them. Maybe he had been delayed by that thorough guard when crossing into North Bridge. He obviously didn't know they were staying at The Prancing Pony or he wouldn't be asking if people had seen them. They were going to have to be careful.

Delvin decided to move further away from where he had seen the black magician before talking to people in other bars. When he felt he was far enough away, he tried several bars, but none of the people he spoke to knew of any magician in North Bridge. He also looked in twice at the bar near the Governor's House where he had met Aggie, but there was no sign of her. As he walked past the Governor's House, he saw that it was covered in scaffolding where the damage from the fire of the previous year was still being repaired.

Time was moving on so he made his way back to The Prancing Pony.

Delvin looked into the common room, but there was no sign of the others there, so he went up to the room he shared with Grimbolt and Nippy.

Grimbolt, Jarla and Nippy were all there looking slightly despondent.

"Did you find anything?" asked Jarla. "Sheffs! You smell of beer. How many bars have you been in?"

"I've been in a few," replied Delvin. "I wanted to talk to as many locals as possible." He looked across at Grimbolt, a serious look on his face. "I saw the black magician. He is out there looking for us. He must have followed us from Hengel."

"Does he know we are at this inn?" asked Grimbolt.

"No, he was asking people if they had seen us so he doesn't know where we are." Delvin went on to describe his encounter with the black magician.

"That complicates matters," said Grimbolt thoughtfully.

"Maybe we should hunt the black magician," said Jarla. "We don't seem to be doing very well finding the one in North Bridge."

"One thing at a time, Princess Jarla," said Grimbolt. "Sir Delvin, did you find out anything about the North Bridge magician on your bar crawl?"

"Not really. Nobody seems to know of any magician working in North Bridge. Did you find anything?"

"We found an advertisement for a lady who reads people's fortunes. We checked her out. She's been doing it for years, so I'm pretty certain she's not the magician we're looking for. There was also a children's entertainer, but he's been doing it for ages as well."

"I talked to some kids," said Nippy. "They've not heard of any new magician."

"Did you find your friend, Sir Delvin?" asked Grimbolt.

"No," replied Delvin. "I looked in at the bar where she used to drink but there was no sign of her. It was a bit early though. She might come in later."

"Right," said Grimbolt. "I believe we should concentrate on the North Bridge magician. The only way we could hunt the black magician is for one of us to act as bait to lure him out, and that would be dangerous. We do though need to keep a look out for him. One of the people he asks about us, may have seen us come here. If that happens, and we catch sight of him around here, that would change things. Then it would be worth going after him. But in the meantime, we'll continue looking for the North Bridge magician."

"Sir Delvin, try that bar again later to see if your friend comes in. If she does, it would be well worth you talking to her, since we seem to be running out of other options. But first, you'd better sober up."

Delvin nodded and lay down on one of the beds. The others continued talking, trying to think of other ways of finding the magician. Soon Delvin was asleep.

Delvin was woken a few hours later by Grimbolt shaking his shoulder.

"Wake up! you need to get some food in you before your next bar crawl." Grimbolt gave his lopsided smile.

"What time is it?" asked Delvin.

"Evening," replied Grimbolt.

Delvin slowly got off the bed and stretched. His head felt thick. He went over to the washstand and splashed water on his face. Then gathering his wits together, he followed Grimbolt down the stairs to the inn's common room.

Jarla and Nippy were already there, and they had ordered bread, cheese and cold meats. Delvin sat down, and Grimbolt brought him a large glass of water.

Delvin drank his water and ate a few mouthfuls of bread and cheese. He realised he hadn't had any lunch and was quite hungry. Jarla looked at him pityingly over her glass of wine, while Nippy happily tucked into his food.

"How are you feeling?" asked Grimbolt.

"Quite a lot better," replied Delvin as he started on the cold meat.

After finishing his meal, Delvin got up and straightened his clothes. Then after checking Freda was being well looked after, he made his way to the bar near the Governor's House where he had previously met Aggie. All the way there he was careful to keep to the shadows in case the back magician was nearby.

Delvin looked around the bar and saw Aggie sitting at a corner table. She was a little older than Delvin and had short dark hair, a large chin and a slightly crooked mouth that gave her face character. They had met the previous year when he and Jarla had been trying to stop the war between Hengel and Argent. She had worked in the Governor's House before it had burnt down.

Delvin smiled towards her and ordered himself an ale at the bar. Aggie had seen him, and with a smile got up and came over.

"Back in North Bridge?"

"I couldn't keep away," replied Delvin grinning. "What would you like to drink?"

150

"I'll have a wine," said Aggie. "Come and sit down with me at my table over there." She went back to her table in the corner.

Delvin took the drinks over to the table.

"We won't be overheard here," said Aggie. "Right, tell me who you really are. You came here when the war with Hengel was taking place. The Governor's House then burnt down, the war ended, and you disappeared. Now I hear Hengel has been invaded, and you are back. You said you were a children's entertainer, but you haven't set up as one. Who are you?"

Delvin took a deep breath. "I am a children's entertainer, but I also work for the Duke of Hengel and the Duke of Argent. The Guild of Magicians have been trying to take over Hengel and Argent. I have been trying to stop them."

"Ahh," said Aggie. "That starts to make sense. Why are you in North Bridge now?"

"We have heard that there's a magician from the Guild of Magicians here in North Bridge. We are here to try to deal with him."

"Who are we?"

"I am here with Major Grybald."

"And?"

"My apprentice Nippy."

"And?"

Delvin realized Aggie was very astute, and he would need to tell her everything if he was going to get her to help.

"And Princess Jarla of Hengel."

Aggie roared with laughter.

"Really?"

"Yes really. But you mustn't tell anybody. She's travelling in disguise."

"I've heard all sorts of stories about her. Is it true she has killed seven people?"

"It's actually more than that."

"How many?"

"I know of about thirteen."

"What! There may be more?"

"I've only known her for about a year."

"And she hasn't killed you yet?"

"I think she wanted to once or twice."

Aggie was now shaking with laughter.

"How can I help?"

"We are trying to locate this magician. We haven't had any luck so far."

"I haven't heard of any magicians in North Bridge. I think I would have, since I am now working for a merchant's widow who is very superstitious. If she had heard of a magician or anyone who could read fortunes, she would have got them to read her fortune. You said you were a children's entertainer. You don't happen to read fortunes, do you?"

"Well, yes, actually I do."

"Well, that solves how we are going to get you into her house," said Aggie with a lascivious grin.

Delvin grinned back.

"Right," said Aggie. "Let's go there now. You don't have to go back to Princess Jarla tonight, do you? She doesn't want you for her... amusement?"

"Sheffs no," said Delvin.

"Good," said Aggie getting up.

Delvin followed Aggie out of the bar. They made their way to the Commercial Quarter. Aggie's employer's house was an impressive stone building set a little back from the road. It had four windows either side of a large front door that was flanked with pillars. Aggie took Delvin to a side door that led down some stairs into the servant's quarters.

Through the door was the servant's hall, a large room with a big pine table in the centre. Dressers bearing mugs and plates lined the walls. A smartly dressed white haired gentleman greeted them as they came in.

"Mistress Aggie, you are back early, I was not expecting you until later."

"Magister Femmel, may I introduce Magister Delvin? He reads fortunes, and I thought the mistress might like her fortune to be read."

"Indeed, she might. Wait here, I will go up and ask her."

"I charge four carls for private readings," said Delvin. He thought he had better make it sound like he was reasonably highly priced.

Femmel simply nodded and went out of the room.

Delvin and Aggie grinned at each other.

Femmel was soon back and indicated that Delvin should follow him. They went up the stairs into the main part of the house, across a wide entrance hall and into a comfortably furnished drawing room. Seated by the fire was a lady of about sixty, with grey hair and dressed in a sumptuous gown that would have been fashionable some twenty years earlier.

Delvin bowed to her, and she indicated the chair opposite hers.

As Femmel withdrew, Delvin began his fortune telling. He still had his pack of cards in his pocket from when he had told fortunes in Cavid. He followed largely the same routine as he had done when he had told fortunes for Lady Cavid and her guests. Except this time, he started by reading the lady's palm. He made statements and asked questions that drew information out from her. He then gradually fed the information back as if he had read it in her palm. While doing it he also found out what she wanted to hear, so when he moved on to the cards, he was able to weave a suitable story around the cards she stopped at.

When he had finished, she rang a small bell and Femmel appeared.

"Thank you, that was wonderful... Femmel, pay the magister his fee and give him an extra two carls."

"Yes, my lady," said Femmel bowing.

Delvin bowed and Femmel led him back to the servant's quarters where he gave him six carls.

154

"You've done well there," said Aggie who was waiting for him. "Maybe I'll have to take up fortune telling."

They waited till Femmel had left on an errand then Aggie said, "Follow me."

They went out of the servant's hall, up the back stairs and into Aggie's room at the top.

Sometime later, Delvin lay contentedly next to Aggie who was asleep and gently snoring. He was thinking back over the events of the previous few days, when a faint message came into his head. *'Now our army is not coming this way from Hengel, do you want me to stay here or go to Argent?'* Then a reply that seemed slightly stronger than the first message. *'Stay there for the moment. You might still be needed to stop Hengel's army.'*

It was the magician thought Delvin. But why was the first message weaker than the second? It was being projected from much closer, so it should have been stronger. Then he realized. The magician in North Bridge was projecting towards Norden in a direction away from him, whereas the magician in Norden was projecting in his direction. He thought again. The merchant's house was quite close to North Bridge's wall. Either the magician was between the merchant's house and the wall or was close to North Bridge but outside the wall.

Delvin was excited, and it was some time before he was able to get to sleep.

Chapter 17

Delvin woke up early. He gave Aggie a lingering kiss and rapidly got dressed. Creeping down the stairs he surprised the kitchen maid who was just getting the rolls out of the oven. He grabbed one of the rolls with a grin and was out of the door juggling the hot roll in his hands before she could say anything.

The first thing he did on leaving the merchant's widow's house, was to check what buildings were between the house and the town wall. There were not many, and most of those were warehouses. He examined them as closely as he could, and came to the conclusion that it was unlikely that North Bridge's magician was living in any of them. That meant that he was somewhere outside the walls.

He made his way back to The Prancing Pony and got there just as Jarla was entering the common room for breakfast.

"Where have you been? Not with another of your ladies?"

Delvin ignored the question.

"I've an idea where the magician is."

"Where?" said Jarla sitting down at the table where Grimbolt and Nippy were already eating their breakfasts.

Delvin sat down with them and ordered himself a cup of hot leaf and a roll.

"I think he is outside the town walls opposite the Commercial Quarter." Delvin went on to explain about the messages he had overheard, but was purposefully hazy about what he had been doing in the widow's house.

"Right," said Grimbolt. "The next question is, how do we get at him?"

All four of them looked blank.

"Ideas Delvin?" asked Jarla.

"We need to lure him out into the open," said Delvin thinking quickly. "We could have some sort of bait."

"Bait?" asked Jarla.

"Yes, like fishermen use worms or I believe big cat hunters use goats."

"What bait would you use?" asked Jarla dangerously.

"Well, you're the one they seem to want, they did try to kidnap you."

"So, now you want me to be a worm or a goat," said Jarla glaring menacingly at him.

"Jarla isn't going to be bait," interposed Grimbolt.

Jarla who had begun to move towards Delvin, now stopped. But she remained glaring at him.

Delvin thought quickly then had another idea.

"If I went out of the town a little distance, between where I think the magician is and Norden, I could send a message that might seem to have come from Norden."

"That sounds better," said Grimbolt. "What would be the message?"

"We would need to lure him somewhere specific. Maybe we could get him to go to Hengel to find out what had happened there. Then he would have to cross the bridge, and we could wait for him on the bridge."

"That might work," said Grimbolt thoughtfully. "The magicians might not know what happened to that magician in Cavid, since it was quite sudden, so they might send someone to find out."

"How would we recognize him?" asked Jarla.

"We could ask him to meet the black magician so they could go into Hengel together," suggested Delvin. "If Grimbolt wore a black cloak. That would make him look like the black magician. And we know the black magician is around here at the moment, so it would fit."

"Wouldn't the black magician pick up your message as well as the other magician?" asked Jarla.

"I'd be a reasonable distance out of town and project it very faintly, so it shouldn't get as far as the town of North Bridge where the black magician is."

"I'm not sure I like it," said Grimbolt. "I wouldn't be able to look in his direction. If I looked towards him, he would see from my face that I wasn't the black magician. And I don't fancy having a magician walking up behind me, with me looking the other way, and without me knowing he was there."

"We need an early warning," said Delvin. "How about if I influenced the guards on the bridge to close the bridge. Then he would have to use his magician's stone to get past them. I would then detect it, and I could warn you."

"Sounds a bit complicated," said Grimbolt dubiously.

"We don't know what he looks like," said Delvin. "The only way we'll know it's the magician is if we can get him to use his magician's stone. Unless anyone else has any ideas."

No one did, so they eventually decided that they would have to try Delvin's plan.

They decided that the best time to try to ambush the magician would be two hours after noon. Delvin saddled his horse and set off to go outside the town to send the message to him. Grimbolt meanwhile went to find a shop to buy a big black cloak.

Delvin was only briefly questioned by the guard on the town gate. He said he was visiting a friend at a farm not far up the road. He needed to get back in good time for the ambush, so he couldn't say that he was visiting Argent or anywhere further afield, as it would have looked very odd if he was then back after only an hour or two.

Delvin rode up the road for about four miles. He was well out of sight of the town, and he hoped, far enough away to be sure he'd travelled beyond the magician and so was between the magician and Norden.

The country outside North Bridge was mainly fields. Some had cattle grazing, while in others crops were growing. There were occasional small woods, and streams that splashed over the road on shallow fords.

Delvin came to a clearing in a wood that was by the road and dismounted. He tied up his horse and took out his magician's stone. Then facing North Bridge, he sent a message. He made it as faint as possible, so it would seem to have come from Norden, and also faint enough that it wouldn't be detectable in North Bridge by the black magician. *'I want you to go to Hengel to find out what happened there. Meet the black magician by the centre drawbridge of the bridge over the River Septim. Meet him there two hours after noon. Someone in Hengel may have a stone, if so, it may need the two of you to overcome him.'*

A few moments later there was a strong message from the direction of North Bridge. *'Alright.'*

Good thought Delvin, it looks like the plan had worked. The North Bridge magician was indeed outside the town like he had thought, and he had believed that Delvin's message had come from Norden.

Then another message then came into Delvin's head. *'I thought you wanted me in Argent for the invasion. I am already on my way. Shall I continue or return to North Bridge?'*

Delvin was shocked. The black magician must have picked up his message, and this was now his reply.

A sudden realization hit Delvin. If the black magician had managed to pick up his message to the North Bridge magician, it meant the black magician was close by, and probably only just behind him on the road out of the town. He urgently needed to get off the road and hide.

Delvin quickly untied his horse and led him into the wood, trying to get as far away from the road and as deep into the wood as possible. After about a minute he felt he had gone in far enough and was well hidden from the road. He tied his horse to a strong branch, then crept back so he could keep a watch on the road.

160

He had only just got off the road in time. As he peered through the branches, he saw a figure wearing a black cloak and riding a large black horse, ride past on the road to Argent.

As he watched, a reply came from far away. It must be coming from Norden thought Delvin. *'Continue on to Argent. I want you to make sure there's no problems with the invasion. Lord Querriol is not experienced, so I have told him to stay on the ships. Lady Anbroom may need your help in the city if they have a stone. Once the city is in our hands, head back to North Bridge. Lord Benbark may need your help there. But keep up your search for Delvin. I want him dead, and I want that boy.'*

After a few moments another message came from the direction of North Bridge. *'If the black magician is going to Argent, what do you want me to do?'*

Another message came from Norden. *'Continue as before.'*

Delvin thought quickly. He must wait for the black magician to get out of range before sending any message. But how could he lure the North Bridge magician on to the bridge without getting him to meet the black magician?

Delvin had an idea. Facing towards North Bridge and away from where the black magician had gone, Delvin projected a very faint message, hoping the black magician was far enough away that he wouldn't pick it up.

'Hengel has someone with a stone. I don't want them intercepting our messages, so I am sending a messenger.

Meet him on the bridge as before. He will be wearing a black cloak.'

Would this work? thought Delvin. He waited for several minutes concentrating as hard as he could, but to his relief, no further messages came. It looked like his message had been accepted as coming from Norden and that the black magician hadn't picked it up. That meant the plan to ambush the North Bridge magician was still on.

Delvin untied his horse and led him back onto the road, then remounted and rode back to North Bridge. As he rode, he started thinking more about the rest of the messages he had intercepted. The black magician was on his way to Argent, that was good. But what was that about him helping the invasion?

On getting back to the inn he told the others about the messages.

"Invasion?" said Jarla. "Did he say when that would happen?"

"No," replied Delvin.

"We need to let the duke know," said Jarla.

Grimbolt looked at her. "Both dukes know the mercenaries are threatening Argent and will almost certainly invade. There's nothing more they can do until they know when the invasion is going to take place. Telling them it is going to happen won't change anything. They know that already."

Jarla reluctantly agreed.

Grimbolt went on, "We need to concentrate on this North Bridge magician. If we mess this up, he'll be on his guard and there may not be another chance."

Chapter 18

They were all set on the bridge. Grimbolt was by the tower supporting the Argent side of the central drawbridge and was wearing a long black cloak. He was facing the Hengel side of the bridge with the cloak's hood pulled up over his head. They had thought the North Bridge magician might have been given his description, so he was keeping his face hidden. Jarla was in the shadow of the opposite tower, and Delvin was by the first North Bridge drawbridge. He wanted to be as close to the bridge's entrance as possible, to make sure he didn't miss any projection North Bridge's magician might make to get past the guards. Nippy had been left back at the inn, much to his disgust.

As soon as he had crossed onto the bridge, Delvin had sent a very tight message to the guards at the bridge's entrance to close the bridge to anyone coming from the direction of North Bridge. He was confident that would force North Bridge's magician to use his stone to get past them. Then, when he detected the stone's use, he would wave towards Jarla who would warn Grimbolt that the magician was coming.

Now they had to wait.

With the bridge closed, a queue of people, riders and carts was starting to build up.

Delvin strained his senses for any projection from the North Bridge magician, his nerves taut with the tension of waiting.

Time passed. It was well past two hours after noon and Delvin hadn't detected any projections.

Delvin was worried. Had the magician realized the message Delvin had sent him hadn't come from Norden? Then Delvin froze. A figure was climbing a set of iron rungs set into the side of the central drawbridge tower, and he could see a rowing boat tied to the pier at the bottom of the tower.

Delvin thought quickly. The magician must have decided to row to the tower rather than use his stone to get onto the bridge. Did that mean he realized the message he had received was false? Whatever else, Grimbolt must be warned, or the black magician would surprise him.

Delvin began to run towards Grimbolt. He needed to get him away from the edge of the bridge.

"Oi!" he shouted.

Grimbolt looked momentarily up. Delvin gestured frantically for him to move towards the middle of the road. Grimbolt moved away from the edge of the bridge and turned looking quizzically at Delvin.

Moments later the climbing figure came over the bridge's parapet. Grimbolt was still facing Delvin, so didn't see the figure who had drawn a long wicked looking knife.

The figure stepped towards Grimbolt and struck him in the back with his knife. At the same time a message came into Delvin's head. *'You are paralyzed.'* Grimbolt froze. Delvin projected a counter message. *'You are not paralyzed.'* Grimbolt shuddered as he was released from the paralysis and turned, just in time to parry a knife thrust aimed at his throat. Grimbolt sprang back and drew his own knife.

"I thought that message was false," sneered the figure. "You'll have to do better than that... I see you have a stone. I'll let Norden know, then the black magician can kill you and take it off you."

He saw Delvin running towards him and Jarla moving in from the side.

"Do you think you can capture me? Your plan was pathetic, you can't follow me in my boat."

With that, the magician climbed onto the parapet, was over it and onto the iron rungs in a moment, then he jumped off them into his boat which was tied against the bridge five feet below.

There was a crash as his feet hit the boat. Delvin rushed to look over the parapet. The boat was a wreck. Where the magician had landed, he had gone straight through the planks, and there was a gaping hole. The wood must have been rotten thought Delvin. The boat itself was sinking and was already half submerged. There was no sign of the magician. The river was flowing fast, and the fragments of wood from the boat rapidly disappeared under the bridge.

"Check the other side to see if he comes up," said Grimbolt.

They ran across the bridge and looked down into the swirling water. The fragments of wood were now some distance downstream, but there was no sign of the magician.

"Check the base of the tower."

They leaned over the bridge's parapet as far as they could, but could see no sign that the magician had managed to get onto the pier beneath the tower.

"Looks like he has gone," said Jarla who was now peering downstream into the distance. "Did he have time to send a message before he jumped?"

"No," said Delvin.

"That's good," said Grimbolt. "That means the magicians don't know that he's dead. They'll think that they still have a magician in North Bridge."

"Are you alright?" Delvin asked Grimbolt. "He stabbed you in the back."

"Just a bit bruised," replied Grimbolt. "I didn't fancy having my back to him when he came, particularly after being shot back in Hengel, so I wore my mail shirt, and it was just as well that I did."

"How is your shoulder?" asked Delvin.

"Not too bad, just aches a bit," replied Grimbolt.

Jarla had a grim smile on her face. "With him gone it means they are down to only four stones."

They started to make their way back to The Prancing Pony. As they passed over the drawbridge, Delvin removed his suggestion from the guards that the bridge should be closed. By the time they had crossed the square, the queue to cross the bridge was just starting to move.

They gathered in the inn's common room and sat down at a corner table where they wouldn't be overheard.

"I think we all need a drink," said Grimbolt signaling to the landlord.

Nippy, who had joined them looked up hopefully, but Grimbolt shook his head.

When the drinks had arrived, they waited for the landlord to move out of earshot.

"Right," said Grimbolt. "What do we do next?"

"There's a magician with the fleet threatening Argent," said Jarla. "We hunt him next."

Delvin suddenly became aware of a fairly faint message coming through. He signaled for the others to keep quiet while he concentrated. *'Get ready to stop Hengel's army from crossing the river. They have someone with a stone with them so you will need to be careful. As soon as we have taken Argent and it is fully under our control, I shall send the black magician to back you up. At present he is assisting with the invasion. It should not take long for the three of them to defeat the one stone Argent has. I am waiting to hear their progress.'*

Delvin told the others what he had overheard.

"Does that mean the magicians have started to invade Argent?" hissed Jarla.

"It seems like it, and with the black magician they now have three magicians there," added Grimbolt.

"Argent's army won't stand a chance against three magicians with stones," muttered Jarla. "We need to get there to help."

"We also need to let Duke Poldor and General Gortly know about this," said Grimbolt. "Right, this is what we'll

168

do. I'll get over to South Bridge as quickly as I can and get an officer from the garrison there to take a message to the duke and General Gortly. As soon as I get back, we leave for Argent. The one good thing is that they still think they have a magician here in North Bridge."

They all rose from the table. Grimbolt dashed upstairs to get his things, while Delvin and Nippy went out to the stables to get Grimbolt's horse saddled. Before they had even finished, Grimbolt was back down and strapping his things on behind his saddle. Moments later he was riding out of the yard towards the bridge.

Delvin and Nippy ran upstairs to get their things, and soon all the horses were ready to go. Delvin had Freda safely tucked up in her sling.

Grimbolt was soon back, and the four of them set out for Argent.

Chapter 19

They were soon through the town gate and cantering quickly towards Argent. It was now well into the afternoon and the sun was starting to get low in the sky.

"We'll get as far as we can in the light, then find an inn," shouted Grimbolt. "Sir Delvin, have you picked up any more messages?"

"Yes," replied Delvin. "The magicians are creating illusions of armies that don't exist and are trying to make the Argent soldiers give up. I've been doing my best to counter them, but we are still quite a long way from them, so I don't know how effective it will be."

"All these illusions," muttered Grimbolt grimly. "Illusions should only be in shows like the ones you do with your magic lantern."

They passed the road junction where one road went to Dandel the other to Argent and pressed on.

Evening was setting in. The messages Delvin was receiving were getting stronger, so he guessed his counter messages were getting stronger too.

"I don't think we will quite make Thanley before it's dark," shouted Grimbolt. "We need to find an inn."

Just as the sun was setting, they came to The Green Lion, an ancient inn set back a little from the road with a yard in front of it. They rode into the stable yard behind the inn, and a stable lad came out to meet them.

"I'll see if they have any rooms," said Grimbolt dismounting.

As he approached the rear door of the inn the landlord came out to greet them.

"What may I do for you magisters?"

"We need two rooms," replied Grimbolt.

"We have just two left, magister. I am afraid they are not our best, all our other rooms are full. People are fleeing. No one seems to know what's happening. There are all sorts of rumours. I can let you have them for three carls each plus a carl for each of your horses."

Grimbolt looked up at the sky. It was almost dark.

"Right, we will take them," he said, and paid the landlord.

Jarla muttered about being forced to sleep in poor rooms as they led their horses into the stables.

Grimbolt made sure the horses were being properly looked after and then they made their way into the inn. Delvin again left Freda with the stable lad, giving him a copper for oats and for giving her a run.

The rooms turned out to be everything Jarla feared. A narrow bed and a chair were the only furniture in the rooms, and those had seen better days. Grimbolt got the landlord to bring two pallets and some blankets to the larger of the two rooms, though when those were put on the floor there was little room for anything else.

They went down to the common room.

The common room was quite full, and as the landlord had said, rumours were flying around.

They managed to find themselves a table against one of the walls. A very young and flustered waitress ran up to them.

"What may I get you, magisters, mistress?"

"Two ales, one wine and a lemonade please," said Grimbolt.

"If the young magister would like it, we have fresh apple juice," said the waitress smiling at Nippy. "What's your name?"

"Nippy," said Nippy. "That sounds nice. Yes please." He grinned at the waitress who smiled back.

"What have you to eat?" asked Grimbolt.

"We have brandil pie or cold meats."

"What is brandil pie?"

"It's a local dish. Layers of ham, cheese, onion and potato."

"That sounds good," said Grimbolt. "I'll have that." He looked at the others and they all nodded. "Four brandil pies please."

As the waitress ran off with their order, Grimbolt turned to Nippy and grinned. "I think she fancies you."

Nippy returned his grin with a mischievous smile.

The waitress returned shortly after with their drinks and smiled again at Nippy. Nippy smiled back and gave her a wink.

As they sipped their drinks, they sat back trying to listen in to the conversations around the room. There were all sorts of rumours flying around. Several people had fled from Argent. It seemed the mercenaries' ships had landed

172

in the town at dawn, surprising the garrison and rapidly taking control of the city. No one seemed to know what had happened to the duke or what might happen next.

Their brandil pies arrived. The dish the pies had been baked in had been lined with bread rather than pastry. The hot oven had baked the bread to a crisp golden brown. Inside the pie there were layers of ham alternating with cheese and onion, and the pie was topped with potato slices that had also been baked a golden brown. Mustard and herbs had been added to give extra flavour. They tasted delicious.

All four tucked in and conversation stopped while they ate their meal. They sat back when they had finished.

"It's been a long day," said Grimbolt. "If we're going to be up early in the morning, we should have an early night."

"What are we going to do if we run into the mercenaries?" asked Delvin.

"We'll just have to play it by ear," replied Jarla. "Right, bed."

They made their way up to their rooms. Grimbolt opened the room's window before going to bed so the room did not get too stuffy during the night. Soon after they were in bed and asleep.

Chapter 20

Delvin was woken by being roughly heaved off his pallet and thrown onto the floor. A sword was at his throat.

"What money have you got?"

Delvin tried to get his wits together as he opened his eyes. Standing above him was a soldier dressed in a variety of pieces of mismatched armour. He had a plumed helmet on his head and carried a curved sword that was now at Delvin's throat. It must be one of the mercenaries thought Delvin, his fear rapidly rising.

"I only have a few carls in my breeches pocket," said Delvin desperately trying to keep his voice calm.

Delvin now saw that two other mercenaries were standing over Grimbolt and Nippy, while a third had started checking through the pockets of Grimbolt's breeches, which had been hanging next to Delvin's breeches over the back of the chair.

The mercenary found Grimbolt's purse and grinned as he stuffed it into his pocket. Then he started on Delvin's breeches. He found Delvin's few carls and pocketed them with a dismissive grunt, then he found Delvin's magician's stone. He held it up.

"Some silly good luck charm. Well, your luck's out today." With that, he threw the stone out of the window.

"Tie their hands. The magician wants to question all travelers from outside Argent."

"Let me get dressed first," requested Delvin.

The mercenary grunted which Delvin took for a yes. He slowly got to his feet and put on his clothes being watched carefully by the mercenaries. Grimbolt and Nippy were also getting dressed. Grimbolt watching the mercenaries through narrowed eyes.

As soon as they were dressed their hands were roughly tied behind their backs.

"Names?" demanded the mercenary who seemed to be the leader.

Delvin flashed a warning glance towards Nippy, but he need not have done so.

"Danson," said Nippy.

"Pildam," said Delvin.

"Borthwick," said Grimbolt.

They were marched down the stairs into the common room where all the people from outside Argent were being assembled. Jarla was there glaring furiously, as well as two other travelers. The landlord and his staff were by the bar looking dazed and shocked.

The waitress who had served them the night before saw them come in and put her hand to her mouth.

"Nippy, are you alright?" she gasped.

"Nippy?" said the leader of the mercenaries. "We were told to look out for a Nippy." He strode up to Nippy. "What's your name?"

"Danson," replied Nippy looking him directly in the eye.

"You match the description… There's a big reward for a boy called Nippy or Nippold… He turned to two of the

175

mercenaries. "Gorath, Sadish, you come with me. We'll take him to Rostin and see if we can get that reward." He turned back to the other mercenaries. "You other three, take this lot to that magician in Argent... Go on... Get going. If there is any reward, we'll bring your share back."

The three mercenaries taking the prisoners to Argent looked suspiciously at the three taking Nippy to Rostin. Delvin heard one of them mutter that if there was a reward, they would never see the other three again. His two companions nodded. But despite that, and despite exchanging rebellious looks between themselves, they began to usher the prisoners out of the common room. The waitress who had served them the night before was in tears. Delvin looked back over his shoulder and saw a smirk on the face of the mercenaries' leader.

The prisoners were led out into the inn's yard. The sun had not yet risen, and the area was lit by the half-light of predawn. Delvin glanced up to where his bedroom window opened out. Below the window was a cart loaded with kitchen waste. Had his stone landed in there, he wondered? Was the cart collecting pig swill? He didn't have time to wonder any longer, as they were heaved on to their horses, which a scared looking stable lad had obviously been told to saddle. Moments later they were being led out of the yard on to road to Argent.

Delvin was not a very experienced horseman, and he found it quite difficult riding with his hands tied behind his back.

Whatever was going to happen to Nippy, Delvin wondered? He decided to try to talk to one of the mercenaries and shouted across to him, "Why are they taking Danson to Rostin?"

"Quiet!" replied the mercenary.

"Who offered the reward?"

"I said, keep quiet."

"Is it a lot of money?"

"If you don't keep quiet, I'll make you."

Delvin thought he had better not push it too much further. He did though seem to have touched a raw nerve, and had added fuel to the resentment towards the men who had taken Nippy. He wondered if he might be able to go just a little bit further.

"We met him at an inn," remarked Delvin. "He said that he'd run away from his tutor. There was some talk about a princess too, but I didn't quite understand that."

The mercenary was starting to look quite agitated. He rode over to the two other mercenaries and said something to them. One of the other mercenaries glanced back towards Delvin, and then moved his horse closer to Delvin's horse.

"What was that you said?"

"Only that we met him at an inn and he said he had run away from his tutor."

"What was that about a princess?"

"I don't know. He did mention a princess, but I didn't really understand what he was talking about."

The mercenary rode back over towards the other two mercenaries. Delvin could hear more mutterings among the three of them, and grinned to himself.

They were soon through Thanley, which was just waking up with the dawn.

After an hour they stopped for a rest by a stream. Delvin and the other prisoners were pulled off their horses, before the mercenaries took the horses over to the stream to drink.

"Here," whispered Jarla, "back-to-back."

Delvin moved over so his back was against Jarla's back. He immediately felt her fingers feeling for where the rope on his wrists was. Then a slight vibration as her sharpened fingernails started to saw through the rope. There was a stab of pain as she accidentally cut into his wrist. Delvin gritted his teeth. It was essential he didn't make a noise. He just hoped she wouldn't cut a blood vessel in his wrist.

The three mercenaries were arguing by the horses and not looking in the direction of the prisoners. It seemed that Delvin's comments had got them very annoyed and angry.

Delvin's hands came free, and he immediately started pulling at the knots in the rope tying Jarla's hands. They too were soon free. Jarla had glanced meaningfully at Grimbolt, and he had moved himself slowly towards them. Jarla quickly cut his bonds with her nails.

With the three of them now free, they slowly moved closer to the mercenaries who were now shouting at each other. They kept their hands behind their backs as if they were still tied, and stretched their legs as if they were trying to shake cramp out of them after the ride.

When they had got just a few yards away, Jarla nodded to Grimbolt who nodded back. The next instant they leapt at the mercenaries who were taken completely by surprise.

Delvin realized he was meant to go for the third mercenary, so he leapt at him too. As he flung himself forward, he grabbed the mercenary round the neck, his momentum knocking the mercenary off balance. They fell crashing to the ground with Delvin on top. Delvin grabbed the mercenary's knife from his belt and plunged it into his back with all his strength. The mercenary gave a heave then shuddered and was still. Delvin was in a state of shock. He had never stabbed anyone before, let alone kill them. He staggered to his feet to see Jarla and Grimbolt looking at him. Between them, Jarla and Grimbolt had dealt with the other two mercenaries who were now lying dead on the ground.

"You seem to be learning. Maybe now you're not quite so useless in a fight," commented Jarla.

Delvin was still shaken. He was not sure he wanted to be good in a fight.

"Right," said Jarla. "Get those uniforms off them, or whatever it is they call this stuff they're wearing."

"I'll release the other prisoners," said Delvin, wanting a short break to recover.

There were two other prisoners, both of whom were looking shocked at the sudden bloodshed. Delvin soon had them free and rubbing their wrists.

"Why didn't you use your stone?" said Jarla accusingly to Delvin.

"The mercenaries found it in my breeches and threw it out of the window," replied Delvin.

"Sheffs! did you see where it went?"

"I think it might have landed in that cart of kitchen waste."

"We'd better see if we can find it," said Grimbolt grimly. "Without that, we won't be much good to Argent."

Jarla nodded back scowling. "I think you're right. We are going to have to go back... Come on Delvin, get the clothes off that mercenary."

Jarla and Grimbolt had already removed the clothes off the other two Mercenaries and were now packing them onto their horses.

One of the freed prisoners approached Jarla.

"What do we do?" he said.

"Take your horses and ride away," said Jarla dismissively.

They needed no second urgings, and he and the other prisoner quickly mounted their horses and were away.

Delvin, although he was still slightly in shock, started removing the clothes from the mercenary he had killed.

"Right, we need to hide the bodies," said Jarla. "We'll dump them in that ditch and cover it with branches."

Delvin finished removing the mercenary's clothes as Grimbolt and Jarla hauled the first body towards the ditch. The ditch was next to the road and was quite deep with water in the bottom of it.

Grimbolt came back to help Delvin heave the last of the bodies into the ditch. Then they covered the bodies with branches that they broke off from nearby bushes. Soon, unless one looked carefully, the bodies couldn't be seen from the road.

Delvin took the clothes and weapons he had taken from the mercenary he had killed, tied them behind his saddle and then mounted his horse. Jarla and Grimbolt were already mounted, and soon they were all cantering back down the road to The Green Lion, the inn where they had stayed the previous night.

When they reached the inn, Delvin immediately saw that the cart which had been outside his window had now gone. He dismounted and started searching around the yard to see if his magician's stone had landed there.

On hearing them enter the yard, the landlord came out and was astonished to see them.

"Magisters, what happened? I thought those men had taken you away."

"They had," said Grimbolt. "We escaped."

Delvin hadn't found any sign of his magician's stone in the yard. He came over to the landlord.

"Have you or any of your staff found a crystal in the yard? Those mercenaries took it off me and threw it out of the window. I really need to get it back."

"No, I haven't found anything, and none of my staff have said anything about finding a crystal."

"There'll be a reward if they do find it," said Grimbolt.

"There was a cart parked under the window," said Delvin, indicating where the cart had been. "Do you know where that cart went?"

"That cart? That was the swill cart. That's the cart for our kitchen waste. It goes to feed Hanaman's pigs."

"Where can we find Hanaman?" asked Grimbolt.

"His farm is a league up that track there," said the landlord pointing to a track leading off the main road.

"Come on," said Jarla.

"Just a moment," said Delvin. He quickly went into the stables. The stable lad was there.

"Is my rabbit alright?" asked Delvin.

"Aye," replied the stable lad, and went over to a corner of the stables and returned with Freda.

"Thanks," said Delvin, taking her and smiling at the stable lad. He gave Freda a quick stroke as he went back out into the yard.

"I'm going back up to our room to get any of my things that the mercenaries didn't take," announced Delvin.

"I'll do the same," said Grimbolt. Jarla nodded and they all three went upstairs.

Amid the chaos of the room, Delvin found his sling and put Freda in it. He then retrieved a few other items the mercenaries had left.

He and Grimbolt went back down to the yard. Jarla was already there.

"Are you done?" said Jarla impatiently.

"All done," replied Grimbolt. Delvin nodded.

They quickly remounted their horses and set off down the track to Hanaman's farm.

The farm soon came in sight. There were a large number of pigs in a series of pens behind the farm house. The cart stood empty by the pens.

As they dismounted a stout, ruddy faced man approached them.

"How may I help you, magisters?" he said.

"We were staying at The Green Lion down the track there," said Grimbolt. "It was taken by mercenaries. They threw something of ours into the swill cart. I was hoping we might find it."

"Aye, I heard about them attacking the inn. Bad business. What was it they threw in there?"

"A crystal. It has great sentimental value."

"I've fed the swill to the pigs. How big was this crystal?"

Delvin indicated its size.

"Ah, that could be a bit big for them to swallow." He rubbed his chin in thought. "They could have left it in the bottom of the trough… If they got it in their mouths, they could have dropped it out almost anywhere… You are welcome to have a look… here… take this stick to poke around, otherwise you'll likely get real dirty."

He took a stick that was leaning against the side of the farmhouse and handed it to them. They took the stick and went over to the pens. They started by poking around in the swill that had not yet been eaten. They often had to push the pigs away and there were several troughs to check. They also looked under the throughs to see if the stone had got knocked under them by the pigs, but there was no sign of it.

Next, they tried looking around the rest of the pig's pens. The ground had been churned up by the pigs and they quickly got very dirty. But again, there was no sign of the crystal.

Eventually they gave up. Hanaman had been watching them. Grimbolt walked up to him

"If you find the crystal, I'll pay you a reward of ten royals for it," he said.

"Ten royals? I'll look out for it sure enough," replied Hanaman.

"I'll call back," said Grimbolt. He turned to the others. "We'd better be going."

They mounted their horses and returned to the main road. As they passed the inn the landlord was standing outside.

"Any luck?" he shouted.

Grimbolt shook his head.

"What are we going to do now?" asked Delvin. "Are we going to try to rescue Nippy?"

Grimbolt looked up at the sky. It was now approaching noon.

"They have a half day start on us. We won't catch them before they reach Norden."

"No," said Jarla decisively. "We'll go to Argent. Rescuing Nippy will have to wait."

Delvin was not happy about not going after Nippy, but he had to agree that the mercenaries were too far ahead for them to be able to catch up with them.

They turned their horses and headed down the road towards Argent.

After passing through Thanley they stopped by a stream, and washed off the worst of the dirt that they had got covered in at Hanamans's farm. Having got themselves clean, they changed their clothes for the clothes they had taken off the mercenaries. It took a bit of swopping items around between them to find clothes and armour that fitted them and which looked right. But soon they were dressed as mercenaries, and they remounted their horses and continued onwards.

Argent came in sight by mid-afternoon, and they could see its domes and towers rising up above its walls.

Argent was built around a huge natural harbour. Out in the bay the invader's ships lay at anchor. Their black hulls looking like black beetles against the calm blue sea.

On the furthest point of Argent Bay the land rose up as a great rocky cliff over one hundred feet high and was surmounted by Argent Castle, the ancient seat of the Dukes of Argent. Out beyond Argent Castle was a rocky promontory. It was an island at high tide, with cliffs that rose up to a flat and grassy summit. A lighthouse at its end guided ships into the harbour. The dukes no longer lived in Argent Castle. They had long since built a palace on the edge of the city below the castle. The palace was built to resemble a fantasy castle with a series of towers and mock fortifications. It was painted pink, which contrasted curiously with the dark grey of the stone towers and walls of the genuine fortifications of the castle on the cliff above. The city was protected by massive walls that connected to the castle and ran round the landward side of the city, with regular towers and a deep ditch giving further protection. At the other end of the wall to the castle was another fortification, the Harbour Fort. This was a lower building than the castle. It had been built out into the sea, so that its seaward walls rose straight up from the waters of the bay.

Chapter 21

The mercenary guards on Argent's massive city gates hardly glanced at them as they rode through, simply assuming they were other mercenaries.

"Where are we going?" asked Delvin.

"The palace," replied Jarla. "That is almost certainly where the magician and the mercenary general are."

"I suggest we go through the servant's entrance," said Delvin. "I know some of the servants, they should be able to help us."

"Right," agreed Jarla.

They rode through the city towards the palace. Frightened and resentful faces looked out at them from windows and doorways. They heard an occasional muttered insult, and people seeing them coming hurriedly got out of their way, or disappeared into houses or shops. Once a tomato flew towards them. It hit Jarla on the arm splattering her with juice. She scowled in the direction it had come from, but the thrower had already disappeared.

On entering the square in front of the palace they headed to the right, turning down the side to the servant's entrance.

There was a guard on the gateway into the courtyard in front of the servant's entrance. He simply half saluted as they rode past.

"Dreadful security," muttered Jarla.

They rode across the courtyard and dismounted before a large paneled door with iron studs and huge ornate hinges. There was a big iron bell pull hanging down. Delvin took hold of it and gave it a heave. There was a far-off sound of a bell ringing.

The door opened, and a maid looked out. She recoiled on seeing their mercenaries' clothes.

"Send a groom to look after our horses," demanded Grimbolt.

"And send Magister Botherwin to us," added Delvin.

The maid gave a frightened curtsy and rushed off. Shortly after a groom appeared, and looking at them fearfully, took their horses.

Moments later Botherwin came to the door. He was immaculately dressed and looked disdainfully at them.

"Yes?" he asked looking down his nose.

"Magister Botherwin," started Delvin. "Please don't react when I tell you this. I am not a mercenary. I am Delvin, who you also knew as Porvar the magician. I am in disguise. Please let us in and take us to a private room where I can explain everything to you."

Botherwin didn't flinch. He simply said, "Follow me." Then he turned on his heel and disappeared into the building.

They followed Botherwin down a passage and into a side room. Botherwin closed the door behind them.

"Sir Delvin, I didn't recognise you," said Botherwin.

"Let me introduce Princess Jarla of Hengel and Major Grybald," said Delvin.

"Your Highness," said Botherwin bowing. "What are you doing here? Why are you in those dreadful uniforms?"

188

"They were our disguise to get us in here," said Delvin.

"We're here to try to get rid of the magician and the mercenaries," said Jarla. "Do you know what's happened to the duke?"

"He's here in the palace. But he is not himself. It's like he is in a daze."

"He's under the magician's influence," said Delvin. "We need to counteract that."

"How are you going to do that?" asked Botherwin.

"I'm not sure. I do know I'm going to have to get close to that magician. We can't do anything at long range."

"Is the magician's bedroom guarded?" asked Grimbolt.

"Oh yes," replied Botherwin. "Two guards are outside the door and others are at the end of the passage."

"That means we can't sneak into his room at night," mused Grimbolt.

"And I should add," said Botherwin, "the magician is not a him. It is a her. The magician is a lady."

"A lady?" said Jarla in surprise. "Delvin could always seduce her."

Delvin gave Jarla a dirty look and Jarla smiled sweetly back.

"Are there always guards around her?" asked Grimbolt.

"There have been, every time I've seen her," replied Botherwin.

"So, if I shot her with a crossbow bolt, we still couldn't get near her," mused Grimbolt.

"I could probably get close to her if I did a magic show," suggested Delvin.

"What would you do then?" asked Jarla.

"I don't know. Something might occur to me when I see her."

"That's not much of a plan," snorted Jarla.

"It may not be much of a plan, but it's all we have at the moment," said Grimbolt. "I think we'll have to try it. What do you need, Sir Delvin?"

"The main thing I need is a costume. I'll also need one or two other things such as three cups and some coins."

"I do have an embroidered dressing gown," suggested Botherwin, "if that is the sort of thing you want."

"Oh yes," said Delvin. "I'll need some coloured scarfs too, to tie around my head."

"I don't have any coloured scarfs, but I'm sure one of the lady servants will have some."

"We want the absolute minimum number of people to know we are here," warned Grimbolt, "and only people we can absolutely trust."

"I know a lady servant who works here," said Delvin, "and I am sure we can trust her."

"Of course you do," said Jarla rolling her eyes.

"Who is that?" asked Botherwin.

"Hanny," replied Delvin.

"Ah yes Hanny. Well, if you are sure, I can get her for you."

"I've just had an idea," said Delvin, a smile suddenly crossing his face. "I'm not sure if it will work... It will need a bit of luck… Do you have a hat I can borrow? And is there someone who can sew me a small bag?"

"I have several hats," said Botherwin. "What sort do you want?"

"Preferably one that goes with a magician's costume and is quite tall."

"I think I might have one. But as for the bag… I am not sure which of the servants is good at sewing."

"I'll ask Hanny when she comes," said Delvin.

Just then Freda popped her head out of her sling and looked around. Botherwin's eyes opened wide in surprise, but he quickly regained his composure.

"I'll ask Hanny to come here, and I'll get those other things you need," said Botherwin as he bowed and left the room.

Delvin began to think about how he could structure his show and what tricks he could do. He had a pack of cards in his pocket, and with the other items he should be able to put together a good show.

Botherwin returned shortly after followed by Hanny. Hanny looked wide eyed when she was introduced to Jarla and Grimbolt.

"I'll go and get my dressing gown and those other things," said Botherwin bowing again and leaving the room.

Delvin turned to Hanny.

"I'm going to act as Porvar the magician again, and I need to look the part. Botherwin is lending me his dressing

gown. Do you have any brightly coloured scarfs I can tie
around my head?"

"Ooh yes," replied Hanny.

"Great. Are you able to sew?"

"I'm good at sewing. I make my own dresses."

"Wonderful. This is what I need."

Delvin carefully described he bag he wanted Hanny to
make for him. She listened intently then looked up at him
smiling.

"Yes, I can do that."

"Fantastic," said Delvin.

"Botherwin said you were Sir Delvin. Are you really a
sir?"

Delvin nodded and Hanny's eyes grew wide.

"Are you really trying to get rid of the mercenaries?"

Delvin nodded again and Hanny's eyes grew wider
still.

"I'll go and get my scarfs and make that bag for you,"
said Hanny making to leave.

"Don't tell anybody about us. Anybody at all. That's
really important," said Delvin.

"I won't," replied Hanny breathlessly.

Delvin smiled at her and Hanny smiled back then
flashed him a cheeky grin.

"Thanks," said Delvin grinning back.

Hanny curtsied to Jarla and let herself out of the room.

Shortly after, Botherwin returned. He had brought one
of the most splendid dressing gowns Delvin had ever seen.
It was red velvet with blue piping around the edges and

was covered in embroidery. On its back was an embroidered image of a fire breathing dragon. He had also brought a tall blue hat with a wide brim.

"That's magnificent," said Delvin trying the dressing gown on. He picked up the hat and tried that on too. "Perfect," he said.

"When were you planning to perform," asked Botherwin.

"I want to be able to get close to that lady magician," replied Delvin. "I think just after they have finished eating their dinner will be the best time. I can perform close up magic across the dining table."

"I will speak to Magister Balinow," said Botherwin.

"Who is Balinow?" asked Jarla.

"He's the High Steward," replied Delvin.

"Oh, I remember him," said Jarla. "The stuck up one."

Delvin noticed Botherwin trying to suppress a smile.

"I suspect you are hungry," said Botherwin. "It will be noticed if I take some of the main dining room's dinner, and anyway that won't start for a while. The servant's dinner is not until after that. In the meantime, I can find you some bread, cheese and meats. I am sorry that is very plain fare. But if you want to stay hidden, I think it is the least likely to attract attention."

"That will be splendid," said Grimbolt.

Botherwin went out to find them some food.

When Botherwin had brought in the dressing gown, he had also brought the other items Delvin had asked for.

Delvin now worked out which pocket to put the various items in, and the order of the tricks he would perform.

Botherwin was soon back. He was carrying a tray laden with bread, cheese, cold meats, a pie, a bottle of wine, glasses and a flagon of ale. He placed them on the table in the room.

"Thank you," said Delvin and Grimbolt almost together.

"I'll go and see Balinow now," said Botherwin. "I don't think there will be a problem in arranging your show." He bowed and left the room.

Delvin, Jarla and Grimbolt were all hungry. They'd had no breakfast or lunch, and it was now late afternoon. They pulled up chairs around the table and tucked into the food.

When they had finished, they sat back in their chairs. They now had to wait. Dinner for the lady magician and the others in the main dining room would not start for another hour, and it would probably be another hour after that before Delvin could perform his magic show.

They were throwing about ideas for how they might overcome the lady magician when there was a soft knock on the door. It was Hanny. She had brought several brightly coloured scarfs and the bag that Delvin had asked her to make.

Delvin examined them and smiled his thanks.

"These are perfect. Thank you."

"I was thinking," said Hanny. "The duke will be in the dining room. He might recognize you. I thought you might need to be disguised, so I brought some make up. I hope you don't mind."

"Not at all," said Delvin. "That was good thinking."

"It was indeed," said Jarla her eyes sparking. "Can I help you make him up?"

"She's very good," said Delvin. "She has disguised us before."

Hanny nodded and curtsied. Jarla came over and looked at Delvin critically.

Hanny and Jarla discussed how they could change Delvin's appearance. Hanny seemed to have got over her initial shyness in front of Jarla, and Jarla was now in her element. They eventually decided what to do and set about it with gusto. Pads were put in his cheeks to change the shape of his face, grey was added to his hair, his eyebrows were built up with rabbit fur so that they were now bushy, and powder and paint changed his face further.

Jarla and Hanny looked at each other in satisfaction.

"I think that will do nicely," said Jarla. Hanny nodded.

Delvin wound one of the scarfs around his head and placed the hat on top. He put on the splendid dressing gown and tied a second scarf around his waist.

Just then Botherwin came in. He looked momentarily astonished at Delvin's change in appearance, his eyes opening wide. But once again he quickly regained his composure.

"The lady magician, the mercenary general, His Grace the duke and Princess Fionella are eating their dinner at the moment in the Small Dining Room," he said. "They will finish in about half an hour. Magister Balinow has suggested to them that you perform for them when they have finished, and they have agreed. I will take you up in a quarter of an hour. Are you ready?"

Delvin nodded. Botherwin bowed in return and left the room.

Delvin took Freda out of her sling and put her in the bag Hanny had made. Then he took another of the scarfs and put it round the bag to hide it.

Now he just had to wait until Botherwin came for him.

Chapter 22

Botherwin took Delvin up the servant's stairs to the hall where Balinow waited for them. Balinow then escorted Delvin through into the Small Dining Room.

Although it was called the Small Dining Room, it looked big to Delvin. On either side of a huge fireplace were large, highly polished wooden sideboards. In the centre of the room was a table that could have easily seated twelve. Seated next to each other opposite the fireplace, were four people. Delvin's eyes were immediately drawn to a lady sitting at the centre of the table. She was of middle years with long black hair showing touches of grey. She wore a low-cut crimson dress showing off her ample bosom. Resting in her cleavage, Delvin could see her magician's stone hanging on a gold chain around her neck. She had an arrogant expression on her slightly puffy face, and she looked at Delvin with distain.

On her right was a tall thin man of about fifty. He was slightly balding with a calculating look on his narrow face. He was immaculately dressed in a uniform that looked like it might have been designed by himself. It had gold epaulettes and was festooned with gold braid.

On her left was the Duke of Argent. He had grey hair and a neat beard, but his eyes had a vacant look. He was dressed in a green doublet with slashed sleeves, showing purple silk underneath.

On the duke's left was Princess Fionella. Her long blond hair hung down over her shoulders. She too had the same vacant expression as her father. She wore a blue silk dress that beautifully set off her pale complexion.

Delvin took a deep breath as he entered the room holding his bundle of props, including Freda his rabbit who was in the bag which was wrapped up in one of Henny's scarfs.

"Porvar the magician to entertain you," announced Balinow, managing to put a note of superiority into his voice.

Delvin placed his bundle of props on the table in front of the lady magician, making sure no one saw there was a rabbit hidden in it. He removed the three cups from the bundle, took off his hat, bowed, then placed his hat over the rest of the bundle.

"Your Grace, Your Highness, my lady, General, tonight I will show you stunning feats of magic and prestidigitation the like which you have never seen before. You will be amazed, bewildered, astonished and entertained. You will tell your family, your friends, your acquaintances and they will not believe what you tell them... Because I am Porvar the great." He bowed again.

Delvin began with his cups and balls trick. He had made small balls out of rolled up bits of material, and he made the balls disappear from under one cup to reappear under another with bewildering speed.

Next, he performed a trick with cards. He could sense his audience relaxing. That was what he wanted.

He performed a trick with coins.

Now for the important one he thought.

"And now I will show you an amazing materialization."

Delvin turned over his hat, in the process secretly putting his rabbit into it. With a great flourish he took Freda out of his hat and showed her to his audience.

There was an audible gasp. They had not expected him to produce a rabbit. As he held Freda out towards the lady magician, she put out her hand and stroked her.

Delvin placed Freda on the table. She sniffed the air and started bounding towards the far edge of the table.

The lady magician instinctively leaned forward and put out her hand to stop Freda falling off the edge. As she did so, her magician's stone on its chain swung forwards so it was hanging just over the table.

Delvin's hand was already half across the table from where he had placed Freda. In one movement he swept his hand round and grabbed the magician's stone. Instantly he projected *'Paralyze!'* The lady magician, general, duke and princess instantly froze in their positions. Balinow who was standing at the back of the room was also paralyzed.

Still holding onto the stone, Delvin retrieved Freda with his other hand, and gave her the bit of food he had placed at the edge of the table to get her to bound towards it. He breathed a sigh of relief. His plan had worked.

Delvin carefully removed the chain from around the lady magician's neck and placed it around his own neck.

He then released the duke and Princess Fionella from their paralysis and also from any suggestions and compulsions the lady magician had put on them. The duke and princess blinked in surprise and shook their heads as if to shake out any remaining influence. Then Princess Fionella turned to her father and threw her arms around his neck. He returned the embrace with a relieved smile on his face.

"You have released us," said the duke breathlessly. "Is that you, Sir Delvin?" asked the duke, now looking more closely at Delvin.

"Yes, Your Grace," said Delvin. "Now we need to do two things. We need to get all the servants out of the way so no one gets hurt. Then I am going to send a projection to the mercenary general to make him order all his men back to their ships."

"Can you order them to go away altogether?" asked the duke.

"It wouldn't work Your Grace. They have another magician on the ships. He would counteract it. The best I can do is to get them on the ships."

"Right," said the duke. "How can I help?"

"I am now going to release Magister Balinow. I would like you to order him to order all the servants to go to the servant's hall and wait there. I wouldn't want any of them to get in the way of the mercenaries when they leave, and so get hurt."

"Right," said the duke getting up and coming round the table.

Delvin went over to Balinow and released him from his paralysis. Balinow jerked as he was released.

The duke immediately ordered him to get all the servants to go to the servant's hall and to stay there until he rang the bell.

Delvin then projected a strong suggestion to the mercenary general that he must order all mercenaries back to their ships immediately without argument. He must tell nobody what had just happened, he must not do anything that might harm Delvin, the duke, the princess or anyone from Argent, and he must go back to the ships himself. He then released him from his paralysis.

The general looked around, seeming to be fighting the suggestion but failing to overcome it. He got up from the table and marched out of the room.

"Now, Your Grace, Princess, we need to wait until the palace is cleared of mercenaries before we can do anything else."

"It seems you have rescued me again," said the duke. "Are you on your own?"

"No, Your Grace. Princess Jarla and Major Grybald are here too. But it would be dangerous to bring them here before the palace is clear of mercenaries."

They could hear noises and occasional shouts as the general's orders were carried out and the mercenaries left the palace. Eventually it was quiet. They waited a few minutes longer, then Delvin turned to the duke.

"The palace should be clear of the mercenaries now. Do you know if the city's garrison is being held at the barracks?"

"I believe so."

"They are almost certainly being compelled to stay there by a suggestion projected by that lady magician. We need to go and release them. Then they can chase out of the city any mercenaries who are too slow getting to their ships. But before I do that, I need to get out of this costume, and I should also go and get Princess Jarla and Major Grybald. Please could you let the servants know that they can leave the servant's hall, and please could you also get the grooms to saddle some horses for us to ride to the barracks."

"Certainly," said the duke as he tugged the bell pull to summon the servants. "I will come with you to see Princess Jarla and Major Grybald."

Moments later Balinow appeared.

"Your Grace, is it all clear now?"

"It is. Please get the grooms to saddle four horses. Please escort Princess Fionella to her room. And please tell the servants they can now resume their duties."

"Certainly, Your Grace. What shall we do about her?" He gave a disapproving look towards the lady magician who was still frozen in position.

"We can leave her for the time being until our soldiers get back here, then they can deal with her," said the duke, looking with considerable dislike at the lady magician.

Balinow gave a little bow.

Delvin remembered that Balinow had treated him as a servant the last time he had been in the palace. He suddenly had an idea for how to get his own back and grinned to himself.

Delvin projected the suggestion that someone had touched Balinow's right shoulder. Balinow turned to see who it was. Delvin again projected the suggestion of Balinow's right shoulder being touched. Balinow turned again looking puzzled. Delvin sent the projection again, and Balinow turned yet again. Delvin noticed the duke was looking astonished at Balinow turning round and round, so he decided he had better stop.

"Whatever are you doing?" said the duke.

"I thought there was somebody behind me," said Balinow in a confused voice.

"There's nobody there," responded the duke testily.

Just then a message came into Delvin's head, *'Lady Anbroom, why are the mercenaries leaving Argent?'*

Delvin realized in alarm that the message was coming from the black magician. He signaled everyone to wait. After thinking for a moment, he replied, *'Lord Tabsall has a new plan. We are all to go to Rostin.'*

'To Rostin? Why?'

'I don't know the details. I think it is to do with the boy Prince Nippold. He has been captured and is on his way to Rostin.'

'I have finished here. I was about to set out for North Bridge. I have found no sign here of Delvin or Princess Jarla.'

'The plans have changed. Lord Tabsall wants us all in Rostin.'

Delvin took a deep breath. Had he managed to fool the black magician to go to Rostin? If he had, he would be out of the way for a while. He waited for a minute, but there were no more messages.

The duke was looking at him expectantly. Delvin turned to him and told him about the exchanges with the black magician.

"It will be good if you have managed to get that dreadful black magician out of Argent," said the duke.

Balinow had been waiting with the others. Now he bowed and went over to Princess Fionella to escort her to her room.

The duke turned to Delvin. "Lead me to the room where Princess Jarla and Major Grybald are."

Delvin led the way. When he opened the ante room's door, he grinned at the surprise on everyone's faces as the duke strode in.

"Your Grace," said Jarla and Grimbolt almost in unison. Hanny, who was also still in the room, curtsied, her eyes opening wide.

"Princess Jarla, Major Grybald, thank you for your help," said the duke. "Sir Delvin has managed to take the magician's stone off that lady magician." He turned to Hanny. "Thank you too for your help." Hanny was much too overcome to say anything, and simply curtsied again.

"We are going to the barracks to release the soldiers," announced the duke. "I am sure you would like to join us when you have changed out of those mercenaries' clothes. I will see you in the courtyard shortly. The horses are being saddled."

"Thank you, Your Grace," said Jarla and Grimbolt together.

The duke left the room.

"Right, let's get our bundles from the stables so we can get changed," said Jarla making for the door.

Delvin quickly slipped out of Balinow's dressing gown and took off Hanny's scarves. He was about to follow the others when he was stopped by a tug on his arm.

"Would you like to see me later?" asked Hanny with a twinkle in her eye.

"I would love to," said Delvin grinning.

Hanny giggled and gave him a quick kiss on the cheek. Then with a cheeky grin, she picked up her scarves and was gone out of the room.

Delvin followed the others out to the stables and quickly got changed.

They mounted their horses in the courtyard, and together with the duke, rode the short distance to the barracks and army headquarters.

There was no sentry on guard outside the barracks. Delvin guessed there had been a mercenary sentry there earlier, but he had now gone back to the ships.

They dismounted and the duke strode up the steps and through the door into the barracks' hall. There was a flight of stairs opposite the door, and doors led off on either side. An officer sat at a desk just inside the door.

"Sir Delvin, please remove any compulsions from the soldiers here," requested the duke.

"Certainly, Your Grace." Delvin sent out a projection releasing the soldiers from the lady magician's suggestions, making sure it was directed only to Argent's soldiers and not to the mercenaries,

The officer behind the desk gave a slight start. Then seeing the duke was in the hall in front of him, leapt to his feet a look of surprise on his face.

"Your Grace, what may I do for you?"

"Is General Horncliffe here?"

"Yes, Your Grace."

"Get him for me."

"Yes, Your Grace." The officer rushed off up the stairs.

Shortly after, a tall grey-haired man appeared, buttoning up his uniform jacket as he came.

"Ah General Horncliffe," said the duke.

"Your Grace, those magicians used their sheffs awful magician's stones to stop us leaving our barracks again. We really need to sort them out once and for all. I suddenly feel different, has Sir Delvin removed their suggestions, compulsions or whatever they are?"

"He has. He has also made the mercenary general order his men back to their ships. I would like you and your men to make sure they go. Be warned though. The general's men are not under Sir Delvin's influence. I also need some men to accompany me back to the palace to guard it and to deal with the lady magician."

A wicked smile had come over General Horncliffe's face.

"It will be a pleasure, Your Grace." He turned to the officer who had been behind the desk. "I want all men assembled outside immediately, fully armed."

"Yes sir." The officer rushed off.

"If you would care to wait in here, Your Grace, I will have a detachment ready to go back to the palace with you very shortly."

General Horncliffe ushered them into a side room. The room had a large table in the centre with chairs set around it. Opposite the windows, which looked out onto the square, was a large fireplace. General Horncliffe went over to a tall cupboard on the far side of the room and took from it a decanter of wine and a tray of glasses which he placed on the table. Bowing to the duke he left the room.

The duke poured out a glass of wine and offered it to Jarla, then poured out another for himself. They could hear shouts, bangs and the noise of many feet as the soldiers began to pour out of the building.

After only a very short time there was a knock at the door, and General Horncliffe returned.

"My men are beginning to fan out across the city. I have a detachment ready to escort you back to the palace, Your Grace."

"Thank you General," said the duke.

The duke, Jarla, Grimbolt and Delvin followed the general out into the square. Their horses were still in the square with their escort standing next to them. Elsewhere detachments of soldiers were marching out in different directions, their weapons at the ready.

"General, when the city is completely clear, report to me at the palace," ordered the duke.

The duke, Delvin, Jarla and Grimbolt mounted their horses. The duke turned to the officer in charge of the escort. "Right, back to the palace."

The officer saluted and they set off. On reaching the palace, the officer detailed some of the men to guard the gates.

"Sir Delvin, go with the officer and two of his men to release that lady magician. We will want to question her when General Horncliffe gets here. In the meantime, lock her in one of the cellars, and make sure she is chained up, and that there's a guard on the door… Join me in the Green Drawing Room when you are done."

Delvin led the soldiers to the Small Dining Room where the lady magician was still frozen in position. Delvin released her and she collapsed forward. He then sent a projection that she must obey the guards, not try to escape and when questioned, tell everything she knew and tell the truth.

The soldiers marched her away, and Delvin made his way to the Green Drawing Room.

About an hour later Balinow announced the arrival of General Horncliffe. He marched into the room with a satisfied smile on his face.

"The city is clear of mercenaries Your Grace. The Harbour Fort is regarrisoned, and I have also sent a garrison up to the castle. As the enemy fleet is still in the bay, we are building barricades across roads leading from the harbour, in case they try to land again,"

"Excellent," said the duke. "Take a seat General. Right, I think it is time we questioned that lady magician. General, please would you ask your men to bring her up here."

"Certainly, Your Grace."

The General having just sat down, got up again and left the room. He returned after a few minutes with two soldiers holding the chained lady magician between them. She was looking far more bedraggled than when Delvin had seen her at dinner. Her long hair was looking tangled and her dress was covered in stains. But the main change was in her face. Before it had held a haughty superior look. Now it was haggard and there was a look of fear in her eyes.

One of the soldiers brought in a wooden chair from outside and the lady magician was sat on it.

"Sir Delvin, please could you make sure she tells the truth and tells us everything."

"Yes, Your Grace." Although he had already done so earlier, Delvin again sent a projection to the lady magician to answer fully and truthfully.

"What is your name?"

"Lady Anbroom."

"What other magicians with magician's stones are there and where are they?"

Delvin saw Lady Anbroom try and fail to fight the compulsion he had put on her.

"Lord Querriol is on the ships. Lord Tabsall is in Rostin Castle. Lord Benbark is in North Bridge. I don't know where the black magician is. He was here in Argent, but he was about to leave." She looked directly at Delvin. "He is hunting you. He will get you. You won't escape." She gave a smirk.

"We have already dealt with Benbark in North Bridge," said Delvin.

Lady Anbroom gave a look of shock and the duke looked up in query.

"We dealt with him on our way here," responded Jarla.

"Who is the magician's leader?" asked General Horncliffe.

"Lord Tabsall."

"What were the mercenaries' orders?"

"After the failure of Lord Stypin to capture Hengel after his landing in Cavid, we were to capture Argent and then move down to Hengel. Lord Benbark would ensure we could get over the bridge at North Bridge. Then he would join us as we took Hengel. With two magicians, Hengel would not be able to stop us."

"Why did Lord Querriol stay on the ships?"

"He is young and inexperienced. After Lord Drandor was killed, he was given Lord Drandor's magician's stone. He hasn't had it long."

"How many men do you have?"

"Fourteen hundred plus another thirteen hundred who joined us when the fleet that captured Cavid joined us."

"What are the plans now?"

"I don't know. Things have changed."

"What is the name of the mercenaries' general?"

"General Torurk."

They questioned her for a little longer but there was nothing more of use she could tell them.

"Take her to the dungeons in the castle," said the duke. "I'll decide what to do with her later. I don't think there is anything more we can do tonight. We will meet in the morning and decide our next move then."

The duke got up, and as he left the room Balinow appeared.

"I'll show you to your rooms," he said.

Delvin, Grimbolt and Jarla followed Balinow to the main guest bedrooms. Jarla's was the first room they came to. Balinow opened the door and bowed as she went in. He then moved down the corridor and opened the door to Delvin's room. The room was sumptuous. It was far more luxurious than any room Delvin had ever had before. There was a huge four poster bed with scarlet curtains around it. An elaborate dressing table, a matching wardrobe, a matching chest of drawers, a washstand, two easy chairs and a deep pile carpet.

Delvin looked around the room in wonder. As the door closed behind Balinow, he heard a giggle from the bed. Peering out from behind the curtains was the grinning face of Hanny.

"Wow!" said Delvin grinning back at her.

Hanny giggled again.

"I've brought some lettuce and a cucumber," said Hanny with a cheeky grin.

"For my rabbit?" replied Delvin grinning back.

"But of course," replied Hanny.

Delvin felt the day had greatly improved.

Chapter 23

Delvin woke up with a feeling of contentment. He rolled over and saw Hanny looking at him smiling. The sun was up, and beams of light shone through a slight gap where the curtains had not been quite been drawn together. He put his arm around Hanny and gave her a kiss.

Just then he picked up a faint message. *'Invade again!'*

Delvin had not removed the magician's stone from around his neck. Was this a message from Tabsall the magician in Rostin to the magician with the ships in the Bay, he wondered? He lay back and concentrated.

There was a reply. *'They have at least one magician with a stone and probably two, since they have taken Lady Anbroom's stone. I can't overcome two stones with just my one.'*

Another faint message came. *'Wait there while I get Lord Benbark up from North Bridge. Then with two of you, you will be able to invade again.'*

'Can you get the black magician here as well?'

'We'll see. I want him to find Delvin, kill him and take the stone off Princess Jarla. When he has done that, he can come and help you. Wait there until we have enough stones. Then we'll take the city again.'

Just then there was a discreet knock on the door. With a sigh and a slightly rueful smile on his face, Delvin pulled the bed covers over Hanny and rolled out of bed. Then wrapping a blanket around himself, he went to the door.

The duke's valet was outside holding a neat pile of clothes.

"His Grace will be having breakfast in the Small Dining Room in about twenty minutes. I thought you might like a change of clothes." He handed the pile of clothes to Delvin.

"Thank you," said Delvin taking the clothes. He bowed, still clutching the blanket around himself, then closed the door.

"It looks like I have to get up," said Delvin.

"I should be getting up too," said Hanny, stretching and giving Delvin a happy smile.

Delvin washed and shaved and then put on the clothes the duke's valet had brought. They consisted of a smart green doublet and black breeches. Hanny got dressed too and combed her hair before discreetly slipping out, giving Delvin a kiss as she went.

Delvin made his way down to the Small Dining Room. Jarla and Grimbolt were already there eating their breakfasts. Jarla too had a change of clothing. She was dressed in a deep blue dress. Delvin guessed it was one of Princess Fionella's dresses, since it hung rather loosely on her muscular athletic body.

Delvin sat down and a servant brought him a cup of hot leaf. There was an array of rolls, breads, cold meats, cheeses and jams on the table. Delvin helped himself to a roll.

"Did you sleep well?" asked Jarla sweetly, raising an eyebrow.

"Very well thank you," replied Delvin. Jarla gave a slight snort.

Just then the duke entered the room, and they all stood up.

The duke waved his hand for them to sit again, and he took his place at the head of the table. A servant almost immediately placed a cup of hot leaf before him.

"General Horncliffe is checking our defenses and what the mercenaries are doing," announced the duke. "He will be joining us shortly, then we must decide on our next move."

"I overheard some messages before coming down to breakfast," said Delvin. "They were between the magician Querriol on the ships and Tabsall in Rostin."

Everyone around the table looked up and Delvin told them what he had overheard.

"So, they want to invade again, but are not going to do it immediately," mused the duke.

They had almost finished their breakfasts when General Horncliffe came in. He sat down, and a servant brought him a cup of hot leaf.

"Our men are in position throughout the city," he announced. "The barricades are almost complete, and I have men at strategic positions along the harbour in case they try to land again. The mercenaries' ships are still there out in the bay. We tried lobbing a few rocks at them from our catapults on the Harbour Fort, but they just moved their ships out of range, so most of their ships are now close in under lighthouse point. It's as though they are waiting for orders, or trying to decide what to do."

"I intercepted some messages," said Delvin, who then told General Horncliffe what he had overheard.

"So, they are going to stay in the harbour until another magician comes," muttered General Horncliffe, "and when they learn the magician from North Bridge isn't coming, they'll send the black magician."

"We need to move them away before that happens," said the duke.

"How are we going to do that?" asked General Horncliffe. "We don't have a navy capable of taking on their ships and the catapults didn't work."

Delvin took a deep breath. "I have a possible idea," he said. "It's rather far-fetched and I don't actually know if it will work, but even if it doesn't work completely, I think it should work enough to annoy them."

They all looked expectantly at Delvin. He took another deep breath and explained his idea.

"You must be joking," exploded Jarla. "That's the most ridiculous thing I have ever heard."

"It might work," countered Delvin. "I did some experiments back in Hengel… And from them, I actually do think it could work."

"I really don't believe it," said Jarla shaking her head. "You have had some crazy ideas in the past, but this has got to be the craziest."

"Do you really think it might work?" asked the duke.

"I do. If you could get me a piece of paper, I'll show you how I think it might be made."

At a word from the duke, a servant rushed off and returned shortly with a sheaf of paper, a quill and an ink stand.

Delvin drew a rough sketch of the device he was suggesting and explained it in detail while the others looked on intently.

"I suppose it could work," said General Horncliffe dubiously.

"Has anyone any other ideas?" asked the duke.

There was silence around the table.

"In that case," said the duke, "as it is the only idea we have, we will try it. It certainly won't do any harm, and if it works, that will be splendid. We will need to put all our resources into it.

"Sir Delvin, please draw up more detailed plans and work out what is needed. I will summon the masters of all the guilds so they can provide the various skills needed to make this device.

"Major Grybald, please could you go as quickly as possible to Hengel and bring back Sir Delvin's magic lantern. We need to make this device as quickly as we can before the magicians realize that their magician in North Bridge is not coming.

"Sir Delvin, we will meet in the South Chamber in one hour. The guild masters should all be here by then."

The duke got up and they all rose as well. As the duke left the room, the others all looked at Delvin. What had he let himself in for, he thought?

Chapter 24

Delvin and the masters of the guilds all rose as the duke entered the South Chamber. He walked to the head of the large table in the centre of the room and motioned for them all to sit.

The South Chamber was a plain room compared with the other rooms in the palace. Its windows looked out onto the palace garden, and its furniture consisted of a large table surrounded by chairs with two sideboards either side of the fireplace. Its plainness indicated that this was a room for discussions and work and not a room for entertainment.

"Guild-masters," began the duke. "Last night Sir Delvin managed to get the invaders to return to their ships, but they are waiting in the harbour to attack again. They are like a dagger poised at our throat. We need to force them to leave once and for all."

There were nods of agreement all around the table.

"We have tried hurling rocks at them from our catapults on the Harbour Fort, but they simply moved out of range. We need something different. Sir Delvin has an idea that might persuade them to go. It is a very unusual device he is proposing to make, and we cannot be absolutely sure it will work. But before we look at Sir Delvin's device, have any of you got any ideas or suggestions of how we might get the ships to leave?"

The duke looked around the table. The guild-masters looked at each other, and for several moments nobody said anything.

"I don't think any of us have any suggestions, Your Grace," said the master carpenter. The others round he table nodded.

"In that case," said the duke, "we will need to try to make Sir Delvin's device. It is essential we make it as quickly as possible before the mercenaries attack again. That is why I have summoned you. It will need all your skills and resources to build what Sir Delvin is proposing. I therefore ask that you put all your efforts into it. We will build this device in the palace garden here, where we will test and refine it before moving it into its final position. I will now leave you with Sir Delvin to explain his idea to you."

There were nods from all around the table, and the guild-masters all rose as the duke left the room. As they sat down again, they all looked at Delvin expectantly.

Delvin took a deep breath and began to explain the idea for his device.

"Guild-masters," began Delvin. "I want to try and convert the magic lantern that I use in my magic shows, so that it will concentrate a beam of intense light and heat from the sun onto the invaders' ships. If we get it right, it might be able to set fire to the ships' sails. But at the very least, it should be extremely annoying."

"A sort of sun ray shooting device," said the metalworkers' master thoughtfully.

"That's right," replied Delvin. "Let me draw a quick sketch of what I am proposing."

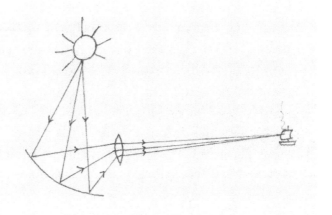

Delvin's quick sketch

"The sun's rays would be gathered by a huge concave mirror. The largest we can make, and reflect them to a point. At that point would be placed my magic lantern lens. The lens would then direct the light so that it formed a parallel beam that could be focused to a small point by moving the lens forwards and back. That point would be directed at the mercenaries' ships. Some of you, when you were children, probably used a lens to concentrate sunlight to a point and burn holes in things. This is the same principle, but on a much bigger scale."

There was silence around the room as the guild-masters considered his idea.

"It just might work," said the master spectacle maker. Others around the table nodded. "There are two key things," he continued. "You need to be able to focus the device very precisely. I think your single lens would work, but it would be difficult to focus exactly. I think it would help if there was a set of lenses to do the focusing beyond your magic lantern lens. I could make them, or you could possibly use the ones in your magic lantern. The second key thing is the mirror." He looked at the master glassmaker.

"We could blow a large concave shape," responded the master glassmaker, "but it would not be perfect and would be too deep. We would need a mould or former of some sort to blow the molten glass against to get the right shape."

"I could turn a shape from wood," said the master carpenter. "If we glued pieces of wood together, we could just about make a mould up to a pace wide, but it would burn if you pressed molten glass onto it."

"How about if we used your wood as a pottery former," said the master potter. "If you made it convex rather than concave, we could press clay against it to make a huge pottery concave former for the glass. We could make it fireproof, so you would be able to press your hot glass against it without it burning." He suddenly looked up as he had another idea. "We could make a rough concave shape out of clay and glue it to a metal backing plate." He turned to the master carpenter. "Then you could turn it to the exact shape on your lathe in the same way you would turn your piece of wood. If we stuck it on to the backing plate with a glue that melted when hot, we could put the whole thing in the kiln."

"We need to do this as quickly as possible, so we need to try both," said the master glassworker.

"We will need a cradle to hold the mirror," said the master carpenter. "The mirror is also going to need to turn on two axes." He looked at the master metal worker.

"I can make a joint that will do that. The part of the device with the lenses is going to have to turn on two axes as well, so it will need a second double joint." He paused thinking. "Both parts, the mirror and the lenses need to be separate, otherwise when you move the lenses, it will move the mirror out of position."

"It's going to be quite difficult to get it to aim exactly," said the master clockmaker. "Both joints are going need a way to give them fine adjustments. I can make screw adjustments for them. It will also need a fine adjustment screw for the positioning of the lens so it can focus precisely. I can make that too."

The discussion went backwards and forwards. The main frame and cradle would be made by the carpenters, and each of the other guilds would contribute their parts. They began to make more detailed drawings, gradually refining and improving their ideas, until after about an hour of discussion, a full plan and design had been agreed upon.

"Right," said the master glassworker. "Let's get to work and see if we can build this thing. I suggest that Sir Delvin acts as liaison between us and coordinates the construction." The guild- masters all nodded their approval.

"Should we give this thing a name?" asked the master metalworker.

"I think we should call it a 'magic sun lantern'," suggested the master glass maker.

"Or 'sun lantern' for short," said the master carpenter.

They nodded their agreement and rose from the table talking animatedly among themselves. Then they thanked Delvin for his idea and returned to their workshops to start making the components needed.

After reporting back to the duke, Delvin visited the various workshops. He was kept busy for the rest of the morning taking messages between them, and working out where in the palace garden the prototype of the sun lantern would be erected.

Delvin had originally thought they could set the sun lantern up on the Harbour Fort, but he quickly realized, that with the mercenaries' ships anchored on the other side of the bay, the long range would make it far less effective. Instead, they would need to erect it on the small island just beyond the castle where the lighthouse stood, next to where the mercenaries' ships lay at anchor. The island was accessible at low tide with a path leading across the sand to it. There were cliffs all around the island, with the path from the mainland leading up a steep slope to the flat plateau on the top.

In the afternoon Delvin took a squad of soldiers over to the island to find the best place to put the sun lantern.

He also wanted to make sure the path was in good repair for carrying the components of the device over to the island, and up onto the plateau. The soldiers were also there to set up defensive positions, so that when they started to use the lantern, the mercenaries couldn't attack and capture it.

Delvin soon found a flat grassy area on the plateau that looked a perfect place for setting the sun lantern. As Delvin stood there looking out over the bay with gulls wheeling overhead, he could see the mercenaries' ships anchored close to the island's cliff face. One ship was bigger than the others. That's probably the flagship he thought. Delvin suddenly had an idea and grinned to himself.

Delvin projected the idea to the gulls that the mercenaries' flagship contained people who were threatening them. He then stood back and watched grinning as the gulls swooped down on the ship, dive bombing the mercenaries on board, pecking at them and covering them in droppings.

Having finished his reconnaissance, Delvin went back down the path to the mainland, leaving the soldiers to prepare their defensive positions.

In the evening Delvin joined the duke and Jarla for dinner and reported on how the preparations were going. The duke seemed very pleased with the progress, though Jarla was still rather sceptical about whether the sun lantern would actually work.

After dinner Delvin went back to the workshops. Some of the guild-masters had decided to work through the night, so he was very tired when he eventually got back to his room. As he shut the door a giggle came from behind the curtains around the bed.

"I've fed your rabbit and given him a run. Cucumber seems to be her favourite, so I've brought another one."

"You and your cucumber," replied Delvin grinning as he got undressed.

Delvin was up early the following morning and gave Hanny a quick kiss as he left the room. He went downstairs and put his head round the kitchen door. A servant was just taking the first batch of rolls out of the oven. With a smile he gave one to Delvin, who had to juggle it between his hands to stop it burning his fingers. He then went to see how the guild-masters were progressing.

A lot of work had been done during the night, and before long the guild-masters and their apprentices were carrying the first components over to the place in the palace's garden where the sun lantern was to be erected.

Under the direction of the master carpenter the main frame was soon assembled, and with the help of the master metalworker, they started testing the pivots and the screws which adjusted its direction.

Throughout the morning Delvin continued taking messages between the different workshops and guild-masters. He then grabbed a quick lunch before visiting the potters. They told him the former for the mirror was drying. It needed to be dry before it could be fired, and they had placed it in a heated room to speed up the drying process. They were hoping it might be dry enough to fire during the following night. They had made a second former that was also drying. After discussions with the glassmakers, they were planning to attempt to use it as a former without firing it first in the kiln. They aimed to have that ready by later that day.

In the late afternoon Grimbolt returned from Hengel with Delvin's magic lantern. Delvin immediately took its large lens and the focusing lenses to the watch and spectacle makers to mount, so that they could be fitted to the device.

That evening the unfired former, which had been burnished so that it was absolutely smooth, was taken over to the glassmakers. The potter's master had a worried look on his face. He would have liked to have left it to dry longer, but he realized the importance of getting the mirror made as soon as possible. The glassmakers had prepared their workshop ready for it, and began melting an enormous piece of glass in their furnace. Everyone held their breath as the glass blower blew a huge ball of glass and kept blowing and turning it as he lowered it onto the former. There was a collective sigh of relief as the former held, and the glassmaker trimmed it off.

"Now we need to make it into a mirror," said the master glassmaker. "There is a new technique. You take a thin sheet of tin, beat it to make it even thinner so it's like paper, flood it with mercury, then slide the glass over it.

We have only recently started using it, but if you get it right, it makes a wonderful mirror."

Delvin measured the glass and rushed over to the carpenters with the mirror's dimensions so they could finish making the cradle to hold it. He then returned to the palace to report to the duke and grab some late dinner.

"When will you be ready to test the sun lantern?" asked the duke.

"We hope to try it first thing in the morning," replied Delvin.

When Delvin finally got up to his room, he was feeling very tired. Hanny was again there to greet him.

"I do know this can't be a long-term thing," she giggled, "but it is fun in the short term." She gave a wriggle of anticipation. "And I do like your rabbit. She loves a little stroke and tickle." She collapsed into giggles again. Delvin grinned back and gave her a kiss.

Delvin was up again well before dawn. He left Hanny still asleep in the bed, and with a candle to light his way since it was still dark, he made his way to the kitchen in the hope of grabbing a roll. But he was too early, since the rolls were still in the oven baking. he would get one later, he thought, as he made his way out to the palace garden.

The guild-masters were all there. Some had again worked throughout the night. A ring of lanterns had been set up around the device to give the guild-masters enough light to see what they were doing. The sun lantern was now assembled, and the guild-masters were making the final adjustments. The previous evening Delvin had set up a sheet on a frame twenty paces away from the it. A cross had been painted in the centre of the sheet so they could aim the sun lantern at the cross.

Delvin was suddenly startled by a voice close to his ear.

"Is it all ready, Sir Delvin?" The duke had come up silently behind him.

"Yes, Your Grace."

Delvin noticed that Jarla and Grimbolt had also come out to see the trial.

The sun began to appear from behind the Grandent Mountains in the distance. The master glassmaker began to angle the mirror to reflect the sun onto the lens, while the master carpenter looked down the aiming-sight he had made, and pointed the lantern at the cross on the sheet.

As the sun rose, a bright circle of light appeared near the cross on the sheet. The master spectacle maker adjusted the focus, and the circle reduced in size and grew in intensity until it was just a handspan across.

"I think it is working," breathed a voice.

The sheet began to smoulder, and then suddenly it burst into flame.

"We need to try the sheet at a greater distance," said the master glassmaker. A servant was sent off to get some more sheets.

Two of the master's apprentices moved the sheet's frame further back, and with a fresh sheet fixed to it, the lantern was focused again.

Over the next hour the masters refined the lantern, making adjustments and improvements until they were satisfied that everything was working as well as it could.

"Well Delvin," said Jarla, as the apprentices put up yet another sheet as a target. "You've managed to wreck a few sheets. I hope you have left enough for our beds... I really didn't think that was going to work."

"I was not sure if it would work either," admitted Delvin.

"Well done, Sir Delvin," said the duke. "That was quite remarkable." He turned to the guild-masters. "Thank you for all your hard work... Right, as soon as you have finished your refinements, the sun lantern needs to be dismantled and taken up to lighthouse point. We in the meantime, will get some breakfast."

The duke led them back into the palace.

Chapter 25

It was late morning by the time they had the sun lantern packed onto mules, and they began to take it to lighthouse point. The tide was going out, and the stretch of sand between the mainland and lighthouse point had just emerged from the sea. On reaching the island the path rose steeply, and the guild masters constantly checked the mule's loads as they climbed the path up to the grassy plateau that Delvin had visited just two days before. The enemy fleet was still anchored close to the cliff where they had moved to when getting out of range of the catapults on the Harbour Fort.

Several squads of men at arms and archers had accompanied them onto the point, and they now took up defensive positions around the island.

The guild-masters carefully unpacked the sun lantern's components from the mules, and with their apprentices began to erect it on the edge of the plateau.

Delvin, the duke, Jarla, Grimbolt and General Horncliffe had followed the procession onto the island. The duke had ordered servants to bring bread, cheese, cold meat, pies and flagons of ale up to the plateau, and the guild-masters ate an impromptu lunch as they worked.

It was past noon when the guild-masters were satisfied that the sun lantern was ready. It was a clear day, the sun bright in the sky.

The duke looked down on the anchored ships and pointed to one slightly larger than the others.

"I think that is their flagship where the magician and the mercenaries' general will be. We will start on that one please guild-masters."

The master carpenter pointed the sun lantern at the ship that the duke had pointed to, and the master glassmaker angled the mirror to reflect the sun onto the lens.

They could see an area of bright light on the side of the ship as the beam of light hit it. Then as the master spectacle maker made fine adjustments to focus the lens, the area reduced in size and grew in intensity. The master clockmaker made fine adjustments to the aim, and the area of intense light moved up to the deck.

A mercenary screamed as the narrow beam of intense light hit him, and he fell writhing to the deck. The beam was moved along the deck catching other mercenaries. One tried to put up a shield to protect himself. The beam stayed on it for a short while. The shield became too hot to handle, and the mercenary had to drop it. The officers by the ship's wheel were looking on in amazement. Then the beam struck them, and they too were yelling and running. Someone must have ordered that the ship set sail as men began to climb the rigging, only to be caught by the beam and fall back screaming to the deck.

A ship lying very close to lighthouse point began to unfurl its sails to try to sail away. The guild-masters moved the sun lantern around and aimed the beam onto its main sail. At that close range, after about a minute the sail began to smoulder, then burst into flames. The ship had started to get underway. The guild-masters directed the beam towards the helmsman, who fell against the ship's wheel, causing the ship to veer to the left and crash into another ship.

A message came into Delvin's head. *'We are being attacked by some heat and light weapon. I don't know what it is.'*

Then a faint reply, *'Get out of range of it, you idiot.'*

A moment later, *'I've told the general. He is trying to.'*

There was confusion in the enemy fleet. The guild-masters were getting more adept at moving the beam from target to target, and as other ships tried to hoist sails, they picked off the helmsmen and the men in the rigging.

As the confusion grew, they could hear shouts, yells, orders and screams from the mercenaries.

Boats had been lowered from some of the ships, and they were starting to row towards lighthouse point and the sun lantern. The beam from the lantern raked one of the boats, and the mercenaries in it flung themselves into the sea to escape it. Another boat got in range of Argent's archers, who were positioned on the cliff ready for just such an attack. The boat was riddled with arrows and slewed to a halt. The next boat began to turn away but not before some long rang arrows made their mark.

Some of the ships were managing to move away, but the sails on two of the ones closest to the lantern had caught fire and smoke billowed across the bay.

Another message came into Delvin's head. The message was weak and faded in and out. *'Magister magician, are you receiving this message?'*

'I am,' replied Delvin.

'I am General Torurk, I am trying to work out how to use these stones.'

'What has happened to the magician Querriol?'

'I remembered how you took the stone off the magician Lady Anbroom. I thought that having one of these stones would be worth more to me than what I am being paid to capture Argent. If I had one, I could make myself king in a place where no one else had a stone. That thought came to me when you started to attack, and I saw Querriol communicate with Tabsall in Rostin... So, I decided to take Querriol's stone.'

'How did you take it?'

'A knife in his back. He was being nicely distracted by you burning everyone, so he wasn't looking at me.'

'What do you plan to do now?'

'I see no point in staying here fighting you, since you have a stone, and I have no advantage over you. I shall sail my fleet to Rostin and get the rest of the money they owe me for capturing Argent. I shall reprovision my fleet there and then sail to Anrovia. They have a nice weak king there. It will be easy for me to take over.'

Delvin ran over to where the duke, Jarla and Grimbolt were watching the enemy fleet as it moved out of range. He relayed to them the messages that he had exchanged with General Torurk.

"So, they are leaving, are they?" muttered the duke. "I don't trust him. When their ships are out of range, we will dismantle the lantern and take it back within the city walls.

234

I don't want a surprise attack at night to capture it. We will also leave a garrison up here." He turned to the guild-masters who were smiling with satisfied looks on their faces. "Thank you, guild-masters. Your work has been extraordinary. I am very grateful."

"We were glad we could help get rid of those mercenaries," said the master glassworker. The other guild-masters nodded in agreement.

"Right," said the duke. "We need to get the sun lantern dismantled and back to the palace before it gets dark." He looked up at the sun which was already starting to get lower in the sky. He turned to Delvin and Jarla. "We will discuss what we do next over dinner."

Chapter 26

Dinner was served in the Small Dining Room. Around the table were the duke, General Horncliffe, Delvin, Jarla and Grimbolt. They were all quite hungry, so it was only when they had finished eating and the servants had left, that they began to discuss their plans.

"I need to go to Norden to try to rescue my apprentice Nippy," said Delvin.

"Is he that important?" asked General Horncliffe.

"He might be," replied Jarla. "The magicians seem to think he's important. They had a reward out for him, quite a big reward. And we think they tried to kidnap him in Hengel."

"Why do they think he is important?" asked the duke.

"They seem to have got it into their heads that he is my son, Prince Nippold," replied Jarla.

"Your son?" said the duke astonished.

"He is not my son," said Jarla emphatically.

"He is an urchin from the streets of Argent," added Grimbolt. "He attached himself to us when we were here at the time of the riots."

"Really?" said the duke laughing. "I've heard of street urchins being cheeky, but this tops everything. Why do they think he is Princess Jarla's son?"

"Because in order to escape, and to stop them killing him and Princess Jarla, I told them he was," said Delvin.

"My guess is they hope to rule Hengel through him," added Jarla.

"Rule Hengel through a city street urchin?" said the duke still laughing.

"Yes, Your Grace," said Jarla. She thought for a moment. "That black magician has been hunting us for some time now. We need to be hunting him. If we don't get him, he'll get us. Sir Delvin sent him on a wild goose chase to Rostin in Norden. I want to follow him. If we can somehow take the black magician's stone off him, now that Querriol's magician's stone has been taken by the mercenary general, it would mean that the Guild of Magicians would only have one stone left." She smiled, a look of determination on her face. "Sir Delvin says he will be heading to Rostin to go after his apprentice. I'll join him."

"Princess Jarla, that will be very dangerous," remonstrated the duke.

"Not as dangerous as waiting here until the black magician finds us and kills us. I would far prefer to be the one doing the hunting."

"I will go with Princess Jarla," said Grimbolt.

General Horncliffe had been silent, but now spoke up. "Your Grace, it is time we invaded Norden. If Princess Jarla eliminates the black magician, they will only have one magician's stone, and Sir Delvin can counter that."

"You may be right," mused the duke. "How long will it take you to organize an invasion?"

"Not long, Your Grace. We will need to leave a strong garrison here in the city, in case the mercenaries change their mind and come back. We can take the men guarding the border with Norden, since if we are invading, we won't need them there. Then we will need to organize supplies, but that shouldn't take long."

"If you need more men my father would probably send some," said Jarla. "The magicians attacked Hengel. I am sure he would like to see them rooted out."

"That would be very helpful," said the duke.

"I will write to him," said Jarla.

"I can write to him as well," added Grimbolt.

"We are decided," said the duke. "We will invade Norden and finish the magicians once and for all. General, please make your preparations. Princess Jarla, Major Grybald, if you would be so good to write your letters, I shall write one too. Then an officer will take them with all speed to Duke Poldor.

"General, please send a message to the garrison in North Bridge, to let the detachment that Duke Poldor sends, get over the bridge and through North Bridge."

"Yes, Your Grace," said General Horncliffe.

"When will you be leaving, Sir Delvin?" asked the duke.

"At first light, Your Grace. Those mercenaries took Nippy my apprentice four days ago. That is quite a start they have. They could well have reached Rostin by now. It is also possible Nippy has escaped. He's quite clever and cunning. If he has escaped, he might need some help."

"I wish you the best of fortune Sir Delvin," said the duke. "Thank you for your help here in Argent. I hope next time we meet it will be in Rostin with the magicians finally defeated."

"Thank you, Your Grace."

Delvin, Jarla and Grimbolt took their leave as they had another early start in the morning.

Hanny was again waiting for Delvin when he went up to his room.

"I am off tomorrow," said Delvin with a rueful smile on his face. "I need to try to find my apprentice Nippy."

"We had better make the most of it tonight then," giggled Hanny. "I know I probably won't see you again, but it has been fun." She gave a little wriggle.

Chapter 27

Delvin was up before dawn. He gave Hanny a brief kiss before going down to the kitchen and grabbing a roll and a cup of hot leaf. Grimbolt and Jarla came into the kitchen shortly after and grabbed a quick breakfast too. By the time the sun was rising over the horizon, they were riding down Royal Road towards the city gate.

"I want another look at The Green Lion where we got captured," said Grimbolt, "and also that farm. If we can find that other stone, we will have a big advantage over the magicians."

They got to The Green Lion later that morning and dismounted in the inn's yard. The landlord came out and looked fearfully at them.

"Magisters, mistress," he began then tailed off.

"What's wrong?" asked Grimbolt.

"A dreadful man in black has been asking about you."

Grimbolt and Jarla looked at each other.

"When was he here?" asked Jarla.

"Yesterday."

"What did he want to know?"

"He wanted to know where you had gone, what you did... everything... I didn't want to tell him... but I couldn't stop myself."

"What did he do then?"

"He looked round the yard like you did, then went to Hanaman's farm like you did. Then he rode off."

"Which way did he go?"

"Towards Argent."

"He must have met those mercenaries," growled Grimbolt. "He'll have made them tell him about capturing us."

"If he went to Hanaman's farm, he must also have found out about Delvin's stone being thrown out of the window," added Jarla. "He's gone back towards Argent. We should go back after him." Her eyes sparkled and there was a grim smile on her face.

"Not a good idea, Princess," said Grimbolt. "How do you propose finding him in a place as big as Argent? And if you did find him, how do you propose dealing with him? Much better to continue on. He'll find out we've left Argent and are travelling towards Rostin, so he'll follow us. We know he'll be coming up behind us, so we can lay an ambush for him. That's the best way to do it. In the meantime, we need to search the yard here again for Delvin's stone, and then if we don't find it, try again at Hanaman's farm."

Jarla reluctantly agreed.

For the next twenty minutes they hunted around the yard, looking in all the corners, on the stable floor, in the bins and anywhere the stone might have fallen. Eventually they concluded it wasn't there.

"Right, Hanaman's farm next," said Grimbolt.

They remounted and rode down the lane to Hanaman's farm.

Farmer Hanaman came out of a shed as they rode into his yard. Like the innkeeper he was looking shaken.

"Magisters, mistress, I can't help you. Please go away and leave me alone. I haven't done anything wrong. Please go."

"We're not here to hurt you," said Grimbolt. "We just want to know what the man in black did."

Delvin touched his magician's stone and projected feelings of reassurance to Hanaman, and a desire to tell them what he knew and to help them.

"He was terrible," said Hanaman. "He made me tell him everything you did... Then he made me tell him where the pig swill was put out. Where the manure was put. He made me rake through all the manure."

"Did he find anything?" asked Jarla.

"I don't know. I was too frightened... and covered in pig muck by then."

"Did you find anything after we had left?" asked Grimbolt. "If you remember, I offered you ten gold royals if you found a stone like the one that I described."

"I did look for it. Ten gold royals is a lot of money... But no, I didn't find anything."

"I'll increase that reward to twenty royals," said Grimbolt. "If you find it, send word to the Duke of Argent. Say Major Grybald offered you a reward of twenty royals."

Hanaman nodded.

Grimbolt turned to Jarla.

"We don't know if the black magician found Delvin's stone, or if it is still hidden somewhere in the muck here."

Jarla grimaced.

242

Just then Delvin noticed that a very large pig had wandered into the yard behind them. He was tempted to use his stone to send a message to it to come up behind Grimbolt and shove him in the back... But then he thought better of it. Grimbolt would probably realize it was him, and he was not sure he wanted to experience what Grimbolt might do to him in return. Also, the possibility that the black magician had found the stone did not put any of them in the mood for a joke.

They had a quick look round the yard and the pig pens themselves, but to no avail. They thanked Hanaman, then remounted their horses and rode back to the main road.

"I hope the black magician didn't find it," said Grimbolt, "If he has two stones, that might make things really difficult."

They rode on. It was a fine day. The crops in the fields that they passed were growing strongly, and the countryside looked peaceful and prosperous. Low hills were dotted with small woods. Fields of crops were interspersed with fields where cows and pigs grazed or dug in the soft earth. Timber framed buildings were clustered around farmsteads, and the smells of the farms and countryside reminded Delvin of the village of Byford where he had been brought up.

They stopped for a late lunch at an ancient inn, its windows peeping out from under a thatched roof that looked almost too thick for the building beneath it.

They ate their lunch outside at a table in the sun. None of them said very much. They were all thinking of the consequences if the back magician had two magician's stones.

They soon came to the road junction. The signpost showing North Bridge one way, Dandel the other. They turned left towards Dandel.

They rode on through the afternoon. The rolling hills began to give way to flatter land. The fields were now mainly crops with occasional windmills rising up above them. Tracks and lanes led off the road to farms and hamlets nestling among the fields.

Before long the town of Dandel came into sight, its walls and buildings rising up above the fields all around. The closer they came the more details they could make out. Dandel was a walled town, but its walls were much lower than the walls of larger towns like North Bridge and South Bridge. Sufficiently tall to keep out brigands and undesirables, but not a serious defensive structure. Its only tower was its gatehouse, and that was like a tall square house with a pitched roof and an arch going through it rather than the battlemented towers of the bigger towns.

The gate was guarded, if that was the word, by an elderly man in a patched uniform. He had probably once been a soldier, but had retired from that to take on the less strenuous job of checking travelers into and out of the town. As Delvin, Jarla and Grimbolt approached, they could see him chatting to some farmers just leaving and waving to another traveler whom he obviously knew.

"Good day magisters, mistress. What is your business in Dandel?" he asked amiably.

"We are just passing through, we are traders on our way to Ablet," replied Grimbolt.

"Go through," said the guard.

They rode under the arch into the town and down the main street. There were a few inns catering to the travelers who passed through and a good selection of shops, their wares hung up outside to show what they sold. The buildings though were mainly undistinguished, with just two stories and timber framed. The main feature of Dandle, and the reason for its existence was its bridge. Dandel was the lowest point that the River Bolla could be crossed, as it wound its sluggish way across the plain towards the sea. A bridge had existed here for centuries. The bridge had gradually been added to over the years, becoming more and more elaborate until the present structure had finally evolved. The bridge was built on many wooden piers and was wide enough for two carts to pass abreast on it. Several buildings had been erected on the bridge itself. These were mainly shops, but the biggest building was an inn called The Royal Bridge. It was in the centre of the bridge and arched over the road. It had been extended out in piers on both sides of the roadway, and beyond the piers the inn extended out still further, overhanging the river itself. Delvin and Jarla had stayed there on their previous visits to Dandel.

"Are we staying here?" asked Delvin.

"We should press on," replied Grimbolt. "I also don't want to stay anywhere too conspicuous. The black magician is almost certainly following us. We don't want to give him any clues as to where we are."

They continued on over the bridge and through the other half of Dandel. The town on the north bank of the river was very similar to that on the south bank, with more inns and shops. The gate in the town wall was similar too. Again, with an ancient ex-soldier checking people in and out. There was a farmer's cart ahead of them, and as they rode up the gatekeeper waved the cart through with a friendly smile, obviously knowing the farmer.

"Where are you headed?" asked the gatekeeper.

"Ablet," replied Grimbolt.

"Go through," said the gatekeeper.

The land beyond Dandel was flat. The neat fields again being mainly given over to crops. They saw occasional windmills, their sails turning lazily in the breeze. They passed several farm carts and travelers on the road, but as the sun dipped, these became less frequent.

"Will we stop at an inn in Ambeldon?" asked Delvin.

"We could probably make it to Ambledon before it gets too dark," replied Grimbolt. "But I want somewhere small where hopefully we won't get noticed."

A few miles short of Ambledon, with the sun now low in the sky, they came to a small thatched inn, The Dunn Cow.

"This looks suitable," said Grimbolt and led them into the inn's yard.

As they dismounted the innkeeper came out to greet them.

"Good evening magisters, mistress. How may we be of service?"

"Do you have two rooms?" asked Grimbolt.

"We do. Three carls per room and a carl per horse for stabling."

"Does that include oats?"

"It does."

"We'll take them."

Grimbolt turned to the stable lad who had come out to take their horses.

"Make sure they are properly brushed."

The stable lad nodded at Grimbolt as he took the horses reins.

Delvin gave the stable lad a smile.

"Please could you look after my rabbit and give him a run and some oats."

The stable lad smiled back and nodded. Delvin gave him a copper and turned to join Grimbolt and Jarla who were on their way into the inn.

The inn turned out to be comfortable. The rooms were low ceilinged with windows peeping out through the thatch. The beds were comfortable too. Each room had two beds, a washstand, chair and a rug on the floor.

After getting themselves washed and cleaned up after their ride, they met in the inn's common room.

The common room was quite full. The customers appeared to be mainly farmers and other locals. Everyone seemed to know each other and there was much laughing and joking.

They took a table in the corner and a waitress rushed up. She was about twenty and gave Delvin a cheeky smile. Delvin smiled back.

"What would you like?" asked the waitress looking at Delvin and giving a little wiggle. Jarla rolled her eyes and shook her head.

"Two ales and a wine please," said Grimbolt glancing at Delvin with a knowing smile. "What have you to eat?"

"We have stew or cold meats."

They all ordered stew, and the waitress rushed off, giving Delvin a wink and another wiggle before she left.

"Sir Delvin seems to have a way with the girls," said Grimbolt laughing.

"He should keep it more under control," said Jarla severely.

"I haven't done anything," said Delvin innocently.

"I don't think you need to," laughed Grimbolt.

"You men. It is all you think of," muttered Jarla.

"What have I done?" asked Delvin.

Jarla simply gave a snort.

Their food and drinks arrived shortly after, the waitress again giving Delvin a wink and a smile.

The stew was excellent and they all tucked in.

"Where do you think it best to ambush the black magician?" asked Jarla between mouthfuls.

"A place where there are trees and rocks, and well away from houses and other travelers," replied Grimbolt. "Over the border in Norden I think would be best."

"I was hoping we could do it before that," said Jarla determinedly, flexing her fingers and tapping her long fingernails on the table.

"We're travelling quite fast, so it's going to take him a day or so to catch up with us," responded Grimbolt.

"You are probably right," conceded Jarla taking a sip of her wine. "How far behind us do you think he is?"

"Not far. He was at Hanaman's farm only a day before us. He'll have gone to Argent, found out we had left for Norden, and followed straight on after us. He might be only two to three hours behind us. That's why we need to keep pressing on as fast as we can."

The thought that the black magician could be so close was a sobering one, and the meal continued in silence as they all thought of how they might keep ahead and eventually ambush the black magician.

When they had finished their meal, Grimbolt suggested they made their way to bed since they wanted to be off early in the morning.

They were up at dawn.

Delvin poked his head around the kitchen door to see if he could get them some rolls. The waitress from the night before was there, just taking a batch of rolls out of the oven.

"Do you want a roll?" she said suggestively, raising an eyebrow and wiggling her hips.

"I'd love to, but don't have time," replied Delvin with a grin.

The waitress laughed and handed him three rolls. As Delvin turned to leave, he felt a hand squeeze his buttock. He turned back.

"Next time," she breathed.

"Next time," replied Delvin.

"Are you flirting again?" said Jarla as he came out into the yard.

"Just being pleasant to the locals," replied Delvin innocently.

They were soon on their way, and before long they entered Ambledon which was just waking up as they rode in.

Ambledon was a large village. It was centred around a large square. Three inns and several shops were set around the square, which had a stone monument on a stepped plinth in its centre. A few of the shops were starting to open their shutters as they passed through.

As they left the village, the flat plain around the River Bolla was left behind and was replaced by low hills and valleys. Although there were still some field of corn, many of the field now held cattle. There were occasional small woods, and streams sometimes ran gurgling over or under the road.

The day had become slightly overcast, but shafts of sunlight occasionally broke through the cloud.

It was not yet noon when they came over a rise and saw the town of Ablet with its large natural harbour nesting below them. Beyond the town they could see the Gulf of Ablet. Fishing boats were dotted across the water and gulls wheeled overhead. They knew that across the gulf in the far distance lay the town of Rostin where they were headed, but it was too far away for the town to be visible.

Ablet was a walled town with two gates. The road coming from the south went through one gate, the road coming from the north went through the other. This meant all travelers heading north or south had to go through the town.

They rode down the hill to the town. The gatekeeper on the south gate letting them through when they said they were heading north. The town's main road led to a large square facing the harbour. Fishing boats were moored at the quayside and several inns lined the square. The main road continued through the square and out towards the north gate. They didn't stop in the town. The gatekeeper on the north gate again let them through with few questions, and they continued on the road heading north.

The country was still low hills and woods and they got occasional glimpses of the sea in the distance. Cattle grazed in many of the fields, and Delvin remembered from when he had been in Ablet before, that cheese was a specialty of the area.

They stopped briefly at a wayside inn for a quick lunch of bread, cheese and ale, then continued on.

It was almost mid-afternoon when they reached Storncross.

Storncross was a large village. In its centre was a village green on which several cows grazed. Two inns faced each other across the green.

They didn't stop in the village, as Grimbolt wanted to get to the border with Norden before it got dark.

The land they were now riding through was much rougher than the land further south. Deep forests sometimes bordered the road, stretching up to the Grandent Mountains that now seemed very close and which towered above them with snow-capped peaks and rocky crags. This was timber country, and in clearings Delvin saw piles of tree trunks waiting to be transported to saw mills.

Much of the land towards the sea was moorland. In the flatter parts, sheep and cattle grazed in fields bounded by dry stone walls. Other sheep, marked with blobs of colour to tell to whom they belonged, looked for patches of grass among the heather of the moors. Isolated farmhouses and small hamlets nestled in valleys, rough tracks leading off the road towards them.

The sun was low in the sky by the time they reached the border with Norden. Just before the border the road wound between huge banks that had been thrown up on either side of the road. Delvin could see crossbowmen looking down at them from the top of the banks. These were part of the defences that the duke had put in place when he had closed the border to try to stop any magicians from entering Argent from Norden. The border itself was a river flowing down from the Grandent Mountains. The river had cut a deep channel in the hillside before flowing on towards the sea, and a single span stone bridge arched over it. Just before the bridge was a square stone fort. The road ran right through the fort, so any traveler had to pass right through it to get to the bridge. The fort effectively controlled who traveled between Argent and Norden.

The guard on the fort's gate stopped them.

"What's your business. The border is closed."

"I have orders from the Duke of Argent," replied Grimbolt holding out a sheet of paper that the duke had given him.

"Wait here. I'll get the captain," said the guard.

The captain shortly appeared and read the paper. He visibly straightening when he saw the ducal seal. Grimbolt knew the paper did not reveal their identities but instructed the captain to offer all assistance.

"Magisters, mistress what may I do for you?"

"We shall be travelling into Norden at first light. Please could you provide beds for us, a meal tonight, and travel rations for our journey onwards."

"Certainly," said the captain. "Please follow me. An orderly will take your horses." He shouted for an orderly who came running out of the stable block. Both the orderly's and the captain's eyes opened wide in surprise when Delvin handed the orderly his rabbit to look after as well.

The captain showed them up to some small guest rooms. They were sparsely furnished, each with a narrow bed, a pile of blankets folded neatly at one end of it, a chair and washstand.

Having dropped their bundles in their rooms, the captain led them down to the mess room. Dinner was about to start. The other officers around the table stood up when they entered. Places had been set for them, and they took their places. Then everyone sat down and the meal was served.

Dinner was quite plain. Slices of roast meat with vegetables and bread. There was water or ale to drink. Delvin and Grimbolt chose ale while Jarla drank water.

Conversation over dinner was quite stilted, since the officers around the table didn't know their names. The duke hadn't given their names in the document he had given Grimbolt, and Grimbolt, Delvin and Jarla had not volunteered their names either. Through the rather limited conversation, they did learn that there had been little activity on the border. When the duke had first closed the border, the garrison had turned away quite a number of travelers and merchants travelling in each direction. But now that it was generally known that the border was shut, there were very few travelers.

After they had finished their dinner, they thanked the captain and retired to their rooms, since again they wished to make an early start in the morning.

Chapter 28

They were up before dawn, and as the sun began to rise over the Grandent Mountains they rode out of the fort and over the bridge into Norden. They hoped they might reach Rostin before nightfall.

They had changed into the clothes and armour that they had taken from the mercenaries so that they didn't stand out too obviously in Norden. When the captain had come down to see them off, his eyes had grown wide when he had seen them in the mercenaries' clothes, particularly as Jarla was now dressed as a man. He had handed them bags with the travel rations that they had asked for, and wished them a safe journey.

The road was very close to the mountains, and there were forests on both sides. After riding for a while, Delvin glanced to his right and saw a huge brown bear looking at them through the trees. He grinned to himself. Could he control it? He quickly rejected the idea of projecting the idea of food. If the bear found there wasn't any food, he might get angry, and an angry bear might not be a good idea. What else could he project that would make the bear friendly towards them? He had an idea.

Delvin projected the suggestion to the bear that they were its bear cubs. That should make it friendly towards them he thought.

The bear looked at them through the trees and then started lumbering towards them. They were riding at a steady canter, so by the time the bear reached the road, they were well ahead.

A mile further on, Grimbolt signaled for them to stop for a break. There was a small clearing with a stream by the road, the water from the stream flowing over the road into a gully beyond.

They dismounted and led the horses to the stream to drink.

Delvin grinned as he saw the bear coming down the road towards them. Both Jarla and Grimbolt were facing away from the bear and hadn't seen it coming.

The approach of the bear had alarmed the horses, and Grimbolt went over to them to try to calm them down, not realizing what had disturbed them.

Delvin let the bear get quite close.

"There's a bear behind you!" said Delvin nonchalantly to Jarla.

"Don't be so silly," retorted Jarla.

"There is," said Delvin.

Jarla looked over her shoulder.

"Sheffs!" she exclaimed, leaping back.

Delvin was roaring with laughter.

"Don't frighten her, she's friendly."

"How do you know it's a she?"

"I don't," said Delvin, suddenly alarmed and wondering if he had brought a fierce male bear in among them.

"It is a she," said Grimbolt turning towards them, still trying to calm the horses.

The bear had stopped when Jarla jumped, and now sat looking at them.

"You need to get it to move away," said Grimbolt looking grimly at Delvin.

Delvin nodded, and still inwardly laughing, projected the thought to the bear that there was some really tasty food well away from them up in the forest.

"What suggestion did you give it," asked Jarla suspiciously as the bear slowly got up and sniffed the air, moving her head back and forth. After a few moments, the bear slowly lumbered off into the trees.

"I suggested we were its cubs," said Delvin slightly embarrassed.

"You idiot!" exploded Jarla. "That's the most idiotic thing I ever heard. I can hardly believe you. Whatever were you thinking of?"

The horses had now calmed down, and Grimbolt gave Delvin an accusing look. "I don't think that was your best idea Sir Delvin."

"That's an understatement," retorted Jarla. "The horses could have bolted, and then where would we have been."

Delvin said nothing. His joke hadn't turned out quite as well as he had hoped.

They remounted and rode on down the road.

"When are we going to set our ambush?" asked Jarla.

"As soon as I see a suitable spot," replied Grimbolt.

A little further on Grimbolt pulled his horse to a halt and looked around.

"I think this is as good a place as we will find," he said looking around.

A stretch of straight road led up to a rocky outcrop.

"We can tether the horses in the trees, hide behind that rock and the straight road means we'll be able to see him coming. Right, let's get the horses off the road and get into position."

They led the horses into the trees. A little way off the road was a grassy dell that was well shielded from the road. They tethered the horses to a tree in the dell and left them happily eating the grass. Grimbolt had taken the travel rations and water bottles from the saddle bags before leaving the horses, and he now handed them out.

"I don't know how long we'll have to wait for the black magician to come along, but I think we might need something to eat while we wait."

They took up their positions behind the rock. Grimbolt had his crossbow loaded and cocked.

After more than two hours of waiting behind the rock Delvin's legs were getting stiff, and he was starting to wonder when it would be time to have something to eat. Grimbolt had been keeping a steady watch on the road, but there had been no sign of the black magician nor any other travelers. All traffic on the road seemed to have dried up after the duke had shut the border following the magician's previous attempt to take over Argent.

Suddenly, to his horror, a message came into Delvin's head. *Do not use your magician's stone or Princess Jarla will die.'* followed by *'You are paralyzed. You cannot move.'*

Delvin turned his head and saw the black magician with a crossbow pointed at Jarla and a cruel sneer on his face. His cloak covered his left arm which he was holding rather stiffly. His face looked scarred and pockmarked. That must have been caused by the swarm of bees I set on him last year, thought Delvin.

"Well Magister Delvin, you are not paralyzed, so you must have a magician's stone. Don't think you can use it to set animals or insects on me this time. Since my encounter with the bees that you set on me last year, I have been practicing projecting to animals. I believe I have now worked out how to detect it, if you try to influence animals. So... very slowly... place your magician's stone on the ground in front of you."

Thoughts raced through Delvin's head. What could he do? If he tried to use his stone, the black magician would shoot Jarla... How had the black magician come up behind them like that?... Why hadn't they seen him coming?

Delvin very slowly removed the magician's stone from around his neck and placed it on the ground in front of him.

"I know you have probably got more than one stone," said the black magician. "We need to get the other ones out on the ground in front of you as well."

"There is only one," said Delvin.

"Nice try," sneered the black magician. "There is the stone that Borlock gave you, Lord Meldrum's stone, Lord Stypin's stone, Lord Benbark's Stone and Lady Anbroom's stone."

Stypin must have been the magician who'd been in Cavid thought Delvin.

"Those other stones got lost," said Delvin. But even to his ears that sounded unlikely.

"Each if you will remove your clothes. One by one. I intend to make absolutely sure none of you has a hidden stone that you can use... You first Magister Delvin. Slowly... No sudden moves."

Delvin began to remove his clothes. Soon he was standing naked.

"Turn around slowly... Good no stone there... Now you." He nodded his head towards Grimbolt.

Grimbolt started to remove his clothes.

"How did you find us?" asked Delvin.

"I said that I've been practicing projecting to animals," smirked the back magician. "I found I could get birds to tell me where things were. They of course can't give me messages, but if I gave them an image and instructed them to return to me when they had seen it, I could see what direction they flew back from. That told me the direction of what I had told them to look for. If I then instructed them to fly there and back, I could judge how far away it was. I have been keeping track of you since you left Dandel, so I knew you had stopped, and guessed you were hoping to ambush me." He gave a cruel laugh.

I should have realized, thought Delvin. The black magician had used a dog as an early warning back in Hengel. Now he was using birds. Delvin mentally kicked himself for not having thought of it.

Grimbolt was now naked and the black magician told him to turn around.

"Nothing there. Well, it looks like Princess Jarla has the other stones… Remove your clothes."

Jarla, glaring furiously at the black magician, began to take off her clothes.

Suddenly there was a crashing from the undergrowth, and with a snarl, a huge bear leapt out towards the black magician, rearing up on its hind legs with a ferocious growl.

The black magician turned, startled by the noise. As he turned, the bear lunged forward and clamped its jaws around his head.

The black magician let out a stifled scream as his head was crushed. The bear shook him as though he was a rag doll and then dropped the now lifeless body on the ground.

Delvin leapt for his magician's stone, grabbed it and began projecting calming feelings towards the bear, sending the thought to her that her cubs were safe and that all was well.

The bear was looking calmer. She looked at Delvin, Jarla and Grimbolt. Then to Delvin's alarm she started walking towards him. Delvin continued to desperately project feelings of calm towards the bear.

Delvin was almost paralyzed with fear. As the bear came up to him, she put out her tongue and licked him across the face. Delvin didn't move a muscle as the bear gave him another lick. Delvin desperately started projecting the feeling to the bear that her cubs were safe, and they could now look after themselves, and that there was some tasty food high up in the forest. To Delvin's relief the bear gave a snort and began to move away.

Delvin watched, hardly daring to breath, as the bear disappeared through the trees. When it was gone, he let out a sigh of relief. He turned to Grimbolt and Jarla and removed the suggestions and paralysis that the black magician had put on them.

"You and your practical jokes," said Jarla as she reached for her clothes.

"It saved us, didn't it?" retorted Delvin.

"Through luck, not through any planning or intention on your part."

Delvin decided not to reply, but simply got himself dressed, as he was still feeling shaken by his close encounter with the bear.

When they had all got their clothes back on, Grimbolt went over to the body of the black magician.

"Right, let's get his stone and see if he found Delvin's old one at Hanaman's farm."

They soon found the black magician's stone which was hanging on a chain around his neck. But although they searched through all his clothes and pockets they couldn't find any other magician's stones, although they did find the black magician's purse which contained over thirty royals. Grimbolt put the purse in his pocket.

"I'll keep the purse for our expenses," said Grimbolt. "Would you like the black magician's stone Princess?" he asked.

"No thank you. I think it best if you take it," Jarla replied. "I am sure Delvin can teach you how to use it."

Grimbolt nodded and hung the black magician's stone around his neck.

"Right," he said straightening up. "We need to get on if we're going to get to Rostin before dark."

"Shall I get the bear to follow us?" suggested Delvin. "She might be useful in Rostin."

"No!" said Jarla and Grimbolt in unison.

"We are trying to be inconspicuous in Rostin," added Grimbolt. "Having a fully grown bear with us will hardly be inconspicuous."

Delvin reluctantly agreed.

"What are we going to do with him?" asked Delvin pointing to the body of the black magician.

"We'll just have to leave him. We don't have a spade, so we can't bury him," replied Grimbolt.

Delvin didn't like the idea of just leaving a body there, so with Grimbolt helping him, he rolled the body into a nearby ditch and covered it with some branches.

They remounted their horses and continued on their way.

Delvin felt a sense of relief, that for the first time for a long time he was not being pursued by the black magician.

They also now had two magician's stones, so the responsibility for using them did not fall entirely on his shoulders.

Soon the forest began to thin, and before long they were riding through a bleak moorland. There were a few cottages and farmsteads sheltering in the valleys, surrounded by small fields of crops, with the odd cow or pig, and with chickens pecking around. Sheep roamed the moorland. Like in Argent they had blobs of coloured paint on their backs showing whom they belonged to. The landscape had a stark and wild beauty. They crossed over an ancient looking stone bridge that spanned a small river. Delvin could see some boats downstream, they had nets out and appeared to be fishing.

In some of the valleys were small hamlets and villages with mainly single-story houses, often with heavy shutters over their windows to keep out the wind. The larger villages had inns, and there was even an occasional shop.

They crossed a bridge over another small river. The land was now getting hillier, the road mainly following the valleys.

They came to a sheltered valley, and Grimbolt called a halt and turned to Jarla.

"We'd better get some practice using the black magician's stone before we reach Rostin. We might need to use it when we get there, and I for one would like to know what I am doing if that happens."

They dismounted from their horses, and Delvin gave Grimbolt and Jarla rough instructions on how to use the magician's stone.

Grimbolt tried it first, projecting instructions to Jarla to put her arm up or down. After a few tries he started to get the hang of it. Jarla then tried, getting Grimbolt to jump up and down. When they were both feeling confident at what they were doing, they tried sending messages to Delvin.

"Once you get the hang of it, it's not too difficult," said Jarla handing the stone back to Grimbolt.

Grimbolt nodded, and they remounted their horses and were on their way again.

The sun was beginning to dip towards the horizon when they came over a rise and saw the Gulf of Ablet below them.

It was a clear evening. The sea sparkled as the sun reflected off the water, and the wisps of cloud were tinged with pink. Below them lay Rostin, its quays and harbour crowded with fishing boats. And just off the harbour lay the mercenaries' fleet. Ship after ship, dark and threatening against the waters of the gulf.

Chapter 29

Rostin lay in a small bay with cliffs on both sides. As Delvin looked down the coast there seemed to be almost continuous cliffs, with Rostin Bay the only part of the coast where there weren't any. He suspected though that there would be other small bays that he couldn't see. The town sloped down towards the sea. At the highest point, furthest away from the sea, built on a rocky bluff, lay Rostin Castle, the stronghold of the Guild of Magicians. A wall surrounded the landward side of the town and connected with the castle walls. There was a large gatehouse leading into the town, and on the far side Delvin could see another gatehouse leading to a bridge over a small river that emptied into the bay. There were further small towers along the walls and larger towers where the town walls met the sea. At one end of the bay a lighthouse stood on a high cliff. The town had a pleasant look, as besides the buildings there were two area of green, like village greens, one to the north and one to the south.

They rode down to the gatehouse. The guard, seeing their mercenary clothing let them through with a wary and resentful look.

They rode down the main street towards the harbour. The shops were putting up their shutters for the night, and the people they passed gave them more sour looks. It seemed to Delvin that the citizens of Norden didn't much like the mercenaries.

As they got closer to the harbour, Delvin could smell the salt in the air. There was also a slightly sweet smoky smell.

"What's that smell?" asked Delvin.

"That's the smokehouses," replied Grimbolt. "Most of the fish they catch here are either smoked, pickled or salted. They send them all over, even as far as Pandoland. Small villages up and down the coast also bring their fish here. It's quite a big business."

A large square faced the harbour. On the right of the square was a large building. Fishermen were hauling crates of fish they had just landed through a door on the building's seaward side. That must be the fish market, thought Delvin. On the side of the square facing the sea were two inns. Grimbolt headed for the largest, The Starfish. A sign showing a huge golden starfish hung over the entrance.

"We are acting as mercenaries, so we need to behave like we own the place," said Grimbolt quietly.

They rode under an arch into the inn's yard, and a stableboy ran out to take their horses. Grimbolt threw him his reins with a brusque order to make sure he brushed and stabled the horse properly. The stableboy bowed, and Delvin and Jarla gave him their reins too.

They marched into the inn and demanded two rooms. The innkeeper bowed and personally led them to two rooms facing the sea. The rooms were comfortable. Each had two beds, a washstand. two chairs and quite a good rug on the floor.

When the innkeeper had left them, Grimbolt turned to Jarla and Delvin.

"After we've got cleaned up, we'll meet down in the common room in ten minutes. We need to try to overhear what people are talking about." He looked at Jarla. "I'm afraid Princess, that as you are dressed as a man, you're going to have to drink ale not wine."

Jarla gave a grimace and went to her room.

Delvin and Grimbolt had a quick wash, and Delvin put his rabbit Freda in her travelling box and gave her some grain that he had saved for her. He hadn't asked the stable boy to look after her, since mercenaries didn't normally have pet rabbits, and it would have been sure to arouse comment.

When Delvin and Grimbolt entered the common room ten minutes later the room was quite full. The inn seemed to be popular with soldiers from the mercenary fleet, since there were quite a number of mercenaries there as well as locals. Grimbolt looked around. His gaze fell on a table where three mercenaries were sitting. They appeared to have already drunk quite a bit of ale. A lopsided smile spread across Grimbolt's face. There was an empty table next to them, and Grimbolt moved towards it. As Delvin followed him towards the table, he suddenly realized the three mercenaries were the ones who had captured them in Argent and who had taken Nippy to Rostin. He tugged on Grimbolt's sleeve and nodded meaningfully at him. Grimbolt smiled back his lopsided smile. He had also realized who the three mercenaries were. Delvin and

Grimbolt sat down at the vacant table with their backs to the mercenaries.

A slightly flustered waitress rushed over.

"Magisters, what may I get you?"

"Three ales," replied Grimbolt gruffly.

The waitress curtsied and rushed off.

Jarla came in just as the ales arrived. She too had noticed the three mercenaries, and she raised her eyebrows, glancing meaningfully towards the mercenaries as she sat down next to Delvin and Grimbolt. Grimbolt nodded back.

"What is there to eat?" Grimbolt asked the waitress as she placed their ales on the table.

"There's dorlish, roast chicken, cold meats or cheeses," she replied.

"Dorlish?" enquired Grimbolt.

"Dorlish is a specialty around here. It's hot smoked fish in a cream sauce."

"I'll have dorlish," said Grimbolt. The others nodded.

"Three dorlish," ordered Grimbolt.

The dorlish soon arrived and was delicious. The cream sauce had a slightly spicy tang and the dish was served with a selection of vegetables.

None of them spoke as they ate. They were all listening to the three mercenaries at the next-door table.

"Your round," said one of the mercenaries in a slightly slurred voice, waving the waitress over.

"Three ales," ordered his colleague.

The waitress brought over the ales.

"That's two carls one bit," she said. "And you still owe eight carls and four bits."

The mercenary felt in the purse hanging from his belt. A look of shock came over his face.

"It's gone. That little varmint must have picked my pocket."

"What, all of it?" asked one of the others.

"Yes!"

"Including the gold for delivering him to the castle?"

"Yes!"

The others started looking in their purses.

"He's took mine too!"

"And mine!"

The waitress was looking worried.

"You owe over three royals between you. You need to pay… I'll get the innkeeper."

"The little… varmint. He's been nothing but trouble the whole way here."

"We should have left him when he ran off, and not gone after him."

"I told you it was him what put that burr under my saddle. Almost broke my arm when the sheffs horse bucked me off."

"What do we do now?"

The waitress had gone back and spoken to the innkeeper. Delvin saw him go over to one of the other tables where an important looking mercenary sat in a large group. He got up and several of the others followed him.

They approached the table where the three mercenaries sat.

"The innkeeper tells me you can't pay for your drinks. Is that right?" said the important looking mercenary.

"We've been robbed."

"You know the orders. Not to upset the locals. Who robbed you?"

"A boy we were taking to the castle."

"A boy? All three of you? That's pathetic." He turned to the men beside him. "Take them out and deal with them." Then turning to the innkeeper who had followed behind, he asked, "What do they owe?"

"Three royals one carl magister."

The mercenary leader scowled and took the money from his purse and paid the innkeeper. Then he returned to his table muttering under his breath.

"We now know Nippy is in the castle," said Grimbolt. "We'll check it out tomorrow and work out how we can get in."

"We also need to know what the mercenaries are intending to do," said Jarla. "Their general said they were going to reprovision and collect their fee, but what are they going to do then? I feel very uneasy having a hostile fleet so close to Hengel."

They managed to listen in to a few more conversations, but all they learned was that the reprovisioning was almost complete, and that the soldiers who had been given shore leave would shortly be re-embarking.

It had been a long day, so when they had finished their drinks, they made their way to bed.

They were up early the following morning, and after a quick breakfast, set out to explore the town and look for ways of entering the castle.

Despite the land border with Argent being shut, the town, particularly around the harbour had a bustle to it. Ships were being loaded with crates of smoked fish and big earthenware jars which Delvin suspected held pickled fish. Small boats were plying back and forth between the harbour and the mercenaries' ships, taking barrels of water and the last few items they needed for their reprovisioning.

They walked up to the castle. The castle was built as a square with large round towers at each corner. Two smaller towers flanked the gatehouse. The towers were all topped with steep conical roofs. Delvin guessed that was so that snow would slide off more easily in the winter.

There was a square in front of the castle. One side of the square was taken up by the castle. There were several shops around the square, and opposite the castle was a small inn. It had tables outside laid with brightly coloured checked tablecloths. Delvin, Jarla and Grimbolt sat down at one of the tables and ordered hot leaf.

They watched the castle from across the square as they sipped their hot leaf. The castle's gate was guarded by two Norden soldiers. There were only two visitors to the castle while they watched. Each of them was questioned closely before they were admitted.

"When we break into the castle, Grimbolt," started Jarla.

"Major Grybald if you please," interrupted Grimbolt.

"Whatever," muttered Jarla. "As I was saying. When we break into the castle, you should say outside with the black magician's stone, so if we get captured, you'll be able to help the Duke of Argent when he arrives with his army. If we're held in the castle, the duke will need to have someone with a magician's stone able to counter Tabsall and his stone."

"I don't like you going into the castle on your own," said Grimbolt.

"I won't be on my own, I'll have Delvin with me."

"Sir Delvin is good at many things, but as you have said yourself, he's no use in a fight."

"We just won't have to get into a fight then," said Jarla smiling sweetly at him.

"I don't like it, and your father the duke wouldn't like you going in there without me," said Grimbolt.

"He'd like it even less facing Tabsall's magician's stone without having a magician's stone himself," responded Jarla.

"That's true," conceded Grimbolt. "But the question still remains, how are you going to get into the castle? Everyone going in is being questioned by those gate guards, so just wearing these mercenaries' clothes is not going to get you past them."

"Those walls are too high to climb," muttered Jarla looking across at the castle. "Delvin, could we use some device of yours to dazzle the guards while we slip through the gate?"

"A mirror would dazzle them, but not enough to let us get past," replied Delvin.

"We really need one of your tricks Delvin, to make us invisible. Any ideas?"

"Making things invisible is all about misdirection," said Delvin thinking hard. "Getting people to look in the wrong direction while disguising the thing as something they expect to see… We have the mercenary clothes, which is something they would expect to see… so we are half way there…" He looked up grinning. "I have an idea."

Chapter 30

Delvin spent the next hour walking around the streets of Rostin. Every time he came across a dog, he very tightly suggested to it there was an interesting smell outside a shop on the left-hand side of the castle square.

When he got back to the square, Jarla joined him. They wandered over to a shop on the right-hand side of the square.

On the other side of the square, about twelve dogs were milling around sniffing. The two guards on the gate were looking at them in puzzlement.

Right, thought Delvin, everything is in position.

Delvin sent a very tight suggestion to the dogs that they should relieve themselves on the guard's boots. He didn't think the magician Tabsall in the castle would pick up the message, since he knew it took practice to detect messages that were directed at animals. Nevertheless, he kept the projection as tight and gentle as possible, also making sure he was pointing himself away from the castle, so the projection would go away from the castle too.

The effect was immediate. The dogs ran towards the guards and started relieving themselves on the guards' boots, with the dogs at the back jostling for position and trying to get through.

The guards shouted at the dogs and tried to shoo them away. At that point Grimbolt came out of a shop on the left-hand side of the square and started shouting at the guards to leave the dogs alone.

The guards were desperately trying to fend off the dogs, and with Grimbolt shouting at them as well, they didn't notice Delvin and Jarla slip behind them from the right, through the gate and into the castle.

Just past the gate was a door into the right-hand gatehouse tower.

"We'll see if we can hide in here," said Jarla opening the door.

The door led into a small guardroom. No one was in there, but it looked like it was used by the gate guards. There was a spiral staircase in the corner, and they climbed up to the next floor. The chamber above the guardroom was empty.

"We'll hide here until everyone's asleep," said Jarla.

"Should we go up another floor?" asked Delvin.

"We know this room is empty. We don't know if the one above is. We stay here," replied Jarla.

They sat down on the floor. Delvin reached into the front of his tunic and brought out Freda his rabbit and started to give her a run on the floor.

"You haven't brought that rabbit again?" said Jarla in exasperation.

"I thought we might need her for making distractions," replied Delvin.

They had several hours to wait before nightfall and for the castle's inhabitants to go to sleep. They had brought food and water with them and ate a cold dinner of bread, cold meat and cheese.

They heard noises from the room below as the guards changed, and still they waited.

The only light in the chamber came from a narrow arrow slit. As the sun went down the room started to become dark. Although there was a moon, not much of its light penetrated the arrow slit.

The noises coming from the square started to die out as people went home to bed. Two hours later Jarla whispered, "Right, let's start to move."

The chamber had no doors leading off it. The only way out was the spiral staircase. Jarla and Delvin felt their way over to it, and as they didn't want to go down to the guardroom below, they climbed up to the next floor. In the chamber above there was a door to one side. On carefully opening it, they saw it led to a short passage running along the top of the thick castle wall. Windows in the passage let in a little moonlight. This must have once been the wall walk thought Delvin.

They crept down the passage and opened the door at the end. The door led into one of the big round corner towers. A wall ran across the centre of the tower dividing it in two. There was an ornate door in the centre of the dividing wall, a spiral staircase on their left and then another door on the other side.

Jarla went over to the door across from them, opened it and peered through.

"This leads to another passage going along the top of the wall," she whispered.

"What's through this one," whispered back Delvin, approaching the door in the centre of the dividing wall.

He carefully turned the doorknob and pushed open the door. As he opened it, he could smell a strong scent of perfume. The room was a bedroom. A little moonlight came through a window in one wall, and by its light, he saw a large four poster bed with elaborate curtains around it. A figure lay in the bed.

"This is not Tabsall's room," whispered Delvin closing the door.

They went over to the door leading to the passage and went through. Moonlight came weakly through windows on their right. There were three doors on the left side of the passage. They carefully opened the first one. It was another bedroom. There was a large four poster bed, a chest of drawers and wardrobe. But the bed was empty. They quietly closed the door.

They tried the second room. Again, there was a large bed and several items of furniture, but again there was nobody there. The third door also led to a bedroom with nobody in it.

At the end of the passage was another door. As quietly as possible they opened it and went through. They were in another of the large corner towers. As before there was a wall running across the middle of the tower dividing it in two with an ornate door in its centre. Again, there was a second door leading off and a spiral staircase, this time a much wider one.

Delvin again carefully opened the ornate door. He again got the scent of perfume, and glimpsed frilled hangings around the bed. He closed the door as silently as he could.

"Another lady's bedroom," he whispered.

They went through the other door into another passage, again with three doors on their left.

Delvin again slowly and gently turned the door handle to the first door and pushed it carefully open. It was another bedroom. In the four-poster bed was a small figure. Delvin crept forward.

The figure in the bed suddenly sat up.

"You'd never make a thief, you're like a herd of elephants," said Nippy grinning, his teeth white in the moonlight.

"Nippy!" exclaimed Delvin. "We've come to get you out and get Tabsall's stone."

"Yer didn't need to rescue me," said Nippy dismissively. "Could have escaped any time I wanted. They think I'm Prince Nippold. I like being a prince."

"You do know you're not a prince?" said Jarla.

"Yeh, I know. But it's fun while it lasts."

"We're trying to find Tabsall's room," said Delvin. "We want to try to take his magician's stone off him while he's asleep. Do you know where his room is?"

"Yeh, next tower," said Nippy. "Do you want me to do it for you? I'm good at thieving."

"No thanks," said Delvin, the thought crossing his mind, that knowing Nippy, if he had hold of a magician's stone, he would probably try it out, and then anything might happen. "Wait here," he said.

Delvin crept out of the room and along to the next tower. Its layout was the similar to the others, with a cross-wall with an ornate door in its centre leading to a bedroom. As carefully as he could, Delvin turned the doorknob and opened the bedroom door.

In the dim light he could again see an ornate four poster bed, with what looked like embroidered drapes. Heavy and elaborate furniture had been placed to either side, and gold framed pictures hung on the walls. Delvin could see a figure asleep on the bed.

He tiptoed closer, trying not to make a sound. Where might he have put his magician's stone thought Delvin?

There was a bedside table on which were a pair of spectacles, but no sign of a stone. Delvin peered at the figure in the bed. Might he be wearing it on a chain around his neck? He bent down to look closer. The person in the bed was a man with white hair, a beard and big bushy eyebrows. His beard moved as he breathed in and out. This must be Tabsall, the leader of the Guild of Magicians, thought Delvin.

The blankets covered the figure's chest, so Delvin couldn't see if there was a magician's stone there, so he bent down to look at his neck to see if there was a chain around it. But despite looking closely he couldn't see any sign of a chain.

He took a deep breath. That just left it being under his pillow he thought. Delvin crouched down low, and as slowly and carefully as he could, began to slip his hand under the pillow.

There was something there... With a feeling of relief Delvin grasped the thing and pulled it out... It was a stone on a chain.

Suddenly the eyes of the man in the bed snapped open and he began to rise.

"What are you d..." The man was cut off in mid-sentence as Delvin projected *'Sleep!'* The man fell back on the bed fast asleep. A fleeting thought crossed Delvin's mind, with two stones, Tabsall's and his own, would the projection be doubly strong?

Delvin stood up, and with a final glance at the sleeping figure on the bed, went back out of the room closing the door behind him.

With a smile on his face, Delvin went back down the passage to Nippy's room.

Jarla and Nippy were waiting there.

"I've got Tabsall's stone," said Delvin triumphantly.

"Right," said Jarla with a gleam in her eye. "That was the last stone they had. Now we need to sort this place out."

"Don't move or I will shoot!" came a voice from behind them.

Delvin tried to project *'Paralyze.'* To the person behind them, but his projection was immediately countered. He spun round to see two women, one of whom was pointing a loaded crossbow at him. How did they have another magician's stone? Surely, he hadn't miscounted, had he?

Were there more magician's stones than the ones he had been told about?

Chapter 31

The women were wearing dressing gowns over their nightclothes. Delvin recognized the women holding the crossbow. She was Lady Carolina. She had been working for the Guild of Magicians the previous year in North Bridge and also at the disused diamond mine. The other woman he didn't recognize. She was a handsome woman of about forty, with long flowing dark hair and a determined expression on her face. She regarded them with a steely gaze.

"Magister Delvin?" said the woman he didn't recognize. "I've heard a lot about you. I wondered when we would meet. And Princess Jarla? those mercenary's clothes don't suit you, my dear… Now very slowly, place your magician's stones on the floor in front of you… Carolina, if they make any sudden moves… shoot them."

Thoughts flashed through Delvin's mind. She must have a magician's stone, he thought, that much was obvious. Otherwise, how had she managed to counteract his projection. But where had that stone come from? He had thought he had accounted for all the stones that had been found. There shouldn't be any others. That is, unless they had found some more. They had certainly been looking for more stones.

Delvin very carefully took the stone from around his neck and placed it on the floor. He still had the stone he had taken from under Tabsall's pillow in his pocket. He hoped they wouldn't realize he had it.

"Give me the crossbow, and get me that stone," said the woman.

Lady Carolina handed over the crossbow. Then she picked Delvin's stone up off the floor and handed it to the woman who put it in her dressing gown pocket.

"Now search them... thoroughly," said the woman.

Lady Carolina went over to Delvin. She exclaimed in surprise when she found his rabbit in her sling. It took her only moments more to find Tabsall's stone. She held it up in triumph.

"You can have that," said the woman. "Now search Princess Jarla."

Lady Carolina hung Tabsall's stone around her neck then searched Jarla.

"Nothing there," she announced.

"We need to find out what the Duke of Argent is planning," said the woman. "You will enjoy doing that... Take Magister Delvin out into the passage and find out everything he knows then come back here."

"We could do it here together," replied Lady Carolina licking her lips in anticipation.

"No, I need to talk to Princess Jarla and Prince Nippold about where we are going. Also, I don't want the carpet in here spoiled if he is sick or if there is any blood. Do it out in the passage. Then when you get back, we need to plan our next move."

"Can I have his rabbit?" Nippy suddenly asked, a hopeful smile on his face.

"His rabbit? Yes, I suppose so. He won't be needing it any more after this."

Nippy got up and went over to Delvin, brushing past the woman as he went. Delvin took Freda his rabbit out of her sling and handed her over to Nippy.

As Nippy took Freda, Delvin felt Nippy push something hard into his hand. With shock Delvin realized it was a magician's stone. Nippy must have picked the woman's pocket as he brushed past her. Delvin held the stone in the palm of his hand. Borlock, who had taught him magic, had taught him how to palm small objects so that no one would know he had them. He was going to have to be careful. The woman and Lady Carolina both had magician's stones. If he tried to use the stone Nippy had passed to him, they would be able to overcome him by using their two stones combined against his one.

'You will do exactly what Lady Carolina says.' The message came into Delvin's mind. That must be from the woman thought Delvin.

"Into the passage," ordered Carolina.

Delvin went out into the passage closely followed by Lady Carolina.

"You are going to tell me everything you know," said Lady Carolina with a hint of excitement in her voice. "This is just a small taste of what you will experience if you don't tell me everything."

Delvin doubled over and cried out as if in terrible pain. He needed to act as if he didn't have a stone. Then he suddenly realized that he not only hadn't experienced any pain, he also hadn't heard a message in his head. Why not, he wondered?

"So, tell me everything. If you leave anything out, you will experience that again and more."

Maybe Lady Carolina didn't know how to use the stone, thought Delvin. No, he immediately dismissed that idea. She had probably been with the magicians for years, so she would certainly know how to use them. Maybe the stone didn't work. He needed to find out.

'You cannot move. You are paralyzed.' He projected tightly at her.

Lady Carolina froze. Delvin looked questioningly at Lady Carolina and removed the stone from around her neck where she had hung it. He looked carefully at the stone. For some reason this stone wasn't working, he realized.

Delvin grinned. Now to deal with that other woman, he thought.

Chapter 32

Delvin burst back through the bedroom door, hoping to surprise and grab the woman before she could do anything. But he was too slow. The woman spun around and snatched up her crossbow, pointing it straight at Delvin's chest.

I need to distract her, thought Delvin. I have to buy myself some time. He tried projecting *'You are paralyzed you cannot move,'*

The woman simply laughed. "That doesn't work on me. Didn't you realize I had a stone?... The interesting question is... How did you escape Lady Carolina? Did you manage to hide another stone that we didn't find?... And how did you overcome her stone?"

I must keep her talking, thought Delvin.

"Her stone doesn't work."

"Doesn't work?" The woman gave a grim laugh. "Did you take that stone from that idiot Tabsall?... Oh, that explains it!"

"What's wrong with Tabsall's stone?"

"Haven't you realized?" She laughed grimly again. "Years ago, I realized what these stones could do. I seduced Tabsall. He had the stone on a chain around his neck. When I stroked his chest, I got my hand under the stone. Then it was touching me and not him... The rest was simple... I have been controlling him ever since... I had a fake stone made, so everyone would think he still had one. You must have taken the fake." She laughed again.

"So, you have been secretly controlling Tabsall all along?" said Delvin incredulously.

"Yes." She laughed again. "Everyone just thought I was Lady Tabsall, his obedient wife."

"Was it you who formed the Guild of Magicians?"

"Yes, I made Tabsall say the words, but it was my idea. That idiot Spendrank didn't realize the power the stones could give you. He just wanted magicians to go around sorting out petty problems. I saw that the stones could give magicians real wealth and real power. Most of the other magicians agreed. There was only Golbrick and Borlock who wanted to go on as before and continue being goody goodies."

Delvin shook his head in disbelief. Behind Lady Tabsall he could see Jarla and Nippy both frozen in position. She must have paralyzed them, he thought. Freda his rabbit had now hopped out of Nippy's arms and was on the bed looking towards the floor.

Delvin had an idea, but he needed more time. He must keep Lady Tabsall talking.

"What about the black magician?" asked Delvin.

"The secret of the stones needed to be kept, and some of the magicians needed a bit more excitement other than just sitting around getting rich. I've always been good at understanding what men want... So, I invented the role of black magician. Those magicians who wanted excitement took turns at being the black magician, and killing anyone who threatened us."

"The secret of the magician's stones is out now," said Delvin. "Lots of people now know about the stones. People in power. You won't be able to take over now."

"That unfortunately is true. You are a very resourceful man Delvin..." She looked around the room. "Norden is finished... The Duke of Argent is invading, and I imagine he has more than one stone after you dealt with Stypin, Benbark and Anbroom. Even if the black magician came back here, the duke would have more stones than us... It's now time to move on... Incidentally, what happened to the black magician? I thought he was going to try to kill you."

"He's dead," said Delvin.

"So, you've got another one. What happened?"

"He was killed by a bear."

Lady Tabsall raised her eyebrows.

"As I said, it's time to move on. I was just telling Princess Jarla and Prince Nippold what we are going to do... You do know don't you, that the mercenary General Torurk killed Querriol and took his stone off him?... Well, Torurk and I are going into partnership. With our two stones and his army and fleet, we can be king and queen of anywhere we choose. I am leaving with his fleet on the morning tide, first thing in the morning. Lady Carolina, Princess Jarla and Prince Nippold will be coming with me. You could join us Delvin. A resourceful man like you, and one with a stone, would be very useful. Just think, with us behind you, you could be a duke ruling your own country."

While Lady Tabsall had been talking, Delvin had seen that Freda his rabbit had hopped down from the bed and was now snuffling around the floor. Now! He thought. He sent a projection to Freda that there was tasty food on Lady Tabsall's bare feet. Freda hopped over.

Lady Tabsall gave a start and looked down as she felt Freda's fur and nose against her feet. In that momentary distraction, Delvin sent a projection to release Jarla and Nippy from their paralysis.

Instantly Jarla leapt at Lady Tabsall and grabbed her round the neck, pressing her long sharpened nails against the veins on either side. The sudden attack made Lady Tabsall drop the crossbow, which went off, shooting the bolt past Delvin and into the wall.

Lady Tabsall sent a projection to paralyze Jarla that was instantly countered by one from Delvin.

"It's time we finished you once and for all," hissed Jarla, increasing the pressure on Lady Tabsall's throat.

"Haven't you realized who I am?" gasped Lady Tabsall desperately.

"You are the person who caused the death of many people including my brother," growled Jarla.

"I am your mother!" croaked Lady Tabsall.

Chapter 33

In shock, Jarla released some of the pressure on Lady Tabsall's throat.

"My mother?"

"I was Duchess of Hengel. When I first saw your father the duke, I had just come to the city of Hengel with my best friend Lady Carolina. Your father the duke was then married to that milksop Beatrice. I decided he would prefer me as his duchess, so I got rid of Beatrice. A touch of belladonna did the trick. Then I seduced him. We were married shortly after and you came nine months later."

"He always mourned Beatrice," muttered Jarla.

"He never knew what was good for him... After Princess Stella was born, I was getting bored with always playing second fiddle to your father. I wanted to be the one making the decisions. I wanted to have real power.

"When Tabsall visited Hengel I observed him. He had a habit of clasping his magician's stone in his hand whenever he used it. Maybe it helped him concentrate, I don't know.

"I decided I would find out if it was the stone around his neck that gave him his power, so I seduced him. It was easy to get my hand under the stone and then clutch it myself. At first, I just experimented with it around the castle. It was fun making people do what I wanted, whether they wanted to or not. I had the fake stone made so people would think Tabsall still had his stone. Then I realized if I wanted power, real power, I needed to control all the stones, otherwise other magicians might come and take the stone off me. With Lady Carolina, I ran off with Tabsall to Norden. I soon got rid of that fool Spendrank and his Magician's Council, and then formed the Guild of Magicians. Everyone thought it was Tabsall doing it... Lady Carolina was a great help. She was my eyes and ears. If any of the magicians started getting out of hand or thought of taking over, she would find out and let me know. Then either I would get rid of them, or she would seduce them, whatever was most effective.

"After a while I missed Hengel... Rostin is perfectly pleasant, but it's a backwater. I missed the excitement of the city, and I missed seeing my children. So, I decided I would take Hengel over, and I would rule it through my children and grandchildren. But I would be the one with the power. I would be the one making the decisions, whether my children liked it or not..." She looked Delvin in the eye. "But you stopped me..." There was a note of both hatred and sadness in her voice.

"So was that why the magicians kept attacking Hengel this last year?" asked Delvin incredulously.

"Yes. Hengel was always the aim. It was where my children were. Argent was only attacked since it was between Norden and Hengel."

Lady Tabsall managed to turn her head and look at Jarla. "Did you wonder why I tried to have you and Prince Nippold kidnapped? I did it because I wanted you here. I had missed you."

There was a shocked silence.

"What do we do with her?" asked Delvin.

"I can't kill my mother," whispered Jarla, her voice shaking. "When is the morning tide?"

"In about two hours," replied Lady Tabsall. "I had just woken up to get ready when I heard you."

"Get yourself dressed," growled Jarla. "We will be watching to make sure you don't do anything silly. Then Carolina can get dressed. We'll escort you down to the ship, and if you ever set foot in Hengel again... I will kill you personally, mother or not."

"Is that a good idea?" asked Delvin.

"Probably not. But I can't kill my mother. Can you kill a woman in cold blood?"

"No," admitted Delvin.

"Right, Let's do it," said Jarla grimly.

They marched Lady Tabsall back to her room where she quickly got dressed. Then Delvin released Lady Carolina from her paralysis and made her get dressed too.

Both of them had large bags packed. With their bags they made their way out of the castle and down to the harbour.

"Come with me," Lady Tabsall pleaded.

"No," replied Jarla in a slightly strained voice,

Lady Tabsall and Lady Carolina boarded the mercenaries' flagship that was tied up at the quay. General Torurk was there to greet them. He gave Delvin a hard look, then went back to preparing the ship to leave.

Delvin looked at Jarla who was just staring blankly at the ship.

"What's your mother's name?" asked Delvin.

"Virelda," replied Jarla with a slight catch in her voice.

Delvin turned back towards the ship which now seemed almost ready to leave.

They waited at the quayside, neither of them saying anything until the ship had cast off and had sailed out of the harbour.

After the ship had passed beyond the lighthouse at the end of the headland, they turned round and made their way back across the square to the inn where they had been staying.

It took them some time to wake someone to let them in. Eventually a manservant came down and drew back the bolts. When they went up to their rooms, Grimbolt was waiting for them.

"How did it go?" he asked.

They told him what had happened, and that Lady Tabsall had sailed off with the mercenary general.

"Do you know where they are going?" asked Grimbolt.

"They didn't say," replied Delvin. "Though Torurk did mention before that he was planning to go to Anrovia."

"Well, I hope he doesn't change his mind and go to Hengel," said Grimbolt seriously.

"I don't think he will," replied Delvin. "They think we have the magician's stones from all those other magicians. They'll go somewhere where they think no one else has a magician's stone so they can take over."

"So, does that mean all the magician's stones are now accounted for?" asked Grimbolt with a note of satisfaction.

"All the ones in Hengel and Argent," replied Delvin. "But Lady Tabsall and General Torurk each have a stone."

"Didn't you take Lady Tabsall's stone off her?" asked Grimbolt in surprise.

"No," replied Jarla. "I thought of doing it. Then it came to me, that if that mercenary general she has gone off with found out she didn't have a stone, he would have probably killed her. And even if he didn't kill her, he would have been able to do anything he wanted with her. I couldn't let that happen. She is my mother."

"Ahh," said Grimbolt thinking about it. "He just might kill her anyway to get her stone off her. He did that to Querriol."

"True," replied Jarla. "Or she might kill him. She's killed people before who have got in her way."

"They seem to be a well-matched pair," said Grimbolt with his lopsided grin. "Where's Nippy?" he asked.

"He's still in the castle. He's enjoying being a prince. We'll fetch him in the morning," said Delvin.

Chapter 34

Delvin woke as the sun was just rising. He had not had much sleep, but he felt elated. Grimbolt had not had much sleep either having waited up for them, and he groaned as Delvin swung himself out of bed.

They got themselves dressed in their ordinary clothes, since they no longer needed to pretend that they were mercenaries.

When they went down to the common room for breakfast, Jarla was already there. She too had changed into ordinary clothes.

"I couldn't sleep," she said. "I had thought my mother was dead all these years."

"What do we do now?" asked Delvin.

"First we check the mercenaries have really gone," said Grimbolt. "Then we had better go and get Nippy."

"The Duke of Argent is on his way with an army," put in Jarla. "We need to get things ready for when he gets here."

They discussed it a bit more while they finished their hot leaf and rolls.

When they had all finished, they got up from the table and went out of the inn's front door. It was a lovely sunny morning, and they strolled across the square to the quayside. There was no sign of any mercenary ships in the bay, and they couldn't see any out at sea either.

"It looks like they really have gone," said Grimbolt.

They went back into the inn. The innkeeper was just coming out of the common room.

"Have all the mercenaries left?" asked Grimbolt.

"Aye, they left last night. I was surprised to see you this morning. I thought you were mercenaries too."

"No," replied Grimbolt. "We just looked like them."

"Well, good riddance to them is what I say," said the innkeeper with feeling. "Will you be staying long?"

"We should be leaving you today," said Jarla.

The innkeeper nodded and went back to his work.

"Right, let's get to the castle," said Jarla.

There were two guards on the castle gate. Delvin sent a projection to them that they were released from any suggestions from Tabsall or anyone else, and that they should now obey him. The guards stood back and saluted as they went in.

The castle's gate led to a courtyard. Straight ahead of them, opposite the gate, was an ornate door with pillars to either side and flanked by a pair of carved stone lions.

As they walked towards the door, an elegantly dressed gentleman appeared from a side door to their left.

"What may I do for you?" he said in a superior voice looking down his nose at them.

Delvin quickly projected the thought to him that he was released from any influence from the magicians, and that he should obey him.

"I am Sir Delvin," started Delvin, "and this is Princess Jarla of Hengel and Major Grybald. Is Prince Nippold up?"

"Your Highness, Sir Delvin, Major," said the gentleman, his attitude instantly changing. "Prince Nippold is having his breakfast in the Small Dining Room. If you will follow me."

He led them to a door in the base of the corner tower on their right. He opened the door with a flourish, and Jarla, Delvin and Grimbolt went in.

Although it had been described as the Small Dining Room, to Delvin it seemed quite large, as it took up the whole of the ground floor of the corner tower. Tapestries hung on the walls giving the room a comfortable feeling. At a large round table in the centre of the room sat Nippy. Before him was an array of cold meats, cheeses, rolls and pastries. He grinned at them as they entered.

"I likes being a prince," he said through a mouthful of bread and meat.

"So I see," said Jarla eyeing the feast set out before him.

"I see you have managed to get yourself sorted out here," said Delvin. "We need to get things ready for when the duke comes. Join us when you have finished. By the way, who is that superior gentleman who showed us in here?"

"That's Morvel. He's the butler," said Nippy, quickly swallowing his mouthful of food.

They left Nippy to finish his breakfast and went back out into the courtyard. Morval appeared out of a door on the other side.

"Ah Morvel," said Delvin, "I need to see all the servants. Please could you lead me to them."

"Certainly, Sir Delvin," said Morvel slightly raising his eyebrows in surprise.

"While you go and see them," said Grimbolt. "I'll get our things from the inn. Where can we stable our horses?" "The castle's stables are just behind the square on the right," said Morvel.

As Grimbolt left, Morvel led them into the kitchen and through the other domestic areas, introducing them to each of the servants. When Delvin met each one, he greeted them and sent projections to remove any previous suggestions from magicians, and also instructed them to obey him.

When they had seen everybody, he told Morval that the Duke of Argent was coming, and instructed him to prepare six rooms. One each for him, Jarla and Grimbolt, plus one each for the duke and the generals.

"We need to see Tabsall," said Delvin.

They went to Tabsall's room and knocked on the door.

"Come in," came a faint voice from inside.

They entered the room. Tabsall had just finished dressing and looked enquiringly at them. Delvin immediately sent a projection to release him from any suggestions or coercions that the magicians or Lady Tabsall had put on him. Tabsall gave a slight jerk.

"Good heavens! What's happened! My mind is free! I was made to do terrible, terrible things." He looked in wonder at Delvin.

"Lady Tabsall has gone," said Delvin. "You are now free to do what you want."

Tabsall sat down on the edge of the bed and collapsed into tears.

"We'll come back when you are feeling better," said Delvin, not quite sure what to do with a person who was crying.

Nippy had joined them while they had been going round being introduced to the servants.

"What are we going to do now?" he asked eagerly.

"With the duke coming, we need to find some better clothes," said Jarla, looking in distaste at the dirty and scruffy clothes they were all wearing. "How much money do you have Delvin."

"Not enough to buy us both new outfits and get us back to Hengel," Delvin replied. "Nippy, that money you stole from the mercenaries, can you lend us some?"

"Can do better than that," grinned Nippy. "Stole Lady Carolina's purse. You can have that... Didn't like her... Money what I took from them mercenaries. They got paid that money for me... So that sort of makes it my money, doesn't it?... Can I keep it?"

"Yes, alright," said Delvin smiling.

Nippy gave him a wide grin and ran off, returning a few moments later with Lady Carolina's purse.

"Why d'you need to buy new clothes anyway," asked Nippy. "Lots of clothes here. I've been exploring."

Delvin and Jarla looked at each other.

"Them other magicians what you done in. They used to live here. Left lots of clothes."

"Show us," said Jarla.

Nippy showed them to the various bedrooms and opened the wardrobes. Sure enough, they were filled with sumptuous clothes.

"Let's see what we can find," said Jarla. Delvin nodded.

The first clothes Delvin selected were far too big for him. The man must have had a vast waist thought Delvin. The next were too short. Delvin eventually found some that were about his size. Jarla who was helping him, kept picking out the brightest and gaudiest items, urging him to try them on. She grinned as she did so, and grinned even more when he did put them on. She found a hat with a large feather in it and insisted he take it. Eventually Delvin selected a set of very smart but fairly sober riding clothes, and at Jarla's continuing insistence, some quite bright evening wear.

"Right," said Jarla. "Now it's my turn. Apart from Lady Tabsall, the only lady magician in the Magician's Guild was that Lady Anbroom, and she was rather a different shape to me. I'm going to need a seamstress. Delvin go and see if that Morvel can find one."

Delvin was about to make a comment when he saw a warning look in Jarla's eye and thought better of it. Instead, he went to find Morvel to ask about a seamstress.

Morvel did indeed know a good seamstress and a servant was sent to summon her.

301

While Jarla was selecting the clothes she wanted, Nippy eagerly showed Delvin around the rest of the castle and what he had discovered. When Nippy took him down to the cellars, Delvin found it not only contained a huge number of bottles of wine, but also an astonishing array of items that had been discarded over the years.

"I think you have showed me just about everything," said Delvin. "We need to find Jarla."

After instructing the seamstress in what she required, Jarla had been looking around the castle too. They found her examining some of the paintings in the State Dining Room.

"These are quite good," she said.

Delvin looked at the paintings. One showed a rural scene that reminded him of the village where he had grown up.

"I quite like this one," he said.

Jarla turned towards him considering him for a moment, then she straightened her shoulders.

"Right," she said, "We need to start getting things organized. The first thing we need to do is to make sure the gate guards, and any other soldiers, are not still under the magician's influence. We don't want them to oppose the duke when he comes."

While she had been talking, Grimbolt had come into the room after dropping off their bundles. "I'll join you," he said.

They made their way to the town's gatehouse and afterwards to a barracks building. At each of them Delvin sent projections releasing the soldiers from the magician's suggestions and influences, and telling them to obey him. Delvin also sent a general projection to the population as a whole to release them from any influences. He was not sure if that would work, but reasoned it wouldn't do any harm.

They returned to the castle for lunch, which was served in the Small Dining Room where Nippy had had his breakfast. The meal consisted of several types of the smoked and pickled fish that Rostin was famous for, together with fresh bread and cheese. The fish was delicious.

"When do you think the duke and the army will get here?" asked Delvin.

"They were keen to get going as fast as possible," replied Jarla. "I think they will be here by tonight. What do you think Grimbolt?"

"Major Grybald if you please Princess… I agree. They should be in Norden by now and well on their way here."

"Right," said Jarla. "After lunch we shall get changed into our smarter clothes, take our horses, and go and meet them."

Chapter 35

Delvin, Jarla, Grimbolt and Nippy rode out of Rostin in the early afternoon. The sun was still shining, though a cold breeze was blowing off the sea, sending the few clouds scudding across the sky. The countryside around Rostin was very beautiful. Heather covered moorland was interspersed with areas of grass where sheep wandered. There were deep valleys with secluded woods and little streams that bubbled over the road. A good place for walks and rides thought Delvin.

The seamstress had completed the alterations in the riding clothes that Jarla had chosen, and she was now dressed in a dark green leather riding habit. Delvin too was dressed in elegant riding gear. A blue doublet with slashed sleeves and leather trousers with long black riding boots.

They had been riding for about an hour and a half when they met two cavalry scouts riding ahead of the duke's army. They pulled up their horses, and the scouts approached, eyeing them suspiciously.

"Princess Jarla of Hengel, Sir Delvin and Major Grybald to see the Duke of Argent," announced Delvin, projecting the thought to the scouts that they were not a threat and should be immediately taken to the duke.

"I'll take them, you go on ahead," said one of the scouts to his colleague. He turned back to Delvin and the others. "Follow me," he said.

They followed the scout down the road and shortly came upon the army's vanguard. A little further on they came to the duke riding with General Horncliffe and General Gortly. The contrast between the two generals was extraordinary. While General Horncliffe was tall and wore an elaborate uniform covered in gold braid, General Gortly was shorter and wore his customary leather jerkin.

As they approached, General Gortly let out a sigh.

"I might have imagined you would be involved Princess Jarla."

"Good afternoon General," said Jarla sweetly.

"Your Grace," said Delvin. "The magicians and mercenaries have left Rostin. The town is ready to welcome you."

"All of them?" asked General Horncliffe.

"Yes General," replied Jarla. "The last of them left by ship on the early morning tide."

"Excellent." said the duke. "I was not looking forward to storming the town with magicians causing us problems."

"How about the black magician?" asked General Horncliffe. "Is he still at large?"

"He's dead," replied Delvin.

The general's eyes opened wide in a questioning look. Delvin was about to say more, but the duke interposed.

"Onwards," he said. "You can tell us all the details later when we get to Rostin."

It was late afternoon when Rostin came in sight. Nippy in his exploring of the castle's cellars, had found a trunk filled with several silver and red Argent standards. Delvin had instructed the gate guards and the guards at the castle to hoist them on the gate and castle towers.

News about the duke's arrival had got out and had spread rapidly around the town. As he passed through the town's gate a small crowd had come out, and they cheered as he rode past.

Rather than taking the shortest route to the castle, the duke rode down to the harbour first, before turning back towards the castle.

"He wants to make sure as many of the population as possible see him," whispered Jarla.

Outside the castle's gate the duke's party dismounted, and soldiers rushed to take their horses.

They passed through the gate, and the guards stood to attention and saluted. Inside the castle, Morvel the butler bowed deeply.

"Your Grace, we have prepared a room for you, and also rooms for you Generals. If you would like to get freshened up after your journey, I can show you to your rooms."

"Thank you," said the duke.

Morvel led them across the courtyard into the Great Hall and up the stairs. Delvin, Jarla and Grimbolt followed on behind. Out of the corner of his eye Delvin had seen Nippy sneak off to the kitchen. Hungry again thought Delvin.

Dinner was being served in the State Dining Room. Delvin had put on the evening clothes he had selected earlier that day. He wore a gold-coloured doublet with the sleeves cut with red silk, and a green hose. The seamstress had completed the alterations to Jarla's dress. She wore a long red silk dress with a deep cut back. Her hair hung loose over her shoulders which slightly softened her features. General Horncliffe wore a splendid dress uniform, and even General Gortly was wearing a uniform. Grimbolt had managed to find a uniform too. He had probably borrowed it off one of the soldiers in the army, thought Delvin.

The party gathered in the Great Hall, before being ushered into the State Dining Room.

The State Dining Room was between two of the corner towers and was dominated by a long highly polished dining table. An arch led from the Great Hall and another arch opposite led to the Small Dining Room. Two large sideboards either side of a massive fireplace took up the wall on one side. Above the sideboards were hung gold framed portraits of long past Lords of Rostin. On the wall opposite the fireplace hung the paintings that Jarla had admired. A thick carpet covered the floor.

Although the long table was easily big enough to seat over twenty, today it was set for just six, as Nippy had decided he would prefer eating in the kitchen with the servants.

The cooks in the castle had been warned the duke was coming and had excelled themselves. The meal was delicious.

Wine was being served with the meal. Delvin was about to ask for ale, but thought he would try the wine first. The wine tasted far nicer than any wine he had previously drunk, and it complemented the food beautifully. He decided to continue with the wine, and reflected that he had never had a meal quite like this before.

Over dinner, Delvin, Jarla and Grimbolt gave the duke and generals an account of what had happened. The duke and generals listened intently, asking several questions. When they came to the part where Lady Tabsall had revealed she had been the Duke of Hengel's wife, the duke's face hardened.

"We had wondered what had happened to her," he muttered.

After dinner the party moved up to the Drawing Room on the floor above. The room had several easy chairs and sofas set around another huge fireplace. Tapestries hung on the walls giving the room an almost cosy feel despite its size. Sideboards around the walls bore sculptures and other works of art.

The duke waved them to chairs around the fireplace.

"Princess, Generals, Sir Delvin, Major," began the duke. "I have been thinking about what we should do with Rostin now it is restored as part of Argent. Traditionally the barony of Rostin was administered by Lord Rostin. But the line died out some fifty years ago. After the last Lord Rostin died, it was administered by a steward. About thirty years ago, rather than leave the castle empty, it was leased to the magician Spendrank who based his Magician's Council here. That was fine. But we all know what happened next when the Guild of Magicians killed Spendrank and took over. I have decided we need a new Lord Rostin. I don't want to make one of those sycophantic nincompoops back in Argent Lord Rostin…, so I have decided that the new Lord Rostin will be you, Sir Delvin."

Delvin had been taking a sip of wine and almost choked.

"You have helped get rid of the mercenary invaders and helped restore Rostin to Argent," continued the duke. He gave a wicked smile. "And as Lord Rostin, if Argent ever needs your services to repel any future invasions, I can call upon you as one of my subjects."

"Your Grace," said Delvin. "Thank you so much for the honour, but I don't know how to be a lord. I'm just a magician… Being a magician is what I enjoy doing… I know nothing about being a lord and running a barony… I just wouldn't know what to do."

"I can show you what needs to be done," said the duke. "Anyway, all the day to day work is done by the steward."

"Your Grace, I am a citizen of Hengel. All my family and friends live in Hengel."

"Oh, you won't have to live up here," said the duke. "You can live in Hengel, and do your magic if that's what you want. You only need to come up here once or twice a year to hold court. As I said, the steward does the rest. Oh, you'll need to visit Argent once a year as well, to show yourself at court and report to me what's been happening up here in Rostin."

Jarla laughed, "I don't think I have ever seen anyone so reluctant to become a lord."

"Thank you, Your Grace," said Delvin still stunned. "You do me a huge honour, and I will try to live up to the trust you have placed in me and do my very best to perform my duties."

"Excellent," said the duke. "A toast to Lord Rostin."

"Lord Rostin!"

They all raised their glasses. Delvin looked from face to face and wondered if he was dreaming.

Chapter 36

Delvin woke early in the morning. His head hurt. He had drunk too many toasts the night before, and he wasn't used to drinking wine. He hauled himself out of bed as he needed to be ready to see the steward after breakfast. The duke had arranged the meeting the previous night.

After splashing water on his face and getting dressed, Delvin went down to the Small Dining Room for breakfast. The generals were already there and greeted him as he went in. He wished them good morning as he sat down. It took two cups of hot leaf and half a roll to make him start to feel normal.

He was just leaving the dining room when the others came down.

"How's the head this morning?" said Grimbolt with his lopsided smile. Delvin smiled wanly back, and Grimbolt laughed.

The steward's room was in the base of one of the corner towers. Delvin knocked on the door.

"Come in," he heard through the door.

He opened the door and went in. Behind a desk sat a tall man of about fifty, with greying hair and a neatly trimmed beard and moustache, and wearing a long dark gown. Beside him was a much younger man, clean shaven and his dark hair neatly parted.

They both stood as Delvin entered.

"My Lord," said the older man. "I am Branton your steward. This is my son Penton, he assists me. My father and grandfather were stewards before me, and should you wish, I am training Penton to be able to follow on after me."

Delvin bowed, and they returned his bow.

"If you would like to take a seat, I will run over the barony's finances."

Delvin sat down.

"The barony's income, my lord, comes from rents on property and land, plus harbour charges and customs charges on goods shipped in. This was the income last year." Branton pointed to a figure in a sheet of paper he handed to Delvin. Delvin's eyebrows rose, the figure was enormous.

"With the money coming in, one tenth goes on administration. That includes upkeep, staffing and all the costs of the castle here in Rostin and of Rostin House in Argent, and it also covers my costs. When the Guild of Magicians were in control, they took all the remainder." He shook his head. "Before the Guild of Magicians, half the remainder went to the Duke of Argent, the other half was available for Lord Rostin to spend as he wished."

"Half of what is left?" asked Delvin incredulously.

"Indeed, Lord Rostin. Will we be going back to the old ways and not the magician's ways?"

"Yes, I believe we should," said Delvin slightly dazed. "Is any of the income spent on improvements to the town or on the people of Norden?"

"That would be up to you. As I said, you can spend your half as you wish. In the past I believe the then Lords

Rostin built the harbour and town walls, but I don't know the details of the finances back then."

Delvin's mind was reeling, the sums were huge.

"I am afraid that until the next rent day there is not much money available," continued Branton. "When Lady Tabsall left, she took almost all the money we had."

"When is the next rent day?" asked Delvin.

"In three weeks," replied Branton.

"I think you mentioned Rostin House. What is Rostin House?"

"Rostin House is the Lords Rostin's house in the city of Argent. We continued paying for the upkeep when the Guild of Magicians were here, even though they never used it. I actually don't think they realized it was part of the estate. A butler and his wife, who is also the housekeeper look after it. In the past, the Lords Rostin spent quite a lot of time in Argent."

The rest of the morning was spent with Branton going over the fine details, leaving Delvin with his head spinning. He decided to go on a short walk before lunch to clear his mind.

The guards on the castle gate saluted as he left the castle. He walked down towards the harbour. He could feel the curious eyes of the people he passed following him as he went. The news of him being made Lord Rostin must have got out, he thought. When he reached the square by the quay, a town crier was making a proclamation.

"Oh yea! Oh yea! Lord Rostin will hold court at the castle, two hours after noon."

Delvin remembered that the duke had asked Morvel the butler to arrange for him to hold court. What would that involve he wondered?

As Delvin looked out to sea and watched the fishing boats out in the Gulf of Ablet, he thought about his life and what he should do. He enjoyed being a magician. He liked the children's laughter when he did magic at parties. He liked the expressions on people's faces when he read their fortunes. He was happy at Mistress Wilshaw's. Her cooking was good. He could use her parlour to entertain clients. He was living with his best friend Greg. He was earning enough as a magician to more than cover his needs. He didn't need great riches. One day he would get his own house, but not yet. And even then, he didn't want a big house with servants. He was happy with his life the way it had been before all this had started. Was everything now going to change? How could he charge two carls for fortune telling, or a few carls for a children's party if he lived in a huge house? People would ask where his money had come from, and that would prove awkward if he was claiming he was just Devin the magician. No, he preferred his simple life as a magician, not the life of a lord. He straightened his shoulders and decided what he would do. He would come up here two or three times a year as the duke had said he should and perform his duties as Lord Rostin. It would be like a holiday. The area was beautiful. He would enjoy the change. But the rest of the time he would be simply Delvin the magician, doing the magic he loved. He decided that for the time being, he would spend the money from the barony on the people of Rostin and the area around.

Having got his thoughts straight, Delvin felt much better as he walked back up to the castle.

When he got back to the castle, lunch was already set out in the Small Dining Room. Cold meats, pies, smoked fish and a selection of breads were laid out on the table. Jarla, Grimbolt and Nippy had already started their lunch. Nippy had a huge pile of food on his plate.

"How did you get on?" asked Grimbolt.

"Exhausting," replied Delvin sitting down at the table.

"You will need to get used to it," said Jarla. "The duke finished his lunch a few minutes ago. He said to meet him in the Great Hall ten minutes before two hours after noon."

Time was already getting on, so Delvin quickly ate his lunch, then got up and made his way to the Great Hall.

The Great Hall extended right across the back of the castle. Arches at each end led into the bases of the two corner towers. The walls were adorned with ancient weapons arranged in elaborate patterns. At one end on a raised dais, a table had been set up with three tall chairs behind it. The duke was already seated at one of the chairs with the steward Branton next to him. He beckoned Delvin over and indicated the vacant chair. Delvin sat down with a slight feeling of trepidation.

Morvel the butler entered the hall.

"Are you ready, Your Grace, my lord?"

The duke nodded.

Morvel left the room to return moments later with a tall grey-haired man wearing a long gown and a chain of office.

"Your Grace, my lord," announced Morval. "May I present Magister Fornishaw, President of the Guild of Fishermen."

Magister Fornishaw approached the table and bowed low.

"Your Grace, my lord. May I first congratulate your lordship... I represent the fishermen of Rostin... I come to ask for your assistance in repairing the lighthouse at the end of the headland. It has not been functioning properly for some years and is in danger of falling down. Without it our fishermen are in danger in poor weather."

"Do you have costs for its repair?" asked Delvin.

"I do, my lord," said Fornishaw handing Delvin a sheet of paper.

Delvin glanced at it and handed it across to Branton the steward.

"What is your opinion on this?" he asked Branton.

"I believe it is important my lord."

"How soon could we do it?"

Branton examined the figures. "In three weeks on the next rent day," he replied. "But it will take most of the money you have coming in."

Delvin addressed Magister Fornishaw. "Please contact Magister Branton to arrange a contractor, budget and start date," pronounced Delvin.

316

"Thank you, my lord," said Fornishaw bowing and backing out.

Several more petitioners came, and Delvin was able to deal with them without difficulty.

When the last petitioner had left, the duke turned to Delvin.

"Excellent," he said sitting back. "You will make a good Lord Rostin."

Delvin smiled back. It had been easier than he had thought. Then he had a thought and turned to Branton.

"Are there any schools in Rostin?"

"There is one school, my lord."

"Is that a school for people who can pay for it?"

"It is my lord."

"I want to set up a school for those that can't afford to pay. Please could you find suitable premises."

"Yes, my lord," replied Branton, a note of surprise in his voice.

"I think you'll make a very good Lord Rostin," muttered the duke.

When court had finished, Delvin made a point of talking to all the castle servants. He then walked to the barracks, he wanted to talk to the soldiers there as well. News had got out about the lighthouse and his plan for a school, and a number of people cheered as he walked past.

At dinner that evening Delvin decided he should go easy on the wine. He had begun to rather enjoy it, but he didn't want to wake up with a headache again.

"How do you like being a lord?" asked Jarla as they ate roast chicken accompanied by an astonishing array of side dishes.

"I'm starting to get used to it," replied Delvin.

"Now you are a lord you need to have a coat of arms and a standard," said the duke.

"I think it should be a white rabbit on a green background," said Jarla grinning.

"I can see that might be appropriate," said the duke laughing. "But it's not quite the lions, leopards and bears that usually adorn shields and crests." He turned to a servant who was just clearing the plates. "Please bring us some paper, ink and quills."

More ideas were flung around the table, and when the paper arrived, they made rough sketches of them. Coats of arms and standards were not something Delvin had much experience of, so he mainly listened to the others. Then he had an idea.

"How about a row of stars, a small one, then a bigger one then a large one. As if it was a burst of magic?"

"That would work," said the duke."

"I think it should have a dark blue background," added Delvin taking a piece of paper and a quill, and quickly sketching it out.

They all thought that Delvin's idea was appropriate, and the duke agreed that it would become Delvin's coat of arms and his standard as the new Lord Rostin.

"Have you thought what to do with Tabsall?" asked Grimbolt.

"Yes," said Delvin. "He is not an evil man. The problem was Lady Tabsall, and that he let himself be seduced by her when she was Duchess of Hengel."

"Which just happens to be treason," said Jarla severely. "Adultery with the Duchess of Hengel or her daughters is treason," she added.

"That's true, but I think he has suffered enough by being under Lady Tabsall's control all these years. Now he has nowhere else to go."

"He could go to prison," muttered Jarla.

"I have decided he can stay where he is, here in the castle. He's an old man and is not going to do anyone any harm."

Jarla gave Delvin a ferocious scowl.

After they had finished dinner, they did not linger long before heading up to bed. They had to be up early in the morning, since they would be on their way back towards Argent and Hengel and wanted to make an early start.

Chapter 37

It was still very early, with the sun low in the sky, as they rode through the streets of Rostin the following morning. The weather seemed to be changing. A brisk wind was blowing, and it felt colder than the previous few days.

Despite the early hour, a surprising number of people had come out to cheer them off. "I think they have heard about your plans for a free school," said the duke.

As they passed through the town gate, they could see that the army, who had been camping outside Rostin, was already on the move.

The two generals were waiting outside the town for the duke and his party. They all joined with the army as it began to move south.

The whole army was mounted so they made quite fast progress. At midmorning they stopped by a large stream to stretch their legs. The stream ran under a small stone bridge, and a grassy bank ran down to it from the road.

They dismounted and led their horses down to the stream to drink.

Delvin and the duke stood on the bank looking into the crystal-clear water. Suddenly the duke spied a fish, motionless against the pebbles at the bottom of the stream and pointed it out to Delvin.

"I came fishing up here in Rostin when I was a child," he said. "Rostin has the best fishing in all the duchies. Now that Rostin is part of Argent again, I'll come up here again… If I may use your castle?" He looked at Delvin expectantly.

"Of course, Your Grace," replied Delvin.

Delvin enjoyed fishing too, and he smiled at the thought of combining fishing with his duties as Lord Rostin.

Delvin suddenly had a thought. Could he use his stone to influence fish? He tried projecting the idea that an amazingly tasty fly was about a foot above the water just next to the duke.

The fish suddenly moved, and a moment later leapt out of the water. The duke was not expecting it and jumped. But he didn't manage to get far enough away to save himself from getting splashed as the fish landed back in the stream.

Delvin desperately tried to keep a straight face.

Jarla had also been looking at the stream, and she too had jumped when the fish had leapt out of the water. She and the duke now both looked at Delvin, neither of them sure if it was him who had caused the fish to jump. Delvin looked back trying to put on the most innocent face he could muster. Eventually Jarla shook her head and turned away.

Delvin breathed a sigh of relief. He had got away with it. Shortly after, they remounted and continued on their way.

They reached the old border with Argent before nightfall. The duke, Jarla, Delvin, Grimbolt, Nippy and the generals were found accommodation in the fort there.

They set out early the following morning and reached Dandel just as the light was failing. The people in Dandel had heard of their victory in taking back Norden, and quite a crowd cheered as they rode through the town. The duke and his party put up at The Royal Bridge, the inn on the bridge over the River Bolla. They were up early again the following morning, and by two hours before noon had reached the junction where one road led to Argent the other to Hengel.

"Are you coming back to Hengel with the us?" asked Jarla.

"No, not just yet," replied Delvin. "The duke wants me to come to Argent for his victory celebration. He says you can't have a victory celebration for taking back Norden without having Lord Rostin present."

"You'll miss our victory celebration in Hengel."

"I have also got things I need to do in Argent. I need to take the magicians' influence off Norden's soldiers who were captured after the magicians tried to take over Argent last year. They are still locked up in the castle in Argent."

"What are you going to do with those soldiers," asked Jarla.

"They can either go back to Norden or they can join Argent's army down here," replied Delvin. "On top of that, my magic lantern is also still in Argent. I need to get that."

"Right," said Jarla. "I suspect my father will want to talk to you when you eventually get back to Hengel, so I guess we will probably see you then."

She wheeled her horse and joined Grimbolt and General Gortly, and with them she took her leave of the duke who thanked them all for their support. Then together with the Hengel part of the army, Jarla, Grimbolt and General Gortly set out on the road to North Bridge and so back to Hengel.

Delvin was sad to see them go. He would have liked to have gone with them, as he missed Hengel. He turned his horse and joined the duke and his army on the road to Argent.

They reached Argent in the afternoon and a huge crowd had gathered. The silver and red flags of Argent flew from all the buildings, and the crowd cheered and waved as they rode past. Children had home-made silver and red flags that they waved enthusiastically. A dais had been set up in the square in front of the guildhall and temple. The duke climbed up on it and addressed the crowd who had now flocked into the square.

"Citizens of Argent, we have now reclaimed Norden as part of our ancient land. I present to you… Lord Rostin." The crowd cheered as Delvin stepped forward feeling rather embarrassed.

They proceeded on to the palace. Delvin had asked if he should stay at Rostin House, but the duke had insisted that he stay at the palace. They dismounted in the palace courtyard, and Delvin was ceremoniously shown to his room by Balinow.

As soon as they had reached the palace, Nippy had headed straight for the kitchen and servant's hall. Delvin watched him go with a smile, since he knew he would be looking for something to eat. Nippy knew several of the servants from their last visit to the palace, so Delvin was sure he would be fine. He had also asked Nippy to find his magic lantern for him, since he didn't think he would have time to look for it himself.

After washing off the worst of the dirt from the journey, Delvin came down and made his way up to the castle, so that he could take the magician's influence off Norden's soldiers imprisoned there. He asked the guards to bring all the Norden soldiers into the castle's Great Hall. When they were all assembled, he removed the magician's influence, then told them they could either go back to Norden or join Argent's army. He left them discussing among themselves what they were going to do.

When Delvin got back from the castle, he went up to his room to get ready for the victory ball that had been planned for that evening. He fed Freda his rabbit, gave her a run and then put her in a drawer that he had taken out of a chest of drawers in his room. He then got washed, and dressed himself in the evening clothes he had brought down from Rostin. He looked at himself in the mirror. In the ex-magician's fine clothes, he looked very different from the lad who had left Byford only just over a year before.

The ball was preceded by a grand dinner. Delvin found himself seated on the duke's left, the duke's daughter Princes Fionella on the duke's right.

Delvin looked at the amazing array of cutlery and glasses in front of him. He gulped. He decided he would need to watch what cutlery other people used, since he had no idea what some of them were for. He would also need to be careful how much he drank, remembering the headache of a few days before.

Course after course arrived and went, Delvin carefully observed what the other diners did and copied them. Although the food was delicious, he found that trying to do the right thing was quite a strain, and he couldn't help thinking that he would have been far more comfortable with a simple meal at an inn.

When the meal was finished, the duke rose and made a short speech hailing the victory in retaking Norden, and again introducing Delvin as Lord Rostin to the assembled company.

They moved through to the ballroom where an orchestra had set up. As Delvin and the duke entered, the first couples were already starting to dance. Delvin had done some country dancing back in Byford, but nothing like the elegant and intricate dances that were being danced here.

A large lady approached them. Her hair was done up in a highly elaborate style, and a diamond necklace glittered around her neck. A pretty and rather overawed young girl followed her.

"Lord Rostin, my I introduce you to my daughter Griselle?... Your Grace," she said taking the duke by the arm. "Shall we leave the young people to get to know each other?"

Griselle looked shyly at him. "Sorry about mother," she said.

"That's alright," said Delvin smiling back at her. "I don't know anyone here, so it's nice to get someone to talk to."

Moments later a portly middle-aged gentleman approached.

"Lord Rostin, Griselle," he acknowledged Griselle with a brief nod of his head then looked back to Delvin. "I am your neighbour, Lord Ablet. It is good to meet you. May I introduce you to my daughter Morrane." Another pretty young girl stepped forward.

"Lord Ablet," said Delvin bowing politely to Lord Ablet. He turned to Morrane. "It's lovely to meet you." He bowed to her and she gave a little curtsy in return.

"I'll leave you young people to talk, perhaps we can catch up later, Lord Rostin." Lord Ablet bowed again and moved away.

The realization hit Delvin that he was now a highly eligible bachelor and was the target of ambitious parents. Still, he thought, he had always enjoyed talking to pretty young ladies. Perhaps he could have a bit of fun.

The next lady to approach him was a haughty looking lady with a rather cowed looking girl following in her wake. Just as the lady was about to speak, Delvin sent a projection to her to hiccough. He almost burst out laughing at the result, as she spluttered an apology and temporarily retreated.

A little later another formidable looking lady found her voice coming out as a squeak. After that Delvin thought he had better stop, or it might become obvious. He therefore let himself be introduced to all the young ladies of the court.

The young ladies were obviously hoping he would invite them to dance, but Delvin knew his rough country dancing would not be appropriate here, so he excused himself on the grounds of tiredness having ridden a long way that day.

As soon as he felt it was polite to do so, Delvin made his excuses to his new acquaintances. He wanted to be up early in the morning to get back to Hengel before nightfall. He approached the duke and thanked him for his hospitality, saying he would be leaving at dawn. The duke smiled and thanked him in return, then Delvin retired to his bedchamber.

When he got back to his room, he was pleased to see that Nippy had found his magic lantern as he had asked and had placed it in his room. Then he checked Freda and made sure she had food and gave her another stroke. It had been a long day, and after climbing into bed he was soon asleep.

Chapter 38

Delvin was up before dawn. He had put away his court finery and now wore his old plain clothes. The grooms had only just woken up when he entered the stables, and Delvin had to wait while they saddled the horses. He had told Nippy to also get ready early, and while Delvin waited for the horses, Nippy disappeared into the kitchen, returning moments later with several rolls and a grin on his face.

They rode out of the palace munching their rolls. The previous day Delvin had made enquiries as to the whereabouts of Rostin House. To his surprise he had been told it was on Royal Road close to the palace. He must have ridden past it on his way to the palace without realising it was there, so he decided that on his way out of the city he would stop and take a look at it.

Rostin House turned out to be a large and impressive stone building, with a wide flight of shallow steps leading up to a black painted front door flanked by pillars supporting a pediment.

Delvin looked up at the building. Whatever was he going to do with a building like that he thought. He was tempted to knock on the door and go in and look around, but he really didn't have time, since he wanted to get to Hengel before the gates closed at nightfall. He turned his horse and headed for the city gate.

When they reached the gate, it had only just been opened, and they had to wait for the line of carts that was slowly coming in. The carts eventually cleared, and after briefly telling the gate guard that they were travelling to North Bridge, they were on their way.

The day was overcast and it had turned slightly colder. The trees in the small woods they passed were coming into leaf and their branches fluttered in the breeze.

In mid-morning they passed through Thanley.

"We'll stop at The Green Lion for a break," said Delvin. "You never know, that farmer Hanaman might have found my old stone."

When they reached the inn, they dismounted and led their horses to a water trough. As they stretched their legs the landlord hurried out.

"Magisters," he began, "I am so glad to see you. I've a message from farmer Hanaman. He said that if I saw you, I was to say that he has found what you are looking for."

"Thank you," said Delvin. "We'll go and see him. Can I give you something for your trouble in passing the message on?" Delvin put his hand in his purse and handed the innkeeper a gold royal.

"Thank you, thank you magisters," said the innkeeper looking very pleased.

Delvin and Nippy remounted and made their way down the track to Hanaman's pig farm. They dismounted in his yard and knocked on the farmhouse door.

A large lady of middle-years opened the door.

"We are looking for farmer Hanaman," said Delvin.

"I'll get him for you," said the lady.

A few moments later, Hanaman came round the side of the building.

"Ah magisters," he said, "did Trellis at The Green Lion tell you I found that stone you were looking for?"

"Yes," said Delvin.

"Well, I did find it. I'll just go and get it for you." He disappeared into the house.

Moments later he reappeared with a stone. "That other gentleman said he would pay me twenty gold royals for it."

"May I see it?"

Delvin held out his hand and took the stone. It was his old stone, the one that Borlock had left him.

"That's the one. I'll give you the twenty royals you were promised," said Delvin. He still had the money that Nippy had stolen from Lady Carolina. He took twenty royals from his purse and handed them to Hanaman.

"One of them pigs must have trodden on it," said Hanaman, a satisfied look on his face. "It were almost buried in the ground. I only saw it by chance."

Delvin thanked him, then he and Nippy remounted and made their way back to the road.

"What are you going to do with that stone?" asked Nippy as they rode down the road.

"I was just wondering that myself," said Delvin. "Grimbolt already has a stone, so Hengel is well protected... I have an idea... I know... I'll give it to Golbrick, you remember, that old magician up at the disused diamond mine. He said if he ever got another magician's stone, he would love to go back to being a travelling magician, keeping the peace and sorting out problems like he used to do. He could use it to do some real good... Another thing... If he sent me regular messages, he could let me know what was happening in neighboring countries before anyone else knew. If I incorporated that into my fortune telling and shows, people would really think I had special powers." Delvin smiled to himself at the prospect.

They stopped for lunch at a roadside inn, and soon came to the road junction and turned right towards North Bridge.

The guards on the gate at North Bridge hardly questioned them. They look hungover thought Delvin. North Bridge seemed to have had a victory party the night before from the evidence of the debris still in the streets. They crossed over the great bridge, and the guards on the Hengel side of the bridge also looked sleepy and sluggish.

They were soon through South Bridge and on the final stage of their journey. It had been threatening to rain all day, and as the walls of Hengel came in sight, the first drops began to fall.

It was early evening as they rode up to the North Gate of the city. Delvin told the gate-guard he was a children's entertainer returning from South Bridge, and he was waved through. They made their way to the castle to leave their horses at the stables there, then they set out on foot back to the East Quarter and Mistress Wilshaw's house in Chandler's Lane. It was still drizzling, and as they crossed the market square, there was the lingering smells of cabbage and other vegetables even though the stalls had now been taken down. It smelt like this when I came back from Cavid thought Delvin as he dodged the puddles.

When they entered Mistress Wilshaw's house, Mistress Wilshaw was about to serve Greg his dinner in the kitchen. On hearing the door open, she looked up and saw them come in.

"Master Delvin, Master Nippy!" she exclaimed. "Now don't you drip all over my clean floor. Get those wet clothes off and I'll dry them for you. Come on now. Get them off. Where have you been? You must tell me all about it."

As Delvin removed his coat, he could see Greg grinning from the kitchen.

"It's just my coat that is really wet, the rest are fine," said Delvin backing away from Mistress Wilshaw who was trying to feel his breeches.

"Now Master Delvin, are you sure those breeches aren't wet as well? If you catch your death of cold, I don't want to be running up and down stairs looking after you." She shook her head and her ample body wobbled.

"I am sure thank you Mistress Wilshaw," replied Delvin who had now backed away as far as the front door.

"Well come and sit down," said Mistress Wilshaw. "You should have let me know you were coming then I could have cooked extra dinner. I'm only going to have just enough."

Mistress Wilshaw went over to the kitchen stove where she began to fill two bowls from a huge pan of stew.

"Ooo! You should have been here yesterday," she said. "You've missed the victory parade. It was wonderful. All those brave soldiers. Fancy, they've defeated those magicians and captured Norden. Now you sit down. Have you been feeding yourself properly? You are looking a bit thin." She placed large bowls of stew in front of Delvin and Nippy. "Now you eat that up, I want to hear all about what you've been doing."

"We've been travelling around the north doing a few magic shows," said Delvin, knowing Mistress Wilshaw wouldn't believe it if he told her the full story. He also didn't want her telling her friends what he had done, since then it would be hard to carry on being just Delvin the magician.

"Lots of people have been calling wanting you to read their fortunes and do your shows," said Mistress Wilshaw. "I'm surprised I'm not as thin as a rake getting up and down to answer the door."

Delvin smiled. "Thank you, Mistress Wilshaw."

Nippy raised his head from his bowl of stew.

"He's now Lord Rostin," he announced.

"Oh! You do tell some tall stories!" said Mistress Wilshaw.

Greg laughed. "You tried to convince us you were Sir Delvin before. Now Lord Rostin. You'll say you are a prince next. You're really not going to catch me out this time... Lord Rostin!" He laughed.

Delvin laughed back.

"Even I wouldn't think I could convince you that I was Lord Rostin," he said grinning.

It was good being back with his friend Greg, and since neither he nor Mistress Wilshaw believed he was Lord Rostin, he could continue to carry on being just Delvin the magician.

Chapter 39

Greg was up early next morning to go to work at The White Bear where he worked in the stables. Delvin got up too. Nippy decided to remain in bed.

"After becoming a knight and a lord, don't go getting made a prince while I'm at work," laughed Greg as he made for the door.

Somehow the news of his return had got about, and by the time Delvin had finished his roll and cup of hot leaf, there was a knock at the door. It was a young girl wanting a love potion. Delvin went up to his room to get one of the small packs containing chalk powder that he sold as love potions.

More knocks on the door soon followed, and by lunchtime he had told the fortunes of three men and two ladies, and sold four love potions. He had been busy almost without a break.

"Ooo, you do seem to be popular," said Mistress Wilshaw as she brought him some bread and cheese for his lunch. "Come on...sit down at the table and when you've finished eating, you can tell my fortune again." She gave a little wriggle of anticipation. "You didn't quite finish it last time."

Delvin remembered the previous time he had tried telling Mistress Wilshaw's fortune. It had started to get embarrassing as she began to want more and more amorous details.

"I'm not sure there is going to be much more to add from what I told you last time," he said, hoping that might put her off.

"Ooo! I'm sure there is," said Mistress Wilshaw giving another little wriggle.

"With all these clients, my powers are going to be exhausted. It's quite draining," he said, desperately looking for a credible excuse.

"Ooo! I'm sure you will have some left," said Mistress Wilshaw putting a hand on his knee.

Just then there was a knock at the door. Saved by the door knocker thought Delvin.

It was Grimbolt.

"Good afternoon Major Grybald," said Delvin getting up to greet him.

"Good afternoon, Lor…," he quickly corrected himself, "Magister Delvin. His Grace wishes to see you… And it is now Colonel Grybald… I've been promoted."

"Congratulations Colonel," said Delvin. "If I'm seeing the duke I'd better get changed."

"Be quick," said Grimbolt.

"Ooo! A colonel," said Mistress Wilshaw, a gleam in her eye. "Come and sit down and have a cup of hot leaf. I do like a soldier."

Delvin ran upstairs and quickly got changed into the outfit the duke of Argent had given him the previous year. He then straightened his hair and went back down to the kitchen.

Mistress Wilshaw had Grimbolt sat down at the table and was questioning him about what he had been doing. Grimbolt was giving non-committal answers, since he knew Delvin wanted to keep secret the fact that he was now Lord Rostin.

"Come on, we mustn't keep the duke waiting," said Grimbolt getting up gratefully. "Thank you for the hot leaf, Mistress Wilshaw."

As Delvin went through the front door, he saw there were two soldiers waiting outside. Why have I got an escort he thought?

They soon reached the Castle. The guards on the gate saluted as they walked through. They entered the main building and went across the Grand Hall up the Grand Stair and into the Lobby. There were no audiences today, so there were no petitioners in the Lobby. The two guards on the entrance to the Throne Room threw the double doors open as they approached.

Delvin was always struck by the magnificence of the Throne Room with its hammerbeam ceiling, its bosses carved as grotesque faces and the panels between painted in bright colours. The narrow windows above the tapestries on the walls sent down shafts of light that made patterns on the floor.

At the far end of the room two figures were seated on tall chairs. In the larger of the chairs sat Duke Poldor. The long spikes in which his black hair had been arranged were adorned with small silver balls. He was wearing a black doublet that was also adorned with silver balls, the whole thing making him look like some exotic and evil insect. On the other chair sat Princess Jarla. She was wearing a sheer red dress with a deep neckline. A single red stone hung on a necklace around her neck. Her dark hair hung loose over her shoulders giving her a hard imperious look.

Delvin approached and bowed. Grimbolt who was next to him bowed also. The two soldiers accompanying them stood behind.

The duke fixed Delvin with a penetrating stare.

"Sir Delvin, or should I say Lord Rostin... You are under arrest for treason."

Chapter 40

Delvin was momentarily lost for words. He managed to croak, "Treason, Your Grace?"

"Treason," repeated the duke, a malevolent look in his eye. "Did you, or did you not, travel around the country with Princess Jarla, heir to the throne, against my express orders, and sleep in inns with her without a chaperone?"

"Yes, Your Grace," croaked Delvin.

"Father!" interrupted Jarla.

"Quiet!" snapped the duke.

"By doing so, did you, or did you not, thereby destroy the reputation and besmirch the honour of Princess Jarla?"

"We did nothing together," exploded Jarla.

"Quiet! I said," snapped the duke again.

Delvin noticed that two large ladies had appeared and were now standing behind Jarla's chair.

"Her honour has been so ruined that no one will now marry her. Lord Cavid has even gone so far as to flee to the far side of the continent to avoid marriage to her. This is your doing."

"I didn't want to marry Lord Cavid," said Jarla furiously.

"Destroying the honour and reputation of the heir to the throne is treason," continued the duke inexorably. "You have admitted you did so... Have you anything to say before I find you guilty?"

Delvin was too dumbstruck to say anything.

"Guilty!" pronounced the duke, a look of satisfaction on his face.

Jarla had tried to rise but had been firmly pushed back into her chair by the two large ladies.

The duke continued, "When a gentleman besmirches the honour of a lady, that gentleman is duty bound to salvage that lady's honour... by marrying her... This is not a request, Lord Rostin. This is a demand. I demand that you immediately marry Princess Jarla to restore her honour."

Jarla was looking wide eyed.

"Father, you cannot be serious."

"The ceremony will take place in... just over one hour's time." There was now a look of triumph on the duke's face.

"But it's Delvin," spluttered Jarla.

"It's Lord Rostin," replied the duke. "An ancient title and a perfectly respectable match. And you seem to get on quite well... After all, you haven't killed him yet."

"Give me time," muttered Jarla.

"Not before he has given you an heir," responded the duke with a wicked smile.

Delvin started trying to project a suggestion to the duke that he had forgotten all about the marriage and that he was not guilty of anything, but to his surprise it was instantly countered and blocked.

"It's no use you trying to use your magician's stone to influence me," said the duke. "I have ordered Colonel Grybald to counter any projections you try to make."

Delvin looked over his shoulder at Grimbolt who had an evil grin on his face.

"I don't want to be married and have someone hanging around me all day," exploded Jarla again.

"He can spend the day hunting," said the duke.

"I don't hunt," said Delvin in a small voice, now totally shocked at what had transpired. He hadn't realized being a lord would have these complications.

"You can find some other occupation to keep yourself busy," said the duke. "What do you enjoy doing, Lord Rostin?"

"I like performing magic tricks," replied Delvin. "Doing children's parties, that sort of thing."

"Ahh!" responded the duke unenthusiastically.

Delvin suddenly had an idea.

"Your Grace, could I be Magister Delvin the magician during the day when I wasn't wanted at the Castle, then become Lord Rostin when I was needed as Princess Jarla's husband...consort? At the moment, in the house where I live, they don't know I'm Lord Rostin, and my clients don't know either. If they knew that I had a title, I wouldn't be able to carry on doing my magic shows, as most of the people I perform for are merchants and tradesmen in the city."

"It wouldn't work," said the duke dismissively. "People would see you going in and out of the Castle and they would recognize you."

Jarla looked up, a spark in her eyes.

"My husband needs to have his own chambers at the Castle," she said. "The postern tower is now just used as a guard room. If you gave that to Delvin as his private chambers, he could slip in and out of the postern gate in the tower without being seen... He could get changed there each time he went in or out, and if he wore a wig when he was in the Castle, it would change his appearance enough so people wouldn't recognize him."

The duke looked at Jarla then back at Delvin.

"Mmm," he pondered. "If you think it will work... It may do... We will try it... Colonel Grybald, arrange for the guard room to be moved from that tower."

"Certainly, Your Grace." Delvin detected a note of amusement in his voice.

"Right, you must get ready for your wedding... Take them both away and get them prepared."

Grimbolt and the two soldiers who had been standing behind Delvin marched him out of the throne room. Out of the corner of his eye, he saw the two large ladies who had been standing behind Jarla march her away too.

The next half hour was a blur of getting washed, scrubbed, perfumed and eventually dressed in a bright red wedding robe. Various wigs were tried on him. Eventually a dark wig with shoulder length hair was chosen. Grimbolt stood back to look at him once they were finished, grinning his lopsided grin from ear to ear.

"You look almost respectable Lord Rostin," he said. "Look happy, you are about to marry the most eligible lady on this side of the continent." He laughed. "Whether you like it or not… Right, let's get him to the temple."

A carriage was waiting in the courtyard. Above it flew a standard of three stars on a dark blue background. It was the first time Delvin had seen his coat of arms. He paused a moment looking at it. Someone has been busy sewing that, he thought. Then Grimbolt and the two soldiers bundled him into the carriage and got in after him. They're making sure I don't escape, thought Delvin.

A proclamation that Princess Jarla was to marry Lord Rostin had been announced throughout the city, and a crowd had gathered to see the happy couple. They cheered as Delvin was driven the short distance to the temple. He was marched to the front, while the carriage went back to the Castle to fetch Jarla.

As Delvin waited at the front of the temple, he reflected with a wry grin, that what had happened in the last few days had been even more extraordinary than the stories he told with his magic lantern. Perhaps he should embellish his stories up a bit to make them more like reality. But if he did, would anybody believe them?

Delvin looked around the temple. Guards had been placed on all the doors. The duke isn't taking any chances, he thought.

When Jarla arrived, she was dressed in a stunning sheer white silk dress, she wore a diamond tiara on her head, and a further large diamond on a gold chain hung around her neck. She was glaring straight ahead with a furious expression on her face.

The next half hour was a blur as the patriarch performed the marriage ceremony, the duke looking on with a look of triumph on his face.

The crowd had grown by the time they came out, and they cheered and waved flags as the coach drove them back to the Castle.

There was to be a grand ball that evening to celebrate the wedding. A banquet had been prepared to take place before the ball in the Royal Dining Room, to which the most important personages in Hengel had been invited.

The room had been decorated with bunting, and although it was not yet dark, the tables were lit with dozens of candles,

Having already experienced the banquet in Argent, Delvin was now more familiar with what to do with the huge array of cutlery and glasses. The food at the banquet was superb, and even included smoked fish from Rostin.

After dinner there was a speech from the duke, who announced his pleasure in cementing the friendship between Hengel and Argent by this union.

Delvin was then called on to speak. He was tempted to perform a magic trick, but though better of it. In the end he simply said how amazing it was to wed such an astonishing bride. Well, that was true he thought.

The ball was taking place in the Throne Room. This had also been decorated with bunting. An orchestra occupied the dais where the duke usually sat, and they played music while waiting for the royal party to come in from the dining room.

When Delvin and Jarla entered the Throne Room, everyone clapped. Delvin looked around at the expectant faces, and realized he and Jarla were expected to perform the first dance. He looked at her in trepidation, remembering the intricate dances at the ball in Argent. She glared back at him.

"If you tread on my toes, I'll kick you," she said.

Delvin solved the problem by just shuffling around. He would have to learn to dance properly, he thought.

After the first dance Delvin began to circulate around the guests. He discovered a surprising number of relieved young noblemen, who had been living in fear of their lives in case they had been made to marry Jarla. He also overheard several animated conversations, at which the odds on him surviving the wedding night, being emasculated, or not living past the first week of marriage were being discussed. Bets were being placed. One of the noblemen was surreptitiously writing down the details of the bets in a notebook.

Jarla had danced with a few of the young nobles, one of whom was rubbing his arms where her long fingernails had penetrated his doublet and pricked his arms.

Delvin raised his eyebrow towards her and nodded towards the noble.

Jarla came over and whispered quietly to Delvin, "That idiot is the one who has been spreading stories about me. He started the rumour that I've killed seven men and that I'm dangerous, so I thought I'd show him... how gentle I really was."

"But you have killed seven men. Actually, I make it more than seven," said Delvin.

"Yes, but he didn't know that."

"I suppose what he said really was untrue, since he got the number wrong," said Delvin with a smile.

"Exactly," said Jarla smiling back.

"It's probably just as well he didn't know the true figure," added Delvin.

"It's probably just as well that you don't know the true figure either," responded Jarla, a glint in her eye.

Delvin gulped and looked at her. She smiled wickedly back at him.

"Did you want to marry one of them?" asked Delvin.

"No, I certainly did not. They're all a load of effeminate idiots. I didn't want to have fools like them thinking they can tell me what to do." She turned to Delvin and looked him up and down. "Actually, you are not too bad. Better than them anyway."

Delvin returned the look. "You're not too bad either."

Jarla smiled and Delvin smiled back, then they both burst out laughing.

"You can be rather annoying though," said Jarla.

"So can you," replied Delvin.

"You know," said Jarla, looking at him critically, "I think this might just work out," Delvin nodded his agreement.

"But you'll have to give up your girl in every town," she added.

"Oh, come on, I haven't had time to meet anyone in Parva yet… Ow!" he exclaimed as Jarla kicked him.

"You do know, don't you," said Jarla, "that now we're married, that makes you a prince?"

"A prince?"

"Yes, the consort of the heir to the throne is a prince."

"I can't be Prince Delvin. Everyone would realize it was me when I went back to being a magician."

"How about Prince Warren," suggested Jarla with a smile.

"I think just Lord Rostin," said Delvin. He grinned inwardly as he thought of what Greg would say if he went back to Mistress Wilshaw's and told him he was now a prince.

"You know," said Delvin, "now I'm your husband, you should have let me deal with that idiot who spread rumours about you."

"I don't need protecting. Anyway, what would you have done?"

With a grin Delvin sent a projection to the young noble in question. The noble suddenly tripped, crashing into a table holding a large bowl of punch. The table collapsed under his weight, and the bowl of punch fell on him covering him in punch. Delvin turned and looked at Jarla with a grin.

Jarla was laughing. "Being married to you might be quite fun," she said.

The mess was soon cleared up and the noble departed to get changed.

347

"Would you like another dance?" asked Delvin.

Jarla looked at him for a moment. "Yes, but you really must learn to dance properly."

After a little while the duke came over, and with an almost malicious smile, said it was time for them to leave the ball and retire to Jarla's chamber.

Jarla and Delvin glanced at each other, and with slight smiles on their faces, left the ball.

Chapter 41

Jarla shut the door behind them and locked it. She turned to Delvin with half a grin.

"It seems my father has got his way after all."

"It looks like he has," agreed Delvin. "When I woke up this morning, I certainly didn't think the day would turn out like this."

"Neither did I," said Jarla smiling. "At least my father hasn't made me marry that nincompoop Lord Cavid."

"Do you think he would have done if he'd managed to catch him?"

"Oh yes. Lord Cavid only just got away in time." They both grinned.

"You know, when I told Lord Cavid his fortune, I forced the queen on him and lots of red cards and said they signified blood. He went as white as a sheet!"

"You didn't?" said Jarla laughing.

Delvin nodded. "You do have that reputation. I overheard a conversation down at the ball. They are taking bets on whether I'll survive the wedding night."

"What are the odds?"

"Three to one."

"Can you get a bet on for me, I could make a killing."

They both laughed and grinned at each other.

"Mind you," said Jarla. "If your performance is no good, I just might kill you anyway." Delvin gulped and Jarla smiled evilly.

"Right," said Jarla, a mischievous look in her eye. "We had better get on with it… By the way… what are the odds against me emasculating you?"

Delvin gulped.

"Strip!" said Jarla with a wicked grin.

Is this the end of the story?
Will Delvin survive the wedding
night? Will Lady Tabsall be content
with not seeing her children?

See also

The Magician's Secret

Book 1 of Illusions of Power

and

The Three Card Trick

Book 2 of Illusions of Power